The coldest place on earth

The coldest place on earth

Published by The Conrad Press Ltd. in the United Kingdom 2022

Tel: +44(0)1227 472 874
www.theconradpress.com
info@theconradpress.com

ISBN 978-1-914913-52-5

Copyright © Kate Barker-Mawjee, 2022

The moral right of Kate Barker-Mawjee to be identified as author of this work has been asserted in accordance with the Copyright, Designs and Patents Act 1988.

Printed and bound in Great Britain by Clays Ltd, Elcograf S.p.A

Typesetting by The Book Typesetters
www.thebooktypesetters.com

The Conrad Press logo was designed by Maria Priestley.

The coldest place on earth

Kate Barker-Mawjee

One

Each house in the row was successively more shabby until, at the very end of Libsky Street, the furthest from Lenin, the final house had surrendered entirely to the weight of winter.

No footsteps dented the snow on the six slatted steps that led up to the front door and the persistent fingers of frost had scratched behind the glass of the windows and begun to force them outwards from the frames.

It was a single-storey house, perched on stilts like all the others in the town. But the horizontal planks that made up the walls were warped in places by the cold so that they leaned at odd angles, and the roof seemed balanced on top, rather than properly fixed to them. The tall metal pipe of the chimney skewered sharply through the tiles, as if its real purpose were to pin the whole structure together.

A thin line of white smoke rose from the chimney. So they were alive at least. She would not have to knock on the door to check on them and she was relieved. Didn't she have enough on her plate?

To the side of the house, set a little distance away, was a kennel and two snub-nosed black dogs on short chains eyed Irina from under bobbing eyebrows, frosted white at their tips.

'Only that one again,' they said to each other and one of them yawned, extending its steaming tongue before curling the tip up into a quivering 'C' and laying its short snout back down onto its paws with a sigh.

Irina stepped forward cautiously into the gloom, smiling slightly in the way women sometimes do if they fear they will make a silly mistake. The paved road stopped abruptly here and it wouldn't do to slip and twist an ankle. Her torch was in her pocket but it was fiddly to operate through her thick mittens and carrying it for too long turned her fingers into a stiff claw.

She would take it carefully.

A thin noise, a high-pitched keening, sounded somewhere to her left.

Irina took a series of small, shuffling steps to turn to face the direction of the sound. She was still trim – under sixty kilos and the same dress size as in her twenties – but, wrapped in her layers of vest, long sleeved t-shirt, flannel shirt, sweater, cardigan and with her thick knee-length reindeer skin coat belted firmly at the waist, she was as solid and unyielding as a rolled up carpet.

Just a fox, she told herself.

She had passed the house now and there was enough moonlight to show around and to the rear where a fresh path had been trampled from the back door to the outhouse.

The door was unlatched and swung back and forth in the wind. That was all.

If she had gone inside she would have seen that the frost coated the hinges, the walls and the wooden seat. If she had peered into the deep hole, she would have seen that the faeces had frozen as it landed, creating a tall brown stalagmite that, once it reached the level of the seat, would have to be hacked down with an axe before the outhouse could safely be used again.

The old folks were stoical about such things, but Irina thought about her indoor toilet and her polished kitchen taps and considered herself lucky that they were in the town's apartment block at least. A blessing.

This down-at-heel house was the furthest out from the town, such as it was, and behind its decaying wooden back stretched the bleak emptiness of nothing and no one.

Irina shuffled back around and pressed on. She was grateful that a snowmobile had come this way before her. She followed the ruts, frozen hard as metal, their indents like the opposite of railway tracks.

As she walked, each exhaled breath formed instantly into a cloud filled with tiny crystals of ice that twinkled briefly before falling back to scratch against her cheeks.

She was breathing heavily, there was a slight incline at this point, and her lungs tightened in protest at the assault of cold.

She kept her pace steady and headed towards the hazy orange light.

It wasn't so far.

A few more minutes.

Nearly there.

The chain link fence around the Tomyator Weather

Station was only waist high; a symbolic barrier rather than a security measure. Out here where the world stretched away forever, people liked to erect fences around things as if to prove that they existed and to anchor them to the surface of the earth.

The gate in the fence was not locked and Irina bumped it open with her padded hip.

It was a small enclosure and she stepped into her own old footprints, just five paces, to reach the tube that housed the thermometer. She leaned in close to see the number and her breath condensed on the glass so that she had to rub it clean with her thumb before she could tell where the thin blue line stopped.

'Minus 45' she said aloud. She always said it aloud to make sure she remembered. But her words were caught by the wind and flung into the darkening sky.

She looked up to see the wind being gathered in the spinning cups, ice cream scoops, and making a whirring sound.

None of the equipment had been disturbed. Who would bother? Occasionally she'd see the perfectly precise imprint of an owl's talons, three sharp puncture marks at the front and a deeper, hooked channel pointing backwards. There were no other visitors as a rule.

But it was a requirement to check so she glanced at each of the padlocked metal boxes in turn. Then, satisfied she had performed her duty for another day, she turned towards home.

The wind was in her face on the way back into town and she drew her scarf up further to fully cover her cheeks, and pulled her fur hat lower to leave the narrowest slit for her eyes. The smoke from the chimneys pointed back in straight streaks towards the Weather Station.

It was fully dark now and she felt the strain of the walk begin to pulse in the muscles of her calves. The legacy of past journeys was counted out in sharp clicks at her ankle. Her mother had hobbled with arthritis by her age, sometimes needing a stick, so she counted herself lucky to have just the odd ache and pain to contend with.

As Libsky Street petered out, a track split left and at the end of it were the dark shapes of the utility buildings that had served the old airstrip. The kids played up there in the summer, even though the asbestos roofs had collapsed in places. They learned to drive on the ruined runway in the loaf vans that somehow coughed back into life in June after their long hibernation.

As she passed the turning, the wind twisted and blew in on itself to deliver a sudden stillness where the only sound was the synthetic squeak of her steps in the dry, hard packed snow.

A similarly wrapped shape, a man, passed by and they flicked their eyes to each other and made the smallest of nods of acknowledgement, but didn't stop to speak.

This wasn't the city. 'How are you?' was a real question in Tomyator.

If she *had* asked he would have stopped and grasped her hand.

'Worried to be honest. My wife's nephew in Minsk has announced he's a homosexual. Says he's always known. Her sisters are in uproar. I don't condemn that kind of thing you understand, I don't think they can fight it if it's their nature, but it's not a happy life is it Irina? They want me to write him a letter. A man-to-man sort of thing. Where to start?'

And it was too cold for that.

So she was thankful to be nearing home when she stepped into a dense pocket of mist and emerged, moments later, in the middle of the town square.

Her chin was on her chest to contain the remaining heat inside her coat and she kept her eyes on the swept-clean paving slabs. The pale yellows and pinks, municipal colours, were inset with smaller blue squares to create a geometric pattern. The colour scheme was intended to be cheerful she supposed, but the blocks had not weathered well and they rose up in some places and sunk in others so that it was easy to trip.

At the centre of the square, the children's slide plunged its rusted legs into a patch of concrete and the ropes of the swings were frozen rods.

Just like the children who looked, pale-faced, from the windows, they seemed to ache for summer.

The light was still on in the store and the neon sign over the entrance, 'Alexi's Essentials' beamed its backwards and upside down message onto the ground. Good, she had her purse. Picking up the milk now would save her a trip in the morning. But as she approached the rough concrete oblong she saw that the metal shutter over the door was drawn down. Through the steamy window Irina saw Alexi himself, heaving boxes onto the counter, towered over by the reluctant round-backed shape of his huge son.

He looked busy. She wouldn't disturb him.

She crossed over the narrow road that wound around the side and to the rear of the store. Little more than a track, it led down to the schoolhouse which had just two rooms; one where the little ones learned to read and to chant their times tables and the other for the teenagers.

These older children had their lessons sent by email from Yakutsk and were supervised – the mothers arched their eyebrows and made their fingers into quotation marks when they said "supervised" – by a long retired teacher who left them to their own devices and tipped suddenly into sleep and snoring several times each day.

The doctor's house, across the road, had no need of a sign and he didn't bother with appointments.

When he saw it was a patient at the door and not a visitor, he changed from his slippers into shoes and slipped the already looped and knotted tie that was hanging on the coat stand over his head, tightening it around his neck, and patting his wisps of grey hair in the mirror.

His consulting room doubled as a living room and as well as the long examination couch and a filing cabinet for patient notes, there were two chairs for he and his wife to watch television and a small table between them piled high with the collection of crossword books they ordered in specially from Moscow.

There was a carved wooden sideboard topped with a crocheted cover and displaying a radio, some heavy crystal glasses and framed photos of their three grown up children; long gone away but all doing very well and thank you for asking about them Irina.

11

He was an experienced medical man and well thought of.

She had liked the way he'd tapped her huge belly and listened thoughtfully to the sound before unwinding his stethoscope and placing it softly, like a kiss, over her heart. People approved of his gentle manner and the way he took his time. He was thorough, they said. Which more than made up for the lack of modern equipment.

His wife kept busy in the kitchen whilst he saw his patients and called cheerful comments through the serving hatch as he performed his examinations.

'You look fit to pop Irina. It must be any day now.'

In the opposite corner of the square, in front of the unoccupied motel rooms, was Lenin, holding his book with one hand and pointing East, towards the Weather Station with the other. It was a large statue for a town that was, by its own admission, much diminished these days and he looked cross to be here at all.

Visitors to the town were struck by the continuing reverence the folk of Tomyator displayed towards Lenin. Most days there would be three or four locals strolling back and forth in front of him, casting thoughtful glances in his direction.

Evidence, they thought, of the quaint backwardness of these Eastern people. They must remember to mention it when they got home. But, as it happened, the point directly in front of his extended arm offered a rare patch of good mobile signal, so people who were expecting a call tended to hang around him to wait for it to arrive.

It showed that things were not always what they seemed,

and Irina, absorbing the stares of prurience and pity from back-packers on their expensive adventure tours, took a small, superior pleasure in keeping the town's secrets from them.

But it was the four storey apartment block that dominated the square. It had twenty units and was agreed by everyone to be by far the most luxurious residence in town. Similar in quality to a block you might see on the edge of Petersburg perhaps. Or if not Petersburg then Yakutsk certainly.

Parked at the side of the building was the oil truck that had arrived from Natzar to fill up the tank for the temperamental central heating system. The engine of the truck rumbled. The driver would not dare turn it off even for a minute. What? And risk getting stuck here for God knows how long? Not likely.

Irina waved to him, and he touched his hat in reply, then she pushed the heavy swing door into the vestibule. The intercom system had been broken for years and so the door was left permanently unlocked.

She stamped her feet to loosen the compacted snow and, hesitating for just a beat, pushed through the second door and stepped into the stairwell.

It was a plunge into a thick, soupy wave of frying onions and dumplings and stews left on the burner to simmer, undercut by the sharper, elemental, odours of the metal handrails, concrete corridors and the studded rubber of the non-slip mats that were glued onto the stairs.

There were spikey high notes of the concentrated pine disinfectant that Alexi carried at the store and the softer bacterial fug of hard-to-dry washing.

The residents would not dare to open their apartment windows for months and, until then, all of their private, domestic smells seeped under the doors and rolled restlessly around the corridors of the block, looking uselessly for some way to escape.

It was so familiar as to be almost unremarkable to her but if she had found the time to think about such things, she would have recognised it as the stale smell of long marriages, resignation and sighs.

They were just one flight up, sixteen steps. She felt the sharp itch of blood returning to her toes, and at the top of the stairs she turned to the left. Their apartment was the closest to the stairwell. It would take too long to fumble for her keys and she knocked on the door instead.

Vasily, her son, pulled it open so suddenly that she stepped backwards, startled.

He had been passing she guessed, and he let it swing out of his hand so that the coat hook on the back of the door clanged against the wall. There was already a deep gash in the plaster that had exposed the raw breeze blocks beneath. Irina would definitely bring it up it with him. Not now though. Later. When he was less preoccupied.

He was staring at his Gameboy and wearing his headphones. His hair touched his shoulders these days and he had tucked it behind his ears. He didn't look at Irina or speak but turned and paced slowly, like a sleepwalker, away towards his room. His narrow shoulders hunched forward and his thin neck bent towards the console.

Irina stepped inside and closed the door, pulling off her mittens and pushing them into the pockets of her coat for safekeeping. She unbuttoned it with stiff fingers and hung it on the hook, turning her head to one side to avoid seeing the damaged wall. Why upset herself?

She brushed the frost from her hat and carried it into the living room to dry in the warm.

Vasily had already eaten. His dirty plate was on the floor and a knife, coated with butter, lay on the carpet next to it.

In her desk drawer was her ring-bound notebook and she picked it up and slid out the pen that was attached by a little leather loop to the cover. She flicked through to find her place, ran her finger down the column to align it with today's date and in her careful, even handwriting wrote, 'Minus 46.'

Two

'At least we have someone booked in today,' she said. 'So that's something.'

This was her look-on-the-bright-side voice. She set down the mug of black tea in front of Oleg and arranged the khrenovina sauce, honey, ketchup bottle, mayonnaise, dish of salt and jar of pickles into the middle of the table.

She had not meant to clatter them together, whatever Oleg might think, but she wasn't sorry that she had. Why should she apologise? It wouldn't hurt for him to notice the trouble she took to keep their home decent.

'That's better,' she said. Her fingertips were tacky from the jars and she felt disappointed with her life for a moment.

The morning would be saved if he would just look up and notice how hard she tried to be sunny. To say, 'Toast and jam. Three slices. That's what you need.' Or, 'You look tired Irina. Let me go and sort out the room. No arguing – I insist.'

If only he would ask if she felt under the weather. Not in a nasty or insulting way though, in a kind way.

But Oleg made no comment and she twisted the cup so that the handle faced him.

'He's from France.'

She wiped her fingers on her apron, hoping he would smile and say, 'A Frenchy? Oh là là.'

Then they could talk together about which part of France he might be from. They might list the cities they could think of, counting them out on their fingers. Paris of course, Marseille, Lyon. What was the name of that one where they had the famous film festival? It was on the tip of their tongue.

Not that you could knock the French on their dress sense. They'd give them that. Oleg might say something about the smart, pale blue twinset Irina had worn to that wedding they went to in Asyma. A cousin of the bride had complimented her on it and said it looked like 'something you'd see on a catwalk'. Remember?

Then they'd talk about food. They would agree – well it was common knowledge wasn't it – that the French were snobbish about their so-called cuisine. Still, someone who eats a snail would have to have a real nerve to complain about a juicy dumpling filled with rabbit. And they'd laugh about it together.

But he was silent.

His hands were clasped on the top of his bald head, pushing the skin into deep ruts between his fingers.

'We need to make a website or something,' he said.

Vasily snorted.

'Website! Do you even know how dumb that sounds? You have literally no idea how to set up a website.'

He examined the dry ends of his hair that he had clamped between two fingers. The colour was still a novelty.

Irina had unwrapped the brown paper package containing the box of dye by mistake, not noticing it was addressed to her son. The first glimpse of the embossed gold writing made her exclaim, 'Oh Oleg,' out loud, thinking, for a second, that her husband had intended to surprise her with a gift. Then she reddened, angry and embarrassed to have been mistaken but mostly disappointed in him so that she felt a kick of dislike at his stupefied expression. 'Schwarzkopf?' she said, turning the box over in her hands. 'Why did you order this?

Vasily had snatched it from her with a yell, half rage and half shame. Later he had emerged from the bathroom with his hair dyed black and a look of furious contempt for his parents that they couldn't decipher. What was his problem? Who said he couldn't dye his hair anyway? He was practically a grown man after all and could do what he wanted with his hair.

'We couldn't manage a website on our own. We wouldn't have a clue, would we Oleg? But you could help us,' said Irina to her son, tucking her hair behind each ear with a quick movement that made her look young for a second.

As a girl she had had a commonplace prettiness made up of unexceptional but regular features that sat symmetrically on a perfectly oval face. 'Yes, I suppose Irina is pretty.' The point was conceded rather than offered up.

But lacking unusually coloured eyes, a bump on her nose or lips that turned up more on one side than the other meant it was difficult for people to recall her face clearly if they tried to summon up an image of her later.

She was agreeable though and smiled easily and that had

appealed to boys. Her prettiness had not faded entirely, but was hardening year on year.

These days it was an effort to be bright, to keep a grip on her irritation, but God knows she did her best. 'Never mind,' she said, even though she did mind and when she said it she looked around to make sure her efforts to be cheery, despite everything she had to put up with, were noticed.

She reminded herself to smile, especially when she didn't feel like it, but her lips remained firmly pressed together as if to contain a complaint she knew would fall on deaf ears.

Irina looked pretty again now because she had allowed herself to hope for a moment and the hard mask had fallen away.

This was something they could work on together, as a family. A website for the motel would be their grand project and she imagined their heads close together over the kitchen table, scribbling notes, talking ten to the dozen, coming up with crazy, funny ideas late into the night. All of them too excited and full of plans to even notice how late it had become.

'You're always on the computer.'

Vasily stared at her.

'On the computer?' he said, incredulous. 'So what? What does that have to do with it?'

Irina pecked up the moist crumbs from the plastic table cloth with the tip of her finger and collected them in her cupped palm; anticipating a further slight from Vasily but pushing onwards towards it, briskly, as if it were inevitable and better to get it over and done with.

Her expectation of disdain and her submission to it was the sacrifice she offered up to the family. 'Here we go again,' she thought to herself, and often, 'I don't deserve this.' But it remained a bewildering fact that deserving didn't seem to come into it for her in a life that seemed, however she approached it, to roll from one scratchy day into the next, delivering disappointments that came as regularly and inexorably as Monday, Tuesday, Wednesday.

According to the long out-of-date magazines stacked on the counter in the coffee shop, the answer was Positive Thinking. Visualise your goals; whether it's the promotion you've been longing for or to catch the eye of that cute guy on the train...

There was some rubbish about rewiring your brain to attract happiness and reprogramming your neurons and synapses, all written in a science-y way that Irina, even though she had been precisely average at science at school, recognised as a silly piece of nonsense.

Irina licked the froth from her spoon and wondered if the writer had really meant to say that unhappy people deserved their own misery. She considered past instances of spite and her small, ordinary deceits and thought them minor in the scheme of things. It seemed a stretch to imagine that they were to blame for their struggles with the motel.

Anyway, hope was necessary to survive. What would become of them if she succumbed to misery and self-pity like Oleg?

It was unthinkable.

So she offered up her optimism, hardly even believing in

it herself, like a dog showing its belly, and she accepted the scornful kicks it earned her in return. All the time, icing up inside at the terrible unfairness of her lot.

Besides, Irina had a stubborn streak so she held on to her pride in being dutiful and in always trying her best. She knew that Oleg and Vasily depended on her to provide cheerful suggestions just as much as they despised her for them. And, in carrying on, she displayed a feminine kind of courage.

She lowered her eyes to the table in a show of submission that said please don't be too unkind and she thought, here we go again.

'I only meant that you were always so good at computer studies at school. I remember your teacher singing your praises – saying you put the others to shame, how quickly you picked it up. She said you knew more than her after a few weeks. If anyone could make a website you could.'

'Computers and websites are not the same thing.'

'But a website is on the computer,' she said.

Vasily put his head in his hands.

'Fuck me,' he said, under his breath.

Oleg slammed his palm hard onto the table, making the jars rattle again.

'Don't be a fucking smartarse,' he said, glaring first at Vasily and then at Irina. And his reddened eyes, glittering wetly through tight slits, betrayed the brutality of his hangover.

'Oh shush,' Irina said, touching him lightly on the back of his hand. 'He doesn't really mean it. I'm the first to admit I'm not as up-to-date on technology as some people.

Although your father's quite right to pull you up about your language Vasily.' She tried a small, tinkling laugh, including Vasily in its scope, to show it wasn't worth falling out over, but her husband and her son just stared at her with the same damnable expression.

'It's your own fault,' said Oleg. 'Always praising him for mediocrity, mollycoddling him. This is where it's got you. He's a useless lazy shit. He won't help you.'

Vasily's sharp elbows were on the table and he rested his chin in his hands. Unaccountably, a sly smile of triumph was pulling at the corners of his mouth. In the end, his contempt for Irina and her injured martyrdom outweighed his anger with his father. They were siding with each other.

She took a breath to compose herself – never mind – and began to gather the plates and cups together in a display of busyness to show her unconcern.

'Anyway, talking of computers, I need to borrow it Vasily. It's email day.'

'Email day,' said Vasily, coughing out a flat laugh, and then shuddering as though the sound of her voice had caused him physical pain.

The computer was in Vasily's bedroom on the small melanin desk they had bought him for his homework. How did he fit his knees under it? He had become gangly and unattractive as a teenager. It is far too difficult a thought to bear, that your own child is unattractive, ugly even, so Irina tidied up some scraps of paper and scooped a tissue into the bin instead.

She settled in front of the screen, smoothing her hair and sitting up straight. She knew they couldn't see her, of course, but this was part of her work and it was important to approach it with a professional attitude.

She typed a single letter 't' and the whole email address appeared in the box. Tanja.kuznetsov@moscowuniversity/meterolgy. ac

'Tomyator Temperatures' was the subject line and she positioned the curser, winking, at the top of the blank screen.

Irina had already opened her notebook in preparation and she began to type. She could hear the high fizz of Vasily's music leaking from the sides of his headphones and the creak of his bed signalling his impatience for her to hurry up and leave him alone.

1 February – minus 49 degrees Celsius
2 February – minus 47 degrees Celsius
3 February – minus 48 degrees Celsius

Vasily had tried to show her how, if she pressed three different keys, she could make a small 'o' that floated to the right of the number instead of writing 'degrees'. But they had to be pressed in a certain order and he performed the movement too quickly so that she had become flustered. Irina couldn't follow it so said she would just stick to the old way thank you. It was only once a month after all so didn't matter if it took her a little longer doing it like that.

Vasily had kicked the leg of the desk and gone out, slamming the door behind him.

Irina took great care to copy the figures accurately from her notebook, running one finger down the screen, with her eyes flicking back and forth between the illuminated numbers and the page.

Satisfied that she was done, she moved the mouse tentatively to point the cursor to the arrow that had to be pressed in order to send the email. She took a breath and clicked. The whooshing sound reminded her of the wind monitors at the Weather Station.

Finished for another month.

Irina did not trust the computer entirely but they were efficient in Moscow and a polite 'thank you' would usually appear in reply after a minute or two. Only then would she be satisfied that she had been successful.

The wait was longer than usual today and Irina sat watching the digital clock on the corner of the screen click from 9.04 to 9.05. 9.06 until it was 9.15 and she felt the first flutter of concern.

Could she ask Vasily to check whether she had sent the email correctly? She remembered his nasty comments at the breakfast table and folded her hands together in her lap instead.

The ping, when it came, made her start.

Hey Irina,

I'm happy to write to you after all this time. I must admit I think about you often. I imagine you up to your armpits slogging through the snowdrifts for us. I see those numbers and shiver. Bbbrrrr! You deserve a medal. Or a pay rise at least. HA HA!

Anyway, I have some exciting news for you. Next month we are digitising the service. Finally some budget has been found! We are sending an engineer to install new equipment that will transmit the temperatures and some extra useful stuff to us via a satellite. To cut a (very) long story short, you won't have to record the information manually anymore. Well it is the Twenty-first Century. HA HA!

Don't worry, you will still be paid. We need someone there to give the equipment a good kick if it plays up – only joking – don't kick it HA HA. We may not find the money to repair it until the NEXT century!!! Seriously, it's useful to have you on standby because you can report a fault or give a manual reading if there's a glitch. You never know!!!! But no more treks into the wilderness for you :).

Well I hope that news is good for you. And thanks again for all of your work over the years. You have helped keep Tomyator on the map. All warm wishes from Moscow.

Tanja

For the first time she understood the weight and significance of the expression, my heart sank. She felt the enormous muscle clench once, a great thud, and the blood rush to her fingers and toes so that they tingled. Her cheeks were stung with a sudden chill as sharp as if someone had opened a window in winter.

She blinked away the blurring of tears in her eyes.

She had never received a message from the office before.

Perhaps a Merry Christmas once or twice. What was the significance of HA HA? Perhaps the whole thing was a silly joke.

Digitising? It seemed mocking in its tone. Like a trick.

She looked down at her hands in her lap, at the veins standing up thick and green, and at each red knuckle tipped with white at its peak. She would be caught and arrested for her deception of course. It would be a scandal.

She would rather be taken away to prison than face a fine. How would they pay it for one thing? But the agony of the looks and the insinuations in the store would be too terrible to bear. She imagined the police arriving at night. They would be thickset and serious. Vasily and Oleg would watch, white-faced, as they handcuffed her and led her to their van.

But Oleg could not possibly manage the motel without her. She would have to make lists of what to buy, the makes and quantities, and provide instructions for the washing machine. She could show him how to make up the beds. She pictured his thick fingers fumbling with the fitted sheets that were a fraction too small for the mattresses.

And then she realised how utterly foolish she was being and, from long habit, she smiled. Silly, silly Irina. There would be no need to teach Oleg how to run the motel because no one would come.

It was almost a relief.

Tomyator would disappear from the guidebooks. It would be wiped off the map as if by a meteor strike. If it were no longer listed as The Coldest Continually Inhabited Town, why would anyone need to know it existed?

She twisted the chair to her left and gazed out of Vasily's window. Past the apartment block's battered grey metal bins were a fistful of wooden houses in the old style. They ran up the slope in a jagged line that marked their avoidance of the seam of granite that made sinking stilts into the ground impossible. Smoke drifted from their metal chimneys.

Beyond the houses, thirty miles or so to the East was Novirsk. Their rivalry was friendly in the main but, unlike Tomyator, they did not have the population to support a café and people who fell sick had to travel long distances to see a doctor.

The folks there would be happy with the news at least she thought. They'd been grumbling about the title for years. Someone always profits from another's misfortune. As if there were a finite amount of happiness in the world and it simply moved from place to place periodically. They would probably extend their store. They'd need a motel for all the new visitors. It would be a boost for them.

To the right of the houses, set in a small dip was the concrete bunker where the town's stores of petrol were kept. It was closed and by the entrance some discarded tyres were piled up and covered with a tarpaulin that was weighted at the corners with grey breeze blocks. There were no people to be seen or even footprints to show that they existed at all. The flapping of the sheet in the wind was the only movement.

'I thought you had so much to do,' said Oleg from the doorway. 'You're just sitting there. Gawping like a half-wit.'

He leaned over her shoulder to read the email.

'What's this?'

His hands on the back of the office chair were heavy and tipped her backwards so that only her toes remained on the floor.

'Notice the bitch doesn't say 'paid the same amount,' he said. 'Thieves.'

Irina read the message again. Should she reply? What was there to say?

She had a dull pain between her ribs and she rubbed it with the heel of her hand.

Three

The Frenchman's name was Pierre and he looked exactly as a Frenchman should; darkish and floppy-haired with a large, Gallic nose and an exaggerated sense of his own charm. He ran his fingertips across the top of the writing desk, poked his head into the bathroom and considered the view of the square with nods and smiles, checking periodically to see whether his little 'aahhs' and tilts of his head that threw his thick, side-parted hair over his eyes as an expression of satisfaction were as delightful to Irina as he imagined they must be.

She could hardly stand the sight of him and his amused poking around. She clenched and unclenched her hands inside her pockets to hide her agitation.

She had expected that it would be wonderful to meet people from other countries. She had fantasised that some of the guests would become friends and ask her to visit. At the very least they'd write to her when they returned home.

'Irina you'll never guess, it's finally happened – I won't tell you how much the IVF set us back except to say that it was more than we could afford – but anyway we're bursting with happiness. It's early days yet and we haven't even told my family but I simply had to share it with you.'

Irina would open the letters at her kitchen table and catch the faint scent of oregano and bay leaves transferred onto the paper from the fingers of writers from Spain or Greece. Hot countries featured most frequently in her daydreams.

They might tuck a photo inside the twice folded sheet and it would drop, a delightful splash of unexpected colour, showing their daughter's engagement party (remember little Eva in her giant pink snow boots) and the marvellous dancing and, oh Irina, how they wished she could have been there to see it.

She imagined herself as the hub of a network of warm thoughts that lit up like points on an illuminated globe; every envelope an invitation to intimacy.

But when it came down to it she did not enjoy meeting new people. She was awkward around strangers and even though she practised saying 'how was your journey?' in German or, 'here is your key' in English, on her way to and from the Weather Station, in company the words would not come out and she was stiff with mortification at her inability to even try. She was furious at herself for having imagined it would be any different.

The guests, if they bothered with her at all, felt the tense silences and it was obvious they thought her odd and unfriendly. She hid the phrase books she had bought under her basket of ironing and felt hot and stupid when she remembered them.

She would not need them now. Oh God. The thought of the money she'd wasted. Not just on the stupid books and cassettes but on the rugs and the framed pictures. The towels. They had forty-five towels. What would they do with them now?

She looked around the room, following Pierre's gaze, trying to see it afresh through his eyes and her heart clenched at its shabbiness. She took in the scuff marks around the walls from carelessly kicked off boots. The padded headboard had two greasy ovals imprinted on it that marked where the heads had rested as guests were reading their books.

She had loved that padded, dusky pink headboard when it was new. But its plump upholstery had lost its tone in middle age and bulged in unexpected places. Every now and then she would notice that another of the fabric-covered buttons had popped off. She searched everywhere for them, even emptying out the wastepaper baskets and picking through the sanitary bin with her rubber gloves on but never found one. Not once.

'They must flush them down the toilet.' she said to Oleg. Maybe they were worried they had damaged the furniture and took them home, fearing that Irina would demand that they pay extra. It was a mystery and it was impossible to find replacement buttons that matched, so there was a hodgepodge of repairs that added to the shabby appearance.

She regretted it bitterly. Not only the state of the rooms but the hundreds, no thousands, of hours she had wasted in her futile efforts to keep them bright and cheerful. Scrubbing the mould from around the shower doors. Standing on chairs to knock dust off the paper lampshades.

Picking their disgusting tangles of hair from the plugholes. A life wasted. Unappreciated. She twisted her small mouth as if at a sharp pain at the thought and was suddenly exhausted by it all so that she sat heavily on the hard chair.

Irina handed Pierre a laminated sheet with the instructions for operating the shower written in eight languages and indicated the section that was in French.

He raised his eyebrows, taken aback at the abruptness of her gesture, but he was an amiable chap and enough at ease with himself to persist with his friendly overtures. He was not so sensitive that he would think too much about it afterwards if the overtures had not worked.

He had already opened his suitcase on the bed and rummaged through it, scattering clothes so that a pair of underpants had fallen onto the floor. Beneath the clothes his suitcase was crammed with packets of instant noodles, chocolate bars and small, wrapped salamis.

He saw her noticing the pants and made an apologetic face and showed her his palms. She saw that his twinkling charm was from habit and understood he aimed it at all women. He didn't care that she had seen his dirty underwear because he didn't care to impress Irina in particular. She was embarrassed to have thought that he might be flirting with her at first. He was just being French, she thought, and disliked them as a race.

Outside, Pierre gasped at the feel of the air on his cheeks and, wanting to win her over because he preferred to be liked, especially by women, slipped his arm through hers and squeezed her to him. She was touched by the gesture and, just like always when she had been uncharitable or wished ill on someone who didn't deserve it, she wondered when she had become so unkind.

Even Pierre seemed un-amused by the store.

Alexi's Essentials was an ungainly oblong constructed of weather stained breeze blocks that exulted in its own ugliness. It was a squat, complacent sort of lump.

So what? its utilitarian construction seemed to say. If you don't like it…

It was the only store in town, and the only store for thirty long and treacherous miles. If the locals disliked it more than the visitors, it was because they were totally dependent on it.

NO CREDIT announced a sign screwed onto the wall.

The people of Tomyator were not the type to ask for credit in the first place so the sign felt like an insult. And what kind of impression would it make on visitors? It makes us look like freeloaders, people said unhappily. They agreed that someone should ask Alexi to take it down but couldn't decide on the best person for the job.

As the discussions gathered force they would begin to remember that they relied on Alexi to order in their favourite brand of coffee or to phone them when the newspaper they liked finally arrived, and they would fall silent.

One or two considered, privately, that Alexi did not have a license to sell alcohol, officially speaking, but, if you were in his good books…

Someone would say, you know, he probably didn't mean anything by it. They'd put their hands in their pockets and look at their boots. He was a decent enough sort of guy by and large. So the sign stayed and gave them something to grumble about periodically; a reassuring point of agreement of the type that is the essential glue of a small community.

Pierre examined the small window with narrowed eyes. It was not used to display goods. Why bother? Instead the metal racks of shelving ran in front of it and showed the backs of packets of soap powder and bottles of disinfectant rudely to the passer-by.

The shop pointed North so there was little sunlight to shine through and there was just enough of a gap between the shelves for Alexi to peer between them and keep an eye on the square, and for passers-by to see intermittent images of him moving around.

To the rear, a shipping container served as an additional storage space for the twice-monthly deliveries. Alexi had made a covered walkway between the two to keep the path free of snow.

In front of the store, Alexi had hauled out a few things in red plastic buckets to make more room inside. Bricks of butter. Some lumps of reindeer meat in cling film. Pelmeni in big clear plastic packs. The kind of items that could handle a little snow or cold.

Pierre paused to look at the Taimen, smiling at the sight of the long fish stacked frozen stiff in the buckets like baguettes.

Irina pushed open the door. The jingle of the bell was not necessary. The store already had a customer and he, and Alexi, turned to see who would be arriving.

'Pierre is visiting us from France,' said Irina. 'Be nice please. Wave. Show him our big, friendly, local smiles.'

The men chuckled and raised their hands to Pierre.

'On his own,' asked the old man and he shrugged sympathetically when she nodded. 'Is it my imagination or has it been slow at the motel this season?'

'A little,' she said.

'Delighted to meet you,' said Alexi, lifting the hinged counter to come forward and shake Pierre's hand. He smiled at him showing broadly set teeth like sticks of cheese. 'If I'd known you were coming I'd have switched around the price labels.'

The old man waiting at the counter laughed and began a loud, moist bout of coughing.

Pierre removed his gloves and unzipped a pocket, taking out a small camera. Pointing at the camera and then at the shelves, he raised his eyebrows into question marks and, having received a double thumbs up from Alexi, he proceeded to take pictures of ketchup bottles and tins of fruit.

The store stretched back further than it appeared from the front. It had two long aisles of products that were so narrow that it was impossible to pass another person without brushing against them and saying, 'oh, excuse me'.

Alexi, feeling exposed, retreated back to his position behind the counter.

He was a small, hard man with long bony hands. Irina imagined him slipping out of his brown grocer's coat at night and into his pyjamas in a single smooth movement like a hermit crab sliding into a new home.

Although he was no taller than Irina he had created an enormous son, Gregor, a year younger than Vasily, who perched on a stool staring into a small games console. No one had ever seen a wife and there was speculation – that had begun as a joke but was now hardening towards absolute, irrefutable fact – that she was a giantess.

An open bag of bright yellow corn puffs glowed at Gregor's elbow.

On the shelves behind Alexi were three brands of cigarettes, two of tobacco and various rolling papers and a selection of disposable lighters. Piled haphazardly next to them were the sundries that did not have a natural home on the main shelves or were too small to display and would get knocked onto the floor by rummaging children. Birthday candles, fuses, needles, watch batteries, tweezers. 'Etcetera, etcetera,' said Alexi with a flourish.

Lining the two aisles were shelves that rose long past head height. The top shelf required a wooden step ladder to access and Alexi left it propped against the counter so that people could take it and help themselves.

Alexi only stored items on the top shelves which were unlikely to cause too much damage if they were to fall onto a customer's head; boxes of tampons, packets of cereal, toilet paper and the like. But these were the things people bought most often. It meant that most visits to the store involved a frustrating wait to reach the item you had come in specifically to buy as another customer dragged the ladder up and down the aisle or climbed, cautiously up its creaking steps.

It was poor organisation. Everyone agreed. But it never felt like the right time to complain, not when a lady was reaching for sanitary towels, so they shook their heads and waited, ruminating about how they'd run things if they were in charge.

Pierre had passed the display of bottles of fizzy drinks the colour of anti-freeze or bile and the canned chick peas, kidney beans, broad beans and seaweed. Now his attention was caught by the fruit concentrates in bottles and cartons and the neighbouring jars of pickles and olives and peppers. He leaned backwards into the pasta to get his shot. His feet were glued in place on the sticky flooring that might once have been linoleum.

'I hope he's planning to buy something,' said Alexi. 'It's the little things in decorated tins they all like. Five to one he'll go for the caviar. Or pilchards! That's another one they can't keep their hands off.'

The old man, the only other customer, returned to his list, holding it at arm's length with trembling fingers and looking first over the top of his glasses and then tipping back his great gnarly head and turning down the sides of his mouth as he tried to focus though the bottom half of the lens.

'Varifocals they call them,' he had said to his wife over their morning coffee. 'More like 'Neverfocals.' He had thought of that joke earlier, in the bathroom, and had been looking forward to saying it. She had nodded, not seeming to be listening so he repeated it, more loudly this time. She nodded again, saying 'uh huh' but seemed distracted. He had sighed and returned to squinting at his newspaper.

'Elena's been complaining that you don't have the tortellini anymore. She's put it on the list again. Her wish list she calls it. Can't you get them in?'

Pierre had picked up a bar of Alenka chocolate and was turning it over in his hands, reverentially, as if it were a rare artefact.

Alexi scribbled 'tortellini' on a scrap of paper and held it up, to show the old man he'd made a note, before putting it in the pocket of his brown overall.

'I'll try.'

Then he continued loading the old man's purchases into pale blue plastic bags, flicking the beads on his abacus as he worked.

'She's complained about those too. And she's right. A fart would split them.'

Alexi shrugged.

'Bring your own bag then.'

'But we need bags for the rubbish. These are too flimsy.'

'I have bags for the rubbish. Here.'

He picked up a black plastic roll and went to drop it in with the purchases but the old man waved it away.

'Why should I pay? You should be able to use the free bag more than once surely.'

He lifted the blue bag a few centimetres off the counter, experimentally, hoping a split would appear and prove his point. Disgruntled that it held, he continued with his complaint anyway.

'You need to order better free bags.'

Alexi rubbed his narrow chin, in anticipation of his own favourite joke.

'Maybe you should consider taking your business elsewhere.'

The old man sighed and shook his head but he enjoyed

the joke as much as Alexi. There was such a comfort in old jokes. They were an intimacy between tough men who were more likely to waltz naked in the square than say 'I love you' to their friend. There was no need for foolish conversations when they had their jokes.

He looked at his list; his wife would give him hell if he came back without something. He squinted. Alexi was a decent enough sort really. Doing his best like everyone in the end.

Irina took off her gloves and hat in preparation for waiting. She could pick up a few things for the motel. Some bathroom cleaner.

Washing powder. She knew exactly how much was in her purse without having to check.

She had emptied the bag from the vacuum cleaner so many times that the seam had disintegrated and there was more black tape than there was bag. It puffed out exactly as much dust as it sucked up these days. This month she really would have to buy a new one.

She looked around bleakly. The thought of choosing a new vacuum cleaner bag exhausted her.

When she and Oleg had first bought the motel and were full of plans she had ordered a huge box of miniature soaps and two-hundred shampoos in tiny bottles with gold screw cap lids and a gold crest printed onto the clear plastic. The smell was heady and delicious and the shampoo oozed out thickly like melting caramel. But he was right, they were far too expensive really and they agreed they weren't making the money to justify it. The rentals were hardly enough to cover the loan in truth.

So now she refilled the empty miniatures from the five litre bottles of shampoo that Alexi stocked in the store – a sticky job – and the bottles had been rinsed so many times that only the odd flake of gold remained on them.

She thought about the engineer arriving in three days with a sick lurch and, having picked up the giant bottle of Shamtu, replaced it on the shelf.

'Touch it and you have to buy it. It's a new rule,' said Alexi. 'Your young friend there owes me 8,000 Roubles so far.'

'You should charge an entrance fee,' said the old man. 'You're a big attraction.'

He was reluctant to launch himself into the weather and didn't have much to do at home so fussed with his bags for a while before turning to Irina and giving her a frank up and down look.

She had blondish hair and it curled either side of her face to the level of her chin in a style that the younger women liked. What did they call it? A bob. That was it. Not bad looking. Bit skinny round the chops but not bad. She was mid to late forties he supposed and she had an elasticity around her chin that signalled the onset of jowls. She had an upright brittleness. She smiled occasionally but wasn't what you'd call cheerful. The way she fiddled with her wedding ring – there was a nerviness to her.

She was not sturdy like his own wife but she was not weak. He knew that.

'How are things Irina?' he said. 'Oleg keeping alright?'

He made a gesture of drinking, tipping his fist towards his mouth with his thumb extended.

'Oh he's fine,' said Irina. 'Much better in fact. The layoffs were a blow for everyone but we're managing.'

The old man nodded. 'It must be two years since the heating plant was automated. That's a long time to be idle for a young man.'

'Young compared to you, certainly,' said Alexi, leaning over the counter to jab him in his well-covered ribs. 'Why do you think we're always so thrilled to see you? You make us feel like teenagers. It's really very energising.'

The old man glared at Alexi and waved the comment away, delighted by the attention.

'He has a few things planned, said Irina. 'Plus he's obviously got the motel upkeep to manage. He's been talking about a website to drum up trade. It's not something I would have thought of but he's always been more entrepreneurial than me.'

The old man scratched his chin. He had never seen Oleg lift a finger at the motel. The burden was left entirely to his wife. And that scrawny boy of theirs wasn't much better.

Four

'Oh my God! I'm so sorry it's so bloody late,' the engineer said. She pulled off her mitten and thrust out her hand to Irina to shake hands like a man.

'There was a problem getting the equipment off the plane and then the car that came had no trailer so we had to run round making a gigantic fuss to find one before the airport closed. You know? But I'm sorry to get you up just to see to me.'

Irina turned away to deflect her loud chatter and began to smooth the bedspread into place. She could not bear to look at her. She blew her nose for something to do and threw the tissue into the wastepaper bin, then retrieved it and put it in her coat pocket.

'It doesn't matter.'

'It does matter. Poor you. It's the middle of the night. I'm the worst guest in the world.'

'You're not the worst guest,' said Irina. Why would this woman assume that? She didn't know the first thing about the kind of guests Irina had to deal with or the trouble they caused her.

But the woman didn't care to listen. She continued with

her loud apologies. Despite her pretence at being flustered and out of sorts, she hung her showy, bright yellow jacket on the back of the door and rolled her suitcase under the window briskly. She was someone who was used to making herself at home in new places and she touched the thermostat and the back of the chair, even placing her hand on Irina's back lightly as she passed her to move about the room.

It was disconcerting. Irina had the sense she should keep her eyes on her, like you'd watch an unpredictable toddler in case they put their finger in a door hinge or swallowed a penny.

The engineer bent forward suddenly, keeping her legs straight and touched her fingertips on the floor, bouncing slightly in place.

She groaned.

'The Road of Bones. They're not kidding are they? It nearly did me in too.'

Her voice was muffled. Her blond hair hung down past her knees and Irina saw that it was dark underneath and tangled and greasy at the roots.

When she stretched upright again she put her hands on her narrow hips and hula hooped. The white sheen of frost nip had disappeared from her nose and cheeks and she was pinkly cheerful.

'Short hamstrings,' she said. 'You'd be amazed the impact they have on your back. Everything's connected in the end isn't it?'

Irina opened her mouth but couldn't think of anything to say and closed it again, feeling dull. Not that the woman gave a damn about her feelings.

She looked around the room with the entitled complacency of someone who has never suffered a real misfortune in their life and who puts that fact down to their own clever choices, rather than a run of good luck.

Irina saw that she was entirely at home inside her long, over educated face.

She could afford her self-assurance for now. You wait, thought Irina. You're what, thirty-five? You'll see.

She was insufferable. She hoped she would die in the night. She held her teeth tightly together to make sure the unpleasant thought was contained. She examined the idea to see whether she really meant it and found that she did but was interrupted in testing it further by the engineer dropping down onto the bed.

The woman bounced vigorously and tested the springs with her two outstretched hands.

Irina winced. No wonder the mattresses were in such a desperate state.

'So is the hotel yours?' she said.

'Mine and my husband's. Just five rooms. It's a motel rather than a hotel.'

The correction was important and Irina delivered it with a stiff, almost pitying shake of the head to show her superior knowledge. Irina wanted the woman to know that she understood perfectly well that hotels in cities were much grander affairs. She wasn't a bumpkin like some of the people here.

'Good for you,' said the engineer and she jumped up from the too soft bed, wincing and saying 'ouch' and rubbing the small of her back. She examined a black and white print of the town square, taken in the boom times, with her fingers linked behind her head.

Next to it was an illustrated map of the town with the main buildings shown as drawings that indicated their function. There was the food store, the coffee shop, a guest house, an outdoor clothing store, the school, doctor's surgery, the vivid green cross of a pharmacy and a Post Office. Around the edges of the town there was the stretch of the tundra with reindeer and their herders and walruses swimming fatly in the Siberian sea, all smiling and out of scale like the pictures in a children's book.

The engineer studied it carefully.

The prints had been on sale at Alexi's store twenty years ago – no one could remember who provided them – someone from the tourist board he guessed, shrugging. Irina had put up framed versions in all five of their motel rooms.

But now the Post Office and the bar and most of the other amenities had closed and she didn't know how to explain their absence to an American.

If one more person asks me where the bar is, just one more person, I'll take these damn pictures down she thought. But when she lifted the first one off the wall it left a clean square, and she didn't have another picture to hang in its place, or the energy to repaint the walls, although goodness knows they needed it.

It seemed awful to her that every action, however inconsequential, must always form part of a chain of events. There was a remorselessness to her life that meant nothing she did ever seemed to be finished satisfactorily.

She longed to look around and sigh and say, there, that's done.

So there they stayed to taunt her and she clenched her teeth together in unhappy anticipation whenever visitors looked at them.

Like almost everyone who visited, the engineer placed her finger on the town and tracked backwards along the winding cartoon road back to Yakutsk and the airport, complete with illustrated plane, calculating the distance, pleased with how far away she was.

Irina recognised that look; congratulating themselves on their daring. Oh look at me. See how bold and out of the ordinary I am. A real adventurer. I'm in the middle of nowhere. Now this was living, they seemed to say, and they were horribly and predictably pleased with themselves.

The woman opened and closed the drawer of the small writing desk before running her fingers over the crocheted cloth that overlaid it.

Irina had arranged a packet of four biscuits, three sachets of Nescafe, paper tubes of sugar and tea bags on the tray next to the electric kettle. In addition there were three plastic packets of milk that she hoped were still good.

'They're long-life, not immortal,' Alexi had said, when she complained about the last batch, but he changed them without charge anyway. He was good like that.

She felt ashamed of them suddenly and of the stale biscuits and the cheap plastic kettle and mostly of their careful, fussy arrangement on a paper doily on the tray. How pointless she must seem to this woman.

'Here is your towel,' said Irina, and the woman took it,

smiling at the awkwardness of the exchange. When she smiled her eyes, which were long and slanted down at the sides, were almost squeezed shut.

'There is hot water between seven and nine tomorrow morning.' She pointed at the bathroom door. Stupid, stupid Irina. Where else would the hot water be?

'Well,' said the engineer, burying her long nose in the towel and sniffing noisily, 'I shall look forward to it.'

Irina pulled up her hood and began to re-button her coat.

'I'm truly sorry,' said the engineer. 'I promise faithfully to be no trouble for the rest of my stay.' And she placed her right hand over her heart.

'It's no trouble,' said Irina. 'I'm only across the square. We have an apartment in the block.' Her comment had a foolish, boastful tone and she regretted it immediately.

The engineer went to the window, pulled apart the curtains, made a tunnel around her eyes with her hands and pressed it to the glass to peer across the foggy precinct.

The apartment block loomed. She scrutinized the four storey building, painted the same dark green as mildew, with a slightly pitched roof and regular rows of small, unadorned windows. It was busy with drainpipes, satellite dishes and overhead electricity wires.

Each apartment had a small balcony enclosed with glass and in one, where a dim light shone, a woman stood, smoking and looking at herself in a hand mirror.

The engineer's jeans had a pattern of white stitching around the back pockets and a small metal tag with a logo that Irina didn't recognise.

'A girl after my own heart,' she said. 'I know some people don't mind roughing it but I'm in your camp – proper heating, running water. I can't imagine doing without. Could you?'

She rubbed at the glass where her breath had steamed it over.

'Which one is yours?' said the engineer. 'I won't feel so lonely if I know you're in there.'

'We're on the first floor, second balcony from the right,' said Irina. She frowned at the woman's back.

You don't seem like the lonely type, she thought.

Five

The engineer had washed her hair and pulled it back, still damp, into a ponytail. Steam rose from her head.

Her eyes were baggy underneath and scratched round the rims in red but she said she'd had no trouble dropping off. The opposite. She'd slept amazingly, wonderfully. She smiled at Irina over her shoulder, satisfied that a good night's sleep was quite the achievement.

Irina shifted her weight onto her good ankle and clenched her teeth.

'Right. Expert opinion needed. Is the walk this long?' the engineer said, crouching down and lifting a hiking boot to show Irina. 'Or this long?' In her other hand she held a larger, sturdier boot, just short of knee high with fur linings and complicated buckles and fastenings.

Irina knew at once that both pairs had been foolishly expensive.

'Those,' said Irina, pointing at the heavier boot, not giving a damn which boots she wore. But then she added, 'Always wear the warmest you have,' because she clung to the idea of herself as a good person, a kind person, and it shook her up sometimes how easy it was to slip into a kind of contempt for others and when that happened she feared she would lose her old self, the real Irina, forever.

Even so, she burned with impatience while the engineer dressed for the walk across the square to the café. And she did not tell her that the too tight socks she had pulled on would slow her circulation and make her feet colder and not warmer.

It was snowing, not heavily but with a nasty malevolence, and the sharp spray of ice was made more vicious by a wind that hurled it violently toward them first but then ricocheted the shards off the paving stones so their faces were stung twice.

The engineer swayed; it had been calm when she had arrived and she was almost knocked over by the unexpected blasts this morning. She steadied herself against the door frame quickly though and without comment and tucked her head down to shield her eyes.

She didn't make a big fuss at least. That was something.

The café was on the opposite side of the square, no more than a hundred metres from the motel room door, but Irina steered them to the left to walk around the edges and hug the shelter of the buildings rather than cutting across its centre.

These were the little tricks she'd picked up over the years. Small habits that saved a precious remnant of heat for a few seconds more, or made a task a fraction easier or less dangerous to complete.

She rarely thought about it in those terms because when she did she realised that her life was a series of small survival techniques and she would wonder how it had come to this. So she pushed the thought away and imagined herself elsewhere; wearing a straw hat and eating an apple cake in a meadow. Or turning the pages of a book on the steps of a museum.

The café was really an ordinary two-storey house wooden house, raised up on stilts, but the small domestic windows on the lower level had been removed and replaced with a large pane of glass, crudely, as a child might saw a hole in the front of a cardboard box to make a shop to play with.

Zeena stood in the window as usual. It was steamy and just showed a blurred suggestion of her narrow body, but she had cleared a clean oval to peep through and her face, topped with a fuzz of red hair like the scribble on a child's drawing, showed in sharp focus through the hole.

'Any new bookings?' Zeena mouthed, pointing towards the motel, whenever Irina passed by the window until Irina could hardly stand it.

She, her husband and their four irregularly featured children lived in the cramped rooms on the first floor but when there were no customers, the children clattered untidily down the narrow stairs and spread out across the three small round tables, surrounded by chairs, to bicker with each other and snatch at the others' drawings or toys.

They had identical red rings around their mouths from excessive licking but each had a unique feature such as a gummy eye or a permanently dripping nose.

Irina was repulsed by their sickly, slack-faced, pallor and their stringy hair but it gave her an unpleasant feeling to dislike children for their looks so she had made an effort to

51

learn their names and to get to know them. She addressed them with a frantic, compensatory, cheerfulness.

The girls did not like her. They were not as stupid as they looked. They recoiled from her bright questions about school or what they were drawing and so she thought them ill-mannered as well as plain. She would have liked to slap their grey faces sometimes and that urge, when it sprang into her mind, made her shudder.

They were two sets of twins born ten and a half months apart which meant that currently Zeena had four seven-year-old girls to look after. A situation sufficiently unusual that a few years earlier a reporter from the Siberian Times had come and taken their photograph and written a folksy article about them. Zeena had framed it and put on the café wall.

The café steps had been swept clean, for once, and Irina led the way, holding onto the wooden rail to steady herself against the wind.

Inside, three mountainous, craggy-faced women from the Sable Farm with stones for eyes ate their cakes rapaciously as if it were the first time they had tasted something sweet. They wore their fur hats. It was not cold inside the café but very cramped and Zeena did not keep on top of the cleaning so there was nowhere to put them down without them becoming sticky or being trodden on.

They turned to look at the newcomers without pausing in their eating and the engineer smiled broadly and raised her hand and gave a friendly wave. 'Howdy,' she said. The women stared at her for a moment, before returning, as one, to the important task of eating.

'They hate me already,' whispered the engineer to Irina, clutching her arm and grimacing. 'Under five seconds. A personal best.'

She didn't really care of course. It was all a joke to her. Irina saw that other people's opinions didn't matter much to the engineer and she envied her for it and despised her at the same time.

Zeena had run from her place at the window to stand behind the grubby glass display case, straightening her apron. She wore thick red lipstick, a mad colour, that clashed unpleasantly with her hair and she had put on her cardigan inside out.

'Welcome,' she called in a voice intended to be gay but revealing instead a life-or-death desperation undercut with a timorous, simpering gratitude that the two had come in at all.

Sometimes Zeena's chin would wobble and her eyes would glisten with tears for no reason. Irina thought it pathetic and depressing. She longed to be somewhere else but realised, with a pang of panic, that she couldn't think where that particular place might be. Not at the apartment with Oleg for sure. Where could she go? She was washed over with a yearning to escape this bleak, stuck, feeling; homesick for somewhere she had never been.

Zeena pointed at the cakes. Her hand trembled, 'The Polygot for the meringue enthusiast, a very good choice. The Medovik turned out well today too, if I do say so myself.'

'Go for the Medovik,' said one of the women seated at the table, craning her thick neck around to look at the engineer. 'It has custard rather than sour cream. We prefer it like that don't we girls.'

She sported a little of the custard at the corner of her mouth by way of proof. The women were not unfriendly after all; they had been weighing up the pros and cons of a response and deducing that this woman must be a Russian rather than a foreigner, considered her worth the effort.

Everyone in town would know of her arrival by nightfall.

'Four weeks of this and you'll have to roll me home,' said the engineer.

'Ooo four weeks?' said Zeena flushing. 'I provide lunch and dinner. All kinds of soups and stews. In flasks if you're out and about. Anything you fancy. Versatility is my hallmark.'

'Four weeks?' said the large woman at the table to her friends – she had lived in Tomyator for her entire life – 'What on earth will she find to do for four weeks?'

The engineer chose two slices of the honey cake and ordered coffees for them both. Zeena flapped them away with her tea towel and announced importantly that she would deliver everything to them direct.

At the table, the engineer propped her chin on her hand. She smiled at Irina, showing all her teeth, in the open-mouthed, unguarded way of people who are confident they will be liked.

'Now Irina, I'm going to ask for a favour,' she said and Irina stiffened, already resentful that this woman assumed that the answer would be yes. She ached to say no. She gathered herself to say no, firmly, and jutted out her small chin in preparation. She would not be taken advantage of.

'I'm after a person, preferably muscular and male, to bring some of the heavier equipment out to the weather station. And I'll need a hand actually setting up a base, that sort of thing. You must know absolutely everyone Irina. I'm depending on you entirely for a reliable recommendation.'

Irina thought of Vasily at home, lying limply in bed. They could do with the extra money. She was sure the engineer would pay. But she ached to delay the work. So she nodded brusquely and said she would have to think about it for a while, then she'd ask around. At least she hadn't jumped to her request and she felt it a small victory.

Zeena brought the cakes and coffees tremulously on a tray, made a deep curtsey and said 'Bon appetit,' in a high, sing-song voice before backing away from them and sliding back behind the counter.

The engineer clamped down a smile at Zeena's oddness, including Irina in her look.

'I'm dying to know more about you Irina. I would be entirely unsurprised to find you harbouring secrets of some kind.' She actually winked over the rim of her cup. 'Tell me about your husband. Is he handsome?'

Irina reached for a paper napkin and folded it, pressing it to her lips although she hadn't yet eaten any of her cake. It was a prim gesture and deliberate. She intended it to signal her affront.

The directness of the question put her in mind of something a child might say. So she responded as one might to a child, with a non-answer in a breezy tone that suggested they would be indulged just this once, but no more of this nonsense would be tolerated.

'I don't know. I thought so once I suppose.'

Her voice was clipped and precise.

She loaded one less sugar than she would have liked into the coffee and when she looked up, the engineer had fixed her pale blue eyes on her and held her gaze, refusing to look away until she continued. Her expression was unusually frank and curious. Irina searched it for mockery but found none.

Irina folded her arms and rested them on the table, before noticing its stickiness and lifting them up again sharply.

'He's middle-aged and bald and fatter than he used to be but he has nice eyes if he smiles.'

'I was sure he would be handsome,' said the engineer.

Irina picked off some jam from an elbow crossly.

'Why would he be?'

'Well, couples are usually equally attractive in my experience and you're attractive so I just assumed. Perhaps he's still handsome but you're immune to it from repeated exposure.' She took a bite of cake. 'Like chickenpox. What do you think?'

Zeena's cake was as good as had been promised and the engineer twisted around in her chair and said 'mwah' loudly at the same time as she kissed the tips of her fingers.

'Oh stop it,' said Zeena, flapping her tea towel at the engineer and looking pleased.

'Our wedding photographer blew up one of the pictures he took to an enormous size, life-sized probably, and put it in his window on an easel. I suppose he thought we were a good-looking couple. Or maybe it was just a good picture.

Anyway, it was there for years, people recognised us from it sometimes in the street. We were like minor celebrities in Yakutsk.'

Irina touched her neck. The skin had become papery and criss-crossed with lines recently. She wondered what Oleg would say about her looks these days.

'Ha! I knew you weren't from here.'

Irina pressed her lips hard together and realised, with some surprise, that she no longer considered herself an incomer and had become defensive about the town. She bristled at the criticism the remark implied.

'We're both from Yakutsk. Oleg's an engineer too. Heating though rather than your kind of work.'

Useful work you silly girl, she thought, with a satisfying twinge of spite.

'I knew I was right. City girls like you and me have an aura. It means we can seek each other out.'

Irina gulped her coffee quickly, in irritation, and it burnt her tongue. So that serves you right then she thought. It left a stale, roughened taste of burnt toast and dust in her mouth.

She supposed the engineer meant her observation to be some kind of a compliment but it made her feel out of place here in Tomyator. An unanchored outsider. A fraud.

'So why did you come?'

Irina looked down at her plate. It had more than one chip and a smear of old grease around the rim.

Her habit was to be careful about the information she revealed about herself. It was easier to say as little as possible and leave people to draw their own conclusions.

They made their minds up in their own way anyway. Even it was never fair or true.

She lifted a forkful of cake and, just as it drew level with her mouth, she noticed a long red hair poking from the sponge. Irina hesitated, but she was damned if she was going to give the engineer another excuse to sneer at the town, so she closed her eyes, pushed the fork into her mouth and swallowed hard.

The un-chewed cake travelled down her throat in a large lump so that her eyes watered slightly but the hair stuck stubbornly on the back of her tongue, tormenting her.

Why had they come?

'His company suggested it. There was a new heating plant and they wanted him to take on a management role. The pay was good, they helped us with the apartment so we had some spare money and we bought the motel.'

She took another sip of coffee, smaller this time, to try to dislodge the hair.

'Things were on the up. So everyone said. They'd found a new seam at the diamond mine in Sahuk district and this was the nearest town. There were plans to open up the American landing strip from the war so Tomyator would have its own airport again.'

Irina put down her fork. She had tumbled out more of the story than she had intended. She preferred not to think about that decision if she could help it and she was surprised at how easily she had been coerced.

She felt the woman's eyes still on her, pressing her.

'Oleg said it was too good to turn down.'

'I knew it. You're an adventurer,' said the engineer,

reaching across the table and squeezing her forearm.

She knew this. She knew that. It was infuriating and Irina pressed down a violent urge to hurl the boiling coffee in her face. Instead she jutted out her chin again, determined to be obstructive but too conditioned to passivity and politeness to find a response that adequately expressed her anger with this woman's presumptions.

She twisted her mouth and gave a small, sharp shake of her head.

'Sorry, but you're wrong. I'm the opposite. It didn't feel like a risk or I wouldn't have agreed to it. Vasily, my son, he was a toddler. I wouldn't have risked it,' she said again.

'And then...' said the engineer.

Oh, it was too much.

All three of the women at the next table had stopped eating and were sitting in silence, the better to listen in to a new conversation. Irina lowered her voice so that the engineer had to lean forwards slightly, and push her hat up and away from her ear to hear her.

'Nothing exciting to tell if that's what you were hoping for,' she said. Her voice had a sour tone. As if she was very pleased to report that her life story was of no interest at all to anyone, thank you very much.

'We came and things were good for a few years. The motel did a good trade with the mining men and all the construction companies. The heating plant was expanding. We were optimistic I suppose. And then the diamond mine didn't live up to its promise. No one bothered to tell us what the problem was of course. Something about it being too difficult to work – I don't know. After a while it was closed altogether. The airstrip project was abandoned. Everyone went away.'

She thought about her first trip to Tomyator.

On the train first. Four hours on an ancient clanking rust bucket that stopped at places so small that, aside from a rough raised concrete platform, there was no sign of life at all. No waiting room or ticket office. No officials. No one got on or off. The train rocked on its wheels as it waited and the wind swept freely across a vast and unvarying landscape of rough grasses washed in grey greens. It slipped over low hummocks until it bashed up against the side of the train, angrily, surprised at meeting a barrier.

Then they reached Oskanyon.

It was the end of the train line and had a stuck-up, self-important air as a result. Oskanyon didn't consider itself a staging post; you had arrived. The driver jumped down onto a proper platform with a waiting room lined with hard red plastic benches and stood with some other men huddled in their coats. They looked through the greasy window, with a despicable disdain, at the twenty or so passengers who got off, filed past the ticket office and dispersed, it seemed, to the winds.

A filthy man with a built-up shoe approached them, slyly, and asked them if they wanted to buy a watch and when Irina said, 'no thank you', he spat onto the platform near their feet.

Irina and Oleg followed the backs of the departing people through the ticket office and into the town. The station was set amongst a collection of ugly, low rise buildings along a too wide main street that included a small supermarket, big enough for there to be a centipede of trollies by the entrance but with only one till for payment. So that was the measure of it.

There was a garage with a repair shop and three rusty fuel pumps, a two-storey office building with a sign that read Expo Minerals. There was a smell of metal and grease in the air. Irina thought of the word 'anvil'.

There was a Post Office with a cash machine blinking in the wall and a small shop displaying sets of pans and mops in its smeared window. Next door the headless mannequins wore coats and trousers that reminded her of the fashions of her childhood and delivered a jolt of surprise that time had passed so quickly and now she was grown up and married. Oddly, and she remembered this moment so vividly, just as she was thinking about being married, she noticed a shop selling wedding dresses. Of all things.

Further along the road, past where the pavement had run out, was a cluster of warehouses; each with a single shutter like a giant mouth. They were closed up and silent. Was it lunchtime? Irina had lost track of time, but the gaggle of forklift trucks scattered around the entrance spoke of their usual industry.

Between the buildings Irina could see a straggle of houses, wooden framed and set, belligerently it seemed, with their backs or sides turned deliberately to their neighbours, stretching no more than a kilometre from the centre. Beyond them, the grey sky and the grey ground merged so there was no horizon.

The town had an unfriendly feeling to her.

A blue bus, with perhaps twenty seats, idled as the driver dozed inside with his cap pulled down over his eyes. The destination plate on the front was blank. She supposed everyone except them knew where it was going.

'This must be the place,' said Oleg, nodding towards the garage. He was trying to be confident to cover up his fear that this would all be a terrible mistake and she would blame him. He was careful to avoid Irina's eyes so that he could hide his doubts from her. So they crossed the broad, slush-filled road, looking right and left for cars that didn't appear and holding hands to give each other comfort that it would be alright. She squeezed his hand to signal that she had faith in him and not to worry. Everything would work out for the best as long as they had each other.

At the garage, Oleg shook hands with their driver and followed him into the heated repair shop to climb into a jeep. It had one door that was a different colour to the rest of the car and ripped seats repaired with thick black tape. The glass in the rear view mirror was held in place by two looped rubber bands.

'You should worry about what's coming up, not what's behind you,' the driver said when he saw her noticing it. He was the kind of man who found it arousing to scare a woman.

His hands on the wheel were lined with black scars where oil had got into his cuts and the skin had healed over the top of them.

They had looped out of the garage, past the sleepy bus and were out of the town within moments and Irina turned to watch it recede with a sick feeling, as if she were leaving her childhood home for the first time.

Oleg had regained his enthusiasm for the trip by now, sorting out the car had been weighing on his mind, and, sitting in the front seat next to the driver he gave excited, quick looks towards the man that made him seem childish and pathetic to Irina.

He looked over his shoulder to her, nodding with pleasure and she forced herself to smile back at him, to please him, consoling herself that at least the company was paying for this. That was something at least. It would be an adventure if nothing else and they didn't have to move to Tomyator if they thought it wouldn't suit them.

Plus it was warm in the car and the jolts in the road were cushioned by the great, soft bounces of the suspension well enough. She would try and focus on the positives.

She looked out of the window at the scrubby vegetation and tried her hardest to consider it wild and magnificent. The ugly, scrawny bushes were blown into paperclip contortions by the wind and she wondered at their pointless resistance to it. Every few miles a small, twisted tree with blackened branches clutched at the air.

She was struck with a silly thought. How lonely to be a tree here. And then her eyes filled with tears at the idea of Vasily back in Yakutsk with Oleg's mother and him crying for her, not knowing where she was.

It wasn't a wholly unpleasant feeling though, this upsurge of yearning to put her arms around her child and to hold him and kiss him and stroke his feathery hair. To give him comfort. She touched the wetness in her eyes with the tips of her fingers and felt that there were proper fat tears ready to roll down her cheeks if she let them. Twenty-three was young to be tied down with a kid these days – all her friends had hinted at it – but they had not experienced this maternal surge and she felt a pleasing prick of superiority at her maturity. Her life had entered a new phase.

She'd tried to explain it to Oleg that night in bed; how some kinds of sadness made you feel fuller in your heart but others emptied everything inside you away, but he was irritated with her and said, 'It would have been crazy to bring him Irina. He'd have screamed his head off the whole time.'

He had missed the point and she was cross with him and could not push away the doubts that played at the edges of her consciousness that Oleg thought differently about things than she did. Or at least didn't think about them as much. They went to sleep without kissing goodnight and her unhappiness then was not in the least bit noble or stirring.

They had passed through a few clusters of houses, too small and formless to be called villages but each with its own bus stop, and then there were no more.

At first Irina tried to repurpose her anxiety over this journey into excitement of a kind. She scanned the horizon searching for some interest that she could remark upon; a building perhaps, or a group of trees on a ridge. But there was nothing to see. The unrelenting sameness of the landscape began to scare her with its size and indifference to her, and to them, in their tiny toy car bouncing along its unyielding surface. She felt they might fly off and into the air at any time and disappear and, if they did, surely no one would ever find them again.

A bird, some sort of hawk, tracked them for a while, hovering just ahead of the car and she wondered how small they would seem to it. Like prey.

Everything became too small or impossibly far away to understand and as she looked up at the bird and then to the endless stretches of the plains she struggled to comprehend the distances and was washed over with a shuddering wave of agoraphobia. Looking out of the window frightened her and so she tried to interest herself in the details of the inside of the car.

She kept her eyes on Oleg and the man who talked together in monotone voices of inconsequential things to do with cars and engines. She looked at the miles ticking by too slowly on the counter on the dashboard, and at the discarded polystyrene cups rolling back and forth quietly at her feet, and she dared not look outside for a while.

The road was good in parts and she would settle back in her seat and say to herself, 'come on Irina, it's not really so bad'. Then, for no reason she could understand and without warning, the asphalt would melt away and they would find themselves bucking over rocks that bounced the car so violently that she imagined her teeth being jolted out of their sockets.

When the road was at its worst the men had talked, in a competitive way to show their toughness and experience of the world, of the ten thousand men, or thereabouts, who had died – frozen, starved or worked to death, to make this road and of their crushed and broken bones mixed in with the rocks and mud to make up its surface.

Thereabouts? She was horrified by this new side of Oleg. Irina held on to the back of his seat to steady herself as they bucked brutally over these dead men's broken bodies and she was sickened by it all.

They passed a boulder that someone had marked with an X in white paint.

'This is half way, folks,' said the man, as though it were a good thing, but Irina put her hand to her mouth to cover a small cry, because it meant they were as far away from the safety of people and a town as it was possible to be. Now that it was too far to go back, she urged the car to go forwards.

It was so very far, and the mountains, when they rose up, were not dramatic, just bulky and in the way.

She supposed they were mountains. The cloud was so low that they may have been hills. They weren't much to look at anyway and by now Irina didn't really care one way or the other.

Whatever they were, the road builders had lost patience with their meanders around these stubborn black and lead-grey granite roadblocks and, in places, had simply blasted a wedge from around the base of black cliffs. It meant they were travelling in a rough tunnel that was open on one side.

Irina feared the crash of rocks from above as much as a precipitous fall into the churning rivers in the valleys below.

But worst of all were the hours that came later, when the

road lay flat over a white landscape, stripped of points of reference, that unrolled pointlessly in every direction.

This was the slowest part of the journey. They travelled at twenty kilometres an hour, and then fifteen, and sometimes at ten.

She hated the way the car crawled, as if it were reluctant to arrive. Irina didn't believe in bad omens or jinxes but the horrible crawling of the car seemed to signal something to her that she could not have put into words.

Every few minutes, the road would simply vanish under shifting tides of snow. Irina clenched the ripped seats with her fingers and tensed her thighs as the jeep inched forward tentatively until the road reappeared, a little to the left or the right of where it had been before.

This is hell on earth she thought.

As the white sky began to darken down and the headlight beams became shapes with hard edges, the driver clapped Oleg on the shoulder and jerked his head to the right.

'I call this the pussy test. You're not a pussy are you Oleg?'

The men said harr harr together in gruff, rumbling voices and Oleg banged his hands on the dashboard to make a drumroll in a way she'd never seen him do before, so that he seemed a stranger to her, and she felt unspeakably lonely.

The driver pulled the wheel to the right and lurched off the side of the road and down, crunching across shale before driving onto a wide, featureless plain. The man tapped the compass on his dashboard and pushed his hat

back on his head the better to concentrate. He licked his lips with a purplish tongue as he turned to glance at Irina.

'Brought your bikini?'

It wasn't a plain at all but a frozen lake and they were bowling across it. Irina could hardly bear the thought of the tumult of deep water banging frantically on the ice from beneath and her throat became tight and constricted as if she were already drowning.

It must only have been two or three minutes before they began to climb the shallow incline that signalled their arrival at the other side. She was relieved for a moment and then infuriated. The lake had not been that large and it could not have saved them much time in driving across it. It was merely an act of bravado intended to impress Oleg.

They'd been on the road for over four hours now. It seemed an impossibly long way to travel without seeing a single person.

The driver rubbed his thumb and forefinger into his eyes and blinked rapidly to keep himself alert. He stretched his arms out rigidly on the wheel and shifted in his seat to ease his back. There was only an hour or so to go and he didn't want to stop.

They wound relentlessly forwards through the black night in a thick silence. Once they saw the glint of eyes from the side of the road. 'Was that a wolf do you think?' asked Oleg, but the driver shrugged and said he didn't know. He was tired of Oleg and Irina, and of this journey now too.

A little later the man had laughed, in a sneering way, at Irina's scream when they had sheered suddenly sideways

and a back wheel spun over a hidden ditch. Oleg, caught between his concern for her and his need to display his bravery, hesitated and then laughed too. He had sided with the man against Irina and she became hot and angry at his disloyalty.

How could she have married a man who was so foolish and easily impressed? He was a coward. He tolerated seeing her afraid because it made his meagre reserves of courage seem greater by comparison.

It made her hate him a little, for the first time, and she sat for the rest of the trip with her face turned to the black window where she could examine the two vertical frown lines between her eyebrows and wonder if she would look like that all the time when she was old.

It was too tiring to maintain so fierce an anger for a long time and she was already exhausted. She began to consider instead, when and how he would say sorry and if he would truly mean it. After a while, she began to look forward to it.

At that time though, when she had been angry, she had been preparing to say she didn't like the apartment to hurt him and that she would not agree to the move. But it was brand new and she had loved the kitchen with its modern stove that lined up perfectly with the rest of the worktop, and the way all of the hinges for the cupboards were hidden neatly inside the doors, and the drawers did not need a yank to unstick them.

There were two big bedrooms and Oleg paced out a space under the window where Vasily's crib would fit perfectly and stretched out his arms to show how much room he would have to play.

A balcony too. What a bonus. It was accessed from the living room and was big enough to fit two garden chairs and was entirely enclosed by glass. A real sun trap the woman from the agency said.

This apartment had a place for everything. The ordered regularity of the fitted cupboards, and the toilet that had a neat plastic handle for flushing rather than the chain they had at home, was soothing and so comfortable that it seemed enough to cancel out the unpredictable terrors of the outdoors.

Oleg had watched her listening to the woman from the agency with a small smile, knowing she was being convinced, and he was pleased. They were still newly married, less than three years, and checked carefully with each other. 'Do you agree? Are you sure? Don't say yes just to please me.' It remained important to them at that time that they were in harmony.

Even then she held on to the idea that they could go back. They could go home. If it didn't suit them.

'You didn't though,' said the engineer, 'go back I mean.'

Oh how Irina had longed to go back to Yakutsk; to the cinema with popcorn that was sweet or salty and where there was even a choice of two different films.

Now and then, for a treat, if Oleg's mother agreed to watch the baby, she and Oleg would go to the Chinese buffet. They would line up to dip bright serving spoons into the succession of metal buckets filled with coloured meats that glistened with oily sauces. They would scoop rice and noodles into heaps on the thick warm plates. Oleg would usually wrap some dumplings in napkins and slip them in his pockets, laughing at her disapproval, and they would eat them later at home. The cold dumplings seemed all the more delicious for being illicit.

They didn't think twice about jumping into their car in one neighbourhood and arriving a few minutes later in another that had a different flavour and different houses and shops. Just like that.

There was an indoor play centre lined with rubbery mats in bright colours where Vasily could tumble around, and Irina could sit with the other mothers and drink tea and make fun of their husbands and swop stories about how exhausting this whole motherhood business was.

More than anything though, she wanted to meet the eyes of someone she did not know and who had not already formed an opinion of her. She ached for the casual surprise of strangers in the street.

Here there was just the inexorable progress of the seasons and the slow but seemingly inevitable decline of the town. But they had their loan to pay on the motel and no one wanted to buy it. So what option did they have but to stay and to hope that things turned around? That something would come up.

'Our business is here,' she said. 'Besides,' and she sat up a little straighter and rubbed at a sticky spot on the table with the corner of her paper napkin, 'it's a wonderful community. City people don't usually understand. Everyone looks out for one another, especially the old folks. It's a good place to bring up a family.'

A film crew from Australia had come a few years ago to make a documentary about life in the coldest town on earth. They said it was going to be educational but they weren't interested in seeing Dr Nevsky's archive of the old council papers. Even though he had some original plans of the town and drawings showing how the first buildings had been constructed. He had nodded, he understood, but Irina could see his feelings had been hurt.

Instead they asked silly questions about the outdoor toilets and encouraged the teenagers to exaggerate about their smoking and drinking and to boast about imaginary sexual conquests.

The woman doing all the talking was a tiny, hard blond thing with a rasping voice and skin that, close up, was the colour and texture of a fine grade of sandpaper.

They sent a videotape of the programme to Alexi when it was finished and Irina watched herself, through her fingers, answering their trivial questions. They had edited out the translator who had stood behind the camera and Irina's words appeared in English on the bottom of the screen. In one scene she had been told to pretend to buy a snow shovel from Alexi who was pale from stage fright and sweating so that his thin hair stuck in stripes on his forehead.

It had been peculiar watching herself from the outside and considering how others might see her. She realised her voice sounded exactly like her mother's but Oleg just shrugged and said 'does it?' when she mentioned it.

Everyone howled at the parts with Alexi, mocking his wooden performance mercilessly and imitating the way his eyes kept darting towards the camera. She hoped someone might mention her own appearance. She was pleased with how natural she seemed, but as she had just been herself, without acting, it drew little comment.

'What's it like living here?' the Australian woman kept asking her. 'What's it like?'

She seemed curious, but Irina could see from her pale eyes, that had a fishy, reflective quality, that she could not absorb any of the meaning of what she saw in Tomyator. And anyway, what she really wanted to know was, 'how can you stand it?'

And when it's put to you like that, what could she do but defend the town and her choice to live in it? And her choice of Oleg and everything in her secret, unhappy life that flowed from those decisions because, ultimately, she had no one else to blame.

She had made her bed.

So she talked about the first real snow that fell fast and eager in September and announced itself with a silence so complete that people felt compelled to speak in whispers for a while.

She talked about the joy of spying a six-week-old wolf cub in Spring, tumbling between the trees to keep up with its brothers and sisters, nosing the flowers as it passed them, and trotting after its mother on their way to the river. Of course they were a problem for the reindeer herders but they tolerated it because it was part of the natural cycle of things.

She talked about the feel of the sun on your face in July – oh the gorgeous glory of it – and your shared commitment to soak up every ray so that the whole town gathered in the square to chat and sun themselves on benches while it lasted.

Sleeves were rolled up and an extra button was undone on their shirts as they angled their faces towards the light and warmth. There was a reawakening of a common purpose and a rekindling of old loyalties that had been tested through the long winter months.

There was a camaraderie that transcended minor fall-outs about a borrowed tool that had not been returned – or at least, not returned in the same condition. Gossipy remarks that had consumed them through the winter months were forgotten. 'What did it matter?' they said. They put all that to one side to burnish themselves in the sun and to agree that they were lucky to be here, together, in this place that was so 'other' than the rest of the world.

There were things she loved about Tomyator. There were. There were. And if she concentrated, and turned her face from things that did not make her happy, then she could survive it intact.

Irina looked into the engineer's frank, inquisitive face and was surprised to see her eyes still fixed on her. They locked together, without awkwardness, as each woman surveyed and assessed the other.

'How extraordinary you are,' said the engineer.

Irina blushed and gestured the silly comment away. That was too much. She was not extraordinary in any way and she feared that the engineer might be mocking her. Anyway, to her astonishment, almost three hours had passed, just like that, and the light was already beginning to fade.

It was too late to set off for the Weather Station now so the engineer said she would pick up some supplies from the store and then return to her room and start on her paperwork instead.

Irina walked back across the square towards home with a lightness around her shoulders. She could not recall the last time she had talked so much and so easily. Better still, it seemed to have earned her a reprieve, even if it was only for twenty-four hours.

Six

G regor sat resolute at the controls of the snowmobile holding the handlebars and facing into the distance, past the petrol store, in an unseeing way. His large, wax-coloured head resembled a hurriedly peeled potato whose eyes had yet to be dug out with a knife. His round back, directed to the crowd, was a statement: as the driver, it was certainly not his job to be loading the sled.

Instead, it was the engineer and the owner of the heated garage who walked back and forth, laden with awkwardly shaped equipment, discussing the order of the stacking as they worked.

It was a still day and they moved quickly but with care on the icy path, billowing vapour that hung in the air until they became indistinct in a fog of their own making.

It was pretty in its own way.

A small crowd of onlookers stamped their feet and huddled together to wonder aloud what in heaven's name could possibly be in all those cases and to offer advice on the best way to load them on the sled attached to the back of the snowmobile.

It was a rickety old thing, the sled, held together in

places with thick wraps of black tape and one of the men poked it with the toe of his boot to see if it could be trusted to make it.

'I'm not holding my breath,' he said and the others smiled and nodded.

They were hoping for failure, not because they were malicious, but there was invariably more to talk about when things didn't go to plan and they were more starved of new subjects for conversation than they dared to admit.

All around the edges of the square, the watchers from the windows hoped for some excitement too. They had pulled up their chairs and settled into them, soothed with hot tea and a sigh, in order to make the most of it.

Ordinarily there wouldn't be much to see in the square. Just their neighbours popping in and out of the store and the children charging at each other and swinging their school bags in great arcs over their heads in battle on their way to or from school. The watchers speculated, at great length, about the ailments of the people creeping over the Square to knock on Dr Nevsky's door. So there was some entertainment to be had there.

But one day sort of slid into the next in a way didn't it? And they longed for something new to happen.

Irina shielded her eyes from the low sun and eyed their dumb, good- natured curiosity with a disdain that showed in the impatient movements of her eyes and the way she returned their friendly remarks with curt, brittle gestures.

If they noticed her irritation they didn't let it bother them. Their heads swung in unison back and forth, open mouthed, as they watched the cases being transported from the garage and onto the sleds.

They put her in mind of a row of cattle, patient and dull, watching a farmer pouring feed along their long trough. She found their contentment provoking. How could they be satisfied with so little? And that thought, the thought that she, Irina, was not satisfied, allowed her to temper her own unhappiness with a triumphant superiority that sustained her in the same way as their comments and chuckles sustained them.

When one of them laughed they all joined in eagerly, even those who hadn't quite caught the joke. She clenched her teeth at the sound of it. Perhaps the engineer was right. She was a city girl. She frowned and stamped her feet. Thank God for that then.

The cases, although heavy, had wide handles so could be held with two hands and heaved onto the back of the sled. The engineer had moved these in place first to form the base of the load. Next was a crate filled with tools that the watchers recognised and named.

'Hello, she's got spanners in there I see. Screwdrivers. Is that a soldering iron?'

They were pleased with themselves when they could identify the tools. There was also a large wooden mallet.

'That'll be for the tent,' they agreed happily.

The engineer lifted on a small heater and four large tins of oil, a trestle table the size of Irina's kitchen table, a folding chair and two shovels and some rolls of plastic tubing onto the sled.

She was not used to the heavy gloves and fumbled with the smaller items but did not become cross or give up.

78

Instead she bit down on her bottom lip, paused for a moment to think and then persevered, until gradually she became used to them and her movements grew more sure.

The engineer worked steadily, but her trips between the garage and the growing mound on the sled left no mark in the snow that had descended heavily in the night and frozen to metal hardness in the bitter early hours.

Irina squinted against the cold, sharp light of the sun that was glinting over the far distant horizon to the left of the apartment block. Ten am or thereabouts she guessed. Like the locals she didn't bother with a watch. They wore too many thick layers to make a wrist watch accessible and a watch carried in a pocket ran fast as the metal inside it contracted. Or else it stopped when the oils in the mechanism froze altogether.

It had taken her five years, at least, to get used to not wondering about the precise time and only recently had she come to understand that here in Tomyator it didn't really matter.

This was the first clear day for weeks and she banged her mittens together and shuffled from foot to foot in the same dance as the curious onlookers. The forecast was for calm but there would be no warmth from the sun. She watched the engineer working, blurred in a haze of her own breath.

Last to come out from the garage was a long canvas sack containing the tent and its metal poles. It was too heavy for the engineer to manage on her own and the owner of the garage had heaved it onto his shoulder and placed his feet carefully to keep his balance under its weight.

The crowd, who stood close together with their backs to

the sun and threw long shadows, speculated cheerfully about whether the sack was more likely to contain the engineer's husband or boss and predicted that it would be the straw that broke the camel's back as far as that flimsy old sled went.

They were looking forward to it.

On the engineer's shoulder was a rucksack that Irina had seen her pack carefully with notebooks, manuals and two small handheld devices. They reminded Irina of oversized mobile phones but with larger different coloured buttons and a small screen.

Whatever they were she found them aggravating. She had a reflexive dislike of things she could not understand.

This was the 'digitising' part of the operation she guessed. Vasily would know the right words but he had refused to help this morning and she felt an acid twist of envy for Alexi who at least had a son who would help.

The snowmobile was as old as the sled and very small, and Gregor's wide buttocks had spread to flow proprietorially over the seat. The plan had been for the engineer to ride pillion to the weather station where he could help her unload, but she had looked doubtfully at the tiny space left uncovered.

'Talk about excess baggage,' said a man, pointing at Gregor's backside, and they chuckled, although not especially unkindly. 'Good job it's not far.'

His wife wrapped her arms around herself and hopped from foot to foot, growing bored with the scene and thinking about warm tea.

'So, tell me, what are you actually planning to do with

all this stuff?' she asked the engineer. 'If it ever makes it there.' She had the blunt, guileless manner that was typical of the Tomyator folk but the engineer smiled at her, pleased to be asked about it anyway.

'In here,' she said, tapping one of the cases, 'are the parts that will make up a solar panel that I'm installing to power the new transmitter. The transmitter, if I do my job right,' she tried to cross her fingers in her thick gloves, 'will beam the temperatures up to a satellite. Exciting don't you think? Why don't you come up and see for yourself when I've got started? I'll show you how it all works.'

The woman looked doubtful.

'Yes, you should come,' said Irina abruptly and the woman looked at her with her head turned to one side, birdlike. She wasn't sure what business it was of Irina's. Everyone knew this girl had come on the orders of Moscow. Irina had always been superior about whatever it was she did at the Weather Station. She supposed she was just trying to cling on to some control while she could.

'I'll see,' the woman said to the engineer. But her expression indicated clearly enough that a needless walk in the dead of winter, just to look at some silly boxes and tubes wasn't high on her list of priorities.

'A palaver for such a short trip,' said the woman to her husband. 'Why didn't she get a couple of the lads to carry the boxes down there?'

'She's only going to the Weather Station' he said, 'not moving to Beijing.' And they agreed it was an enormous fuss about nothing.

They carried on their conversations about the engineer

and her preparations, clucking and making suggestions about how they would do it if it were up to them, over the engineer's head. They were used to visitors being foreign and had forgotten she would understand. The engineer smiled at Irina, tolerating them good naturedly, so that Irina felt taken into her confidence and it was warming.

She watched the engineer strapping the equipment onto the sled using a series of elasticated ropes. Her movements were deft now because she was used to the gloves. The straps were attached so that there were even spaces between them. She circled the sled to find the best points to fix them to and then hunkered down to each one to check it methodically.

Irina watched her, the way she was entirely absorbed in her task, not hesitating to wonder whether she had made a mistake or seeking reassurance that the job had been done well. She moved surely and trusted her own instincts.

'All change eh?'

Irina's neighbour was a repulsively insinuating woman. She leaned in to sniff out news, expecting it always to be bad, and readying herself to recoil from it, as if from a rotten egg.

They shared a party wall at the apartment block and the unwanted sound of her thin, high voice seeping through the bricks was a horrible and unwanted intimacy. At times Irina would have liked to pound on the wall with her fists.

The woman arched her chicken neck in a prissy show of solicitude. She leant close to Irina, whispering as though they were sharing a secret.

'I hear they're modernising. We'll be modernised out of

existence soon you and me. The way things are going.'

In her search for friendship she was drawn to women she suspected were even more unhappy than herself. She hoped they would find a camaraderie in their misery. She heard Oleg's raised voice through the wall and she spoke to Irina with the wheedling tone of a would-be bully seeking out someone weaker than herself.

'We're always the last ones to find out and the first ones to suffer the blow aren't we Irina. It's typical.'

It revolted Irina and she was insulted by the woman's suggestion that they were in any way alike.

'I've known for a while,' said Irina. 'It's been in the pipeline.'

It was a meaningless phrase and the woman raised her eyebrows and made her lips into a small 'O' in amused disbelief. Nothing stayed secret in Tomyator.

Irina, knowing that her own lip had curled, turned her face away quickly, looking towards the engineer.

'Moscow have been talking about digitising for months,' she said, shading her eyes against the sun with her hand 'It's much more efficient. The temperature readings will be beamed to a satellite from the new equipment.'

She turned back to face the woman; she would be civil, but her neighbour had bent forward like a rat on her haunches with her whiskers trembling at the scent of her next meal.

'Oh Irina. My dear, what an awful shame. So they won't need you to read the temperatures any more?'

'No,' said Irina and was glad she was not like this woman who was nourished by the suffering of others.

A frozen dew drop glistened, malicious, on the end of her neighbour's red nose.

'There's no point arguing with Moscow I suppose but that can't be good news. You'll miss the money – who wouldn't? Especially now that the motel is so quiet.'

Irina received just 26,000 Roubles a month from her work for the university. A paltry amount for the effort it took. She had told no one how much she was paid but the residents of Tomyator had gossiped and speculated, often wildly, for years until many suspected she was pocketing hundreds of thousands for her trips.

All that business with Oleg being at home all day, they said. You know why he hasn't bothered to find another job? Here, they would insert a long pause and raise their eyebrows. Because he doesn't need one that's why. Not with the fortune Irina's stashing away.

There was more than a little satisfaction in the town, therefore, that this shameless diddling of the system was finally coming to an end. Karma. Wasn't that what the young people called it?

The woman grasped Irina's thickly gloved hand in both of hers and turned her head to the side in an impersonation of compassion.

'I know Oleg won't be a happy bunny at the moment,' she laughed in a simpering, pained sort of way. 'Well, we know how it is don't we. Remember that I'm only next door. If you need to talk over a tea, or something stronger…' She wrinkled her forehead and scrunched her eyes into a syrupy mask of sympathy. 'You only need to knock.'

'No thank you,' said Irina, pulling her hand away sharply and stepping backwards. Her voice had been too loud, almost a shout, and a few people in the small crowd swung around to stare at them in a mild, bovine manner.

Irina jammed her hands into her pockets.

'They still need a reliable person to be available. They specifically said they need someone experienced to be on hand in case something goes wrong. They've actually said that in an email they sent. Oleg is glad I don't have to make the journey. He worries about me if I'm out too long.'

The woman gathered her bony shoulders together in cynicism.

'That's thoughtful of him,' she said.

'They're paying me still,' said Irina and she tossed her head and showed her teeth to indicate that it was nothing and in fact she was happy about it, but it was a haughty gesture and her neighbour was hotly glad that misfortune had struck. She deserved it. Stuck up Irina.

'Money for nothing you could say. So thank you, but you don't have to worry about us.'

Seven

The crowd, satisfied that they had sucked every drop of marrow from the shinbone of this scene and intent on warming their feet, had left to carry on with their chores. They were pleased, at least, to have something new to chew over once they'd arrived home again.

Gregor kicked the engine into life and departed, jerkily, in a cloud of oily smoke with the blades of the overloaded snowmobile finally piercing the brittle, porcelain skin of the snow.

The sled, against all the odds, remained in one piece and the engineer whooped loudly and danced a victory jig. The smell of the diesel hung in a bluish haze in the air.

Irina and the engineer turned to follow behind and as the spluttering thrum of the snowmobile faded, Irina's eyes flicked around the square, taking in the frozen swing, a pile of snow covered lumber and a collection of empty gas canisters that had been stacked up neatly for collection. She searched urgently for something to say.

Any remark would do. The conversation in the café had delayed the work after all, but she felt herself dull and without colour or depth next to this woman with her certainties and her purpose. What conversations might interest the engineer? The weather? The store? But nothing presented itself. She thought herself idiotic and clenched her fists inside her mittens.

If the woman felt their silence to be awkward she didn't show it. Irina glanced sideways at her and saw that she was brim full of anticipation about the Weather Station and entirely caught up in her own thoughts.

The engineer squinted against the sun and her eyes glittered. Her eagerness to get started at last showed itself in long, energetic strides that Irina had to stretch a little to match. Irina watched their feet striking the hard slippery surface in step and felt herself being marched, carried along, slightly against her will.

The woman's cheeks glowed violently from her earlier exertions in loading the sled but it was still to be seen how well she would cope on the walk to the Weather Station.

As they passed in front of the store the engineer said, 'hang on Irina', and hopped over a bucket in her loping, gangly way to knock on the window and wave to Alexi. She mimed walking with her thickly gloved fingers across her other palm and he showed her a wide grin, and a thumbs up, in reply.

This was only her third day in Tomyator and she was greeting Alexi like an old friend. How easy it was for some people.

Not that Irina coveted her popularity. It was desperate in her view; wanting to be liked by everyone. It showed a weakness of character. She set her lips into a line. Even though it was the harder path to choose, she reassured herself that it was more realistic to be able to rely only on yourself.

She watched the woman's eyes crease in pleasure at Alexi's encouragement and saw that she was buoyed by it. Perhaps, Irina thought, this woman lacked an essential seriousness. The idea that she might be distracted by trivialities encouraged her a little. Maybe she wouldn't be able to complete the work. She was just a girl really with a girlish kind of enthusiasm – it would be too testing. She would go back to Moscow and everything would carry on as before.

At the edge of the square, and perpendicular to it, was the paved road. If Irina and the engineer were to turn right and walk for a few minutes it would begin to wind through a cluster of thirty neat, single storey wooden houses that had been newly built when Irina had arrived in Tomyator.

In those days they had been packed tight with little families whose mothers and fathers walked to work along the road towards the group of low grey sheds, slotted under the horizon, that made up the Sable Farm on the edge of town.

Mothers had called or scolded their children from the top of their wooden steps and shouted hellos to their neighbours when they passed their houses as they went about their chores.

Their street had been lively with children who dashed here and there, always having forgotten to wear their hats, busy with their play. It was a cliché really; children bright-eyed and dashing, but she hadn't imagined it. That was the way it was.

In those days all the children had begged their parents for dogs. There was a craze for dogs. Irina remembered one summer when the street had been filled with puppies.

However often they were told 'no', the children would let them into the houses to leap on the beds and curl up in front of the wood burner. The mothers didn't have the heart to put them back out into kennels. Not when the children loved them so much.

But every now and then they would decide that enough was enough. Doors were slammed as the dogs, that were all great big dirty beasts now, were pushed outside by the mothers who complained about their revolting slobber and hair and the muddy paw prints they left on everything.

The exiled dogs would bark, full of indignation, and pace around at the base of the steps.

Not many of the families bothered with dogs these days.

It was the sounds of that time that people missed the most. Children's voices had a way of carrying between the houses and across the open ground as far as the centre of town. Funny, they said, but you didn't really think about how cheerful children's voices were until you didn't hear them anymore.

The Sable Farm had not done so well in recent years. People made a fuss about fur they said and it wasn't good for business. Transport costs from Tomyator were high and bigger industrial farms opened nearer the cities and they could undercut their prices.

The owner of the farm had moved away from Tomyator years ago, as soon as he could afford it in truth, and he sent messages to be delivered by the beetroot-faced manager,

Sergei, who shuffled from foot to foot and chewed his nails before reading out the emails in a trembling voice.

The employees listened, standing extra still, with their eyes narrowed to try to understand. 'Unforeseeable shifts in currency markets... The unreasonable burden of regulation... Altered sensibilities around animal welfare... Changing times... Market forces... The intransigence of traditional lenders...'

The words all ran into one another and made little sense but it was undeniably bad news and the long and short of it was that there would be no pay rises again this year.

But the prices in the store kept rising just the same. Families decided they preferred their old lives in the city, so now many of the houses were empty, or occupied by the older people who felt it too late in life for them to move again.

The handful of children who were left were in their teens and they eyed the jeeps that drove past their houses, past the farm and onto Yakutsk, with longing and resentment.

Irina opened her mouth to tell the engineer about the Sable Farm and the families but she wasn't sure how to start and then it was all too late because they had turned to the left and onto Libsky Street instead.

It was a long, straight street with a paved road but the older houses that lined it refused to stick to prescribed positions in their plots, or even to face the same direction, so that it had the feel of a collection of dachas rather than the outskirts of a small town.

Each plot was six hundred metres square and some of the houses clung to their boundary lines, to create a large expanse of garden to the front whilst others had settled contentedly in the middle of their plot, like a babushka gathering her skirts and sinking onto a footstool.

None of them directly fronted the road and it gave the street a reserved, modest quality.

Back in the Nineties there had been excitement in the town when restrictions on the size of the houses had been lifted and plots could be purchased outright.

Everyone who could afford it bought their land but, despite all of the talk of expansion and the men comparing their drawings and measurements in the store, only a handful had bothered to add an extra floor. They were used to their little houses in the end. They thought their three or four rooms and a small verandah that looped along the front and around one side to be more than adequate for their needs. Besides, it would be harder to keep a bigger house warm and bedrooms upstairs meant further to trek in the night to the outhouse. No. They wouldn't bother with it.

It seemed enough that they could expand if they wanted to and it gave them a greater sense of attachment to the place.

They agreed it was something nice to think about, as you sat on your wooden steps and rubbed your palm back and forth on a plank that had been worn smooth by the passage of your own children's feet.

Some of the plots were contained within chest height white picket fences but even those that had not marked their territory with rows of wooden staves had lined the border of their property with pots or piles of lumber, all snow covered for now, to stake their claim on the land.

As ownership was a newish development in these parts, it was not taken for granted that it would be around forever. So they enjoyed it and guarded it, deliberately, having the sense that they were making the most of it while it lasted.

That same stubborn optimism was on display in their planting. In the brief hiatus of the bitter year, the residents nurtured their hopeful crops with painstaking patience and love.

The gardeners persevered, all the time knowing that their efforts on their sore knees over pots and raised beds would come to nothing if the summer were too short or failed to appear at all.

Irina pointed out signs of their labour to the engineer as they passed the plots.

Look, there, in a sheltered spot next to the house, were the outlines of the raised beds, covered with snow but pierced with wigwams of bamboo. They would support the tendrils of green beans. If only they proved tenacious enough to complete the climb.

They drew level with a plot that seemed flat and barren beneath the snow, but Irina knew its featurelessness was temporary.

Every year, as the frosts retreated, the owner would unfurl long runs of waist high poly tunnels over specially fertilised, raised ridges of soil to pamper their peppers and courgettes into a rapid and fevered fecundity and they would be the envy of their neighbours.

Visitors would be taken to the larder to admire the

shelves of ripe, richly coloured bottled vegetables and fruits. Inevitably a jar would be pressed upon them. 'We have more than we could ever eat,' they said. Later they would imagine their food on a neighbour's table and wonder how sweet the peppers had tasted, what they had been eaten with and whether the children had enjoyed them more or the grown ups. They smacked their lips and savoured their connection to the soil. It was truly marvellous to be able to eat the fruits of their own labours.

Most of the plots had raised beds of a uniform size – not from any desire for neatness or regularity, but because they were constructed from the same railway sleepers, all pilfered from the line that had run up to the landing strip in the old days.

In these beds, beneath their warm blankets of straw, onions, garlic and carrots swelled slowly, taking their own sweet time to come to maturity. The quick crops of chives and lettuces, planted when the sun appeared, flared briefly and with vitality and were chopped with pocket knives and gobbled down within minutes of being picked.

That the seasons were unpredictable barely merited a mention between the gardeners. Yet an especially harsh or early blast of the cold still managed to take them by surprise on occasion.

Terracotta pots that had been hidden by the first snow were forgotten and left outside through the winter to reappear in surprising places as the coldest temperatures retreated.

'What the devil? I could have sworn I moved you to the

woodshed,' they said to them, brushing off the snow and shaking their heads.

The pots would be cracked from the cold and they would sigh when they found them and smash them into smaller pieces and use them to line the pots that they had remembered to bring safely indoors. They were used to making the best of a bad situation and nothing went to waste.

Irina looked often at the engineer as they walked to see how she liked the town. She was gratified by the way her eyes swept across the scene and how intently she listened to Irina's naming and description of the residents as they passed each property.

She had a peculiar way of listening, with her eyes fixed steadily on Irina and her lips slightly parted, so that she seemed to be consuming her words.

Halfway along the street they came to a ruined house that had collapsed in on itself; the roof folded in half in an expression of sorrow.

It had happened so suddenly it seemed to Irina. One day she had noticed some tiles had slipped from the steeply sloping roof but within weeks of the water creeping inside, it had sagged and fallen entirely, leaving the front of the house unattached and swaying in the wind.

Next year, or perhaps the year after, the house would fall completely and the neighbours would quietly repurpose the reclaimable wood and maybe even move their fence a metre or so into their neighbour's land to claim a few more precious metres of soil for themselves.

If they were growing vegetables it seemed justified.

This was one of a sprinkling of houses in the town that had been bought by the incomers; the sharp-faced men with loud voices who ran the mines or surveyed the land like a plague of tics; ready to suck out all their resources and grow fat on the proceeds.

They figured they would need somewhere as a base for their work and imagined their wives would think it charming to have a summer dacha to visit. Just think about all that space for the kids to run around without getting on anyone's nerves they said to them.

But when they disappeared they had forgotten the homes, not even bothering to list them for sale. It wasn't as if people were queuing up to buy them these days. So there we are.

Irina looked away whenever she passed the house. She hoped the engineer would not ask her about it.

It seemed to her that an uninhabited building, however robust or well made, slipped into disrepair the moment people ceased to care about it. It made her wonder how many of the homes on Libsky Street were kept standing by force of will rather than a sound schedule of repairs.

She saw the engineer looking at the fallen house and Irina felt responsible for it. As if it represented a lack of resolve on her part.

There was hope though, and Irina clung to it.

Across the street was a house with window frames and carved shutters that were newly painted a fresh, mint green. It was the smartest house on the street and certainly the most loved.

She saw that the owners had already been busy this

morning, knocking the icicles from the eaves and sweeping the snow from the wooden sills. Orderly stacks of chopped wood sat under the solidly constructed lean-to. The half barrels on either side of the bottom step would be colourful with flowers for the brief interlude of summer and hanging baskets would appear on the wrought iron arms that jutted from the sides of the door frame.

Through the toughest months of winter, Irina looked forward to the day that she would pass this house to see the grass had sprouted suddenly, awakened, and she would know that before long it would flow in soft waves over the edge of the gravel path that led to the street.

Arctic Willow, brilliant dots, would sprout and display petals so small that one had to hold them at the end of your nose to see their fluted shapes and lift them to the light to see their fragile veined leaves. But it was wrong to think they were delicate, they were ferocious and tough and Irina loved them fiercely in return. They crept around the base of the small fruit trees in pots whose boughs would bend low to the ground, in supplication, laden with hard green apples.

It was optimistic.

'I wish you could see us in the summer,' she said. 'It can be beautiful here.'

It was a stiff little remark but underneath it she was almost overwhelmed with a longing to share her small joy in the changing seasons with someone she thought might understand.

'I wish I could too. Honestly. I just know I'd adore it,' said the engineer. 'But don't you think it's beautiful now too Irina?'

She stopped and pointed along Libsky Street towards the Weather Station.

The road unrolled between the wooden houses whose uneven shapes seemed to have grown organically from the ground to create an antique and imperfect harmony of sorts. They formed a gateway to an impossibly vast stretch of crisp, white, emptiness that shimmered and glowed in the bright sunshine.

The engineer tipped back her head to look up into the azure sky and huffed a puff of her breath upwards. She watched it form into a dense cloud of white crystals that hung in the still air. She raised her hand and cupped it around the cloud as if trying to detect its mass.

'Look. It's a miracle. Evidence that we're alive. I envy you this incredible life here Irina, truly.'

Even though they had been walking, Irina could see the warmth beginning to leak away from the engineer. It was clear when someone was suffering from the effects of the cold.

She recognised it in the stiffening of their steps and a growing angularity around their joints. It was almost as if their own fluids and lubricants were seizing up, like the oils in a mechanical watch.

No visitor to Tomyator was immune to it. There were three stages.

At first, they were thrilled by the sharp adventure of the cold. They laughed in delighted shock at its extremity and angled their faces into the wind deliberately, defying it, thinking themselves equal to the challenge and wondered excitedly about how to describe it to their friends when they got home. 'Like a giant freezer. Imagine the coldest you've ever been. Think about leaping into a bath entirely filled with ice cubes. Like being stabbed with icicles. Eviscerating. Numbing.' In the end it was in vain, because there was nothing to effectively compare it too and they were disappointed that they could not communicate the reality of this feeling to someone in their warm kitchen.

Before long, just a few minutes as a rule, came surprise. They had felt invincible in their expensive jackets and boots. They were almost offended at feeling the thin, chilled tendrils of air creeping between the chattering teeth of their sturdy zips. The cold pinched and plucked in unexpected places; their tear ducts and high up inside their noses. They had thought their thick soles would insulate them from the frozen ground but soon, very soon, they would feel the spiteful pinch of it in their toes.

Later, as the cold turned from a sensation into an ache, and then a pain, they became aware of their own breathing. The cold air could not be kept at bay and began to chill them from the inside out. It was frightening and they took quick looks around them to see how far from a shelter they had travelled. They looked to Irina then for reassurance and she would steer them back to safety.

The engineer did not complain and Irina guessed that she would not. She had not complained about anything so far and Irina liked that about her. She realised, uneasily, that there were a few things she liked about her and she checked herself, damping down her feelings with a conscious effort. It would not do to like her, in the circumstances.

The engineer did not ask how much further it was but the warmth from loading the sled had dissipated now. Irina recognised the dawning realisation of the unstoppable brutality of the cold.

Irina brushed her eyelashes of the frostings of ice and touched the engineer on her arm, gesturing for her to wipe her own eyes.

They began to walk again and the engineer continued to look intently at every house they passed, twisting her whole body from her waist rather than just turning her head, because she had already learned to keep her chin hunched down into her chest to retain the warmth.

They had pulled their scarves up over their mouths again and did not talk for now because they couldn't spare the heat. There was a companionable feel between them as they matched each other step for step and breath for breath. Their silence was comfortable and becoming familiar.

When they passed the last house on Libsky Street, one of the black dogs issued a single bark without rising from his sitting position and the other, judging that there had been sufficient noise, licked its companion's nose and was content to stay silent.

There was smoke coming from the chimney and the ancient woman who lived there with her husband appeared at the window, wrapped in her layers, with a fat white cat cradled in her arms, on its back like a baby.

She held its front leg above the knee and flapped it at them so that it appeared to be waving its paw in greeting. The cat flicked the tip of its tail at the indignity but tolerated it. It was indoors and well fed at least, it reasoned. The two women waved back.

'Just five minutes more,' said Irina as they stepped off the paved road beyond the edge of town and struck out into the open endless space of the snow-covered plains.

The wind had a different quality here.

Beyond the shelter of the houses, fences, wood stores and outhouses, the winds met and massed from all directions, unhindered by obstructions and giddy with the freedom to blast and roll across the landscape unchecked. There was a menace to it Irina sometimes thought. As if the winds had been waiting for her to appear, gathering forces, whispering and conspiring, before swooping down to drag deliberately at her hat and coat.

She'd mentioned it to Oleg once, smiling slightly, because she knew it was a silly idea; that the winds waited for her. She had wanted to tell him that those were the kind of fanciful thoughts that came into her head when she was walking, out there, on her own.

'There's no money for a new coat,' said Oleg, not taking his eyes from the television. 'If that's what you're getting at.'

The sun had separated from the sticky horizon at last and the shadows were shortening.

At this time of year, when the days were so brief, Irina could see the sun's movement up and across the sky and it leant a sense of urgency to the journey.

Both women had frosted eyebrows and a pattern of white crystals on their scarves outlining their mouths and nostrils.

Up ahead, the deep 'phut' 'phut' of the snowmobile sounded and Gregor appeared over the low ridge, eclipsing the sun for a second, before cresting the peak and picking up speed on his descent.

The sled was empty now and bounced raggedly with a side-to-side movement, behind him. He would be back in town in no time. He nodded as he chugged past but stared straight ahead, and left a trail of acrid smoke in his wake.

This was the uphill part and the engineer's breath was audible. Irina was pleased with herself that she, ten years older than the engineer she guessed, and not pretending to be especially fit, could manage the journey more easily. The engineer clearly did not want to admit the difficulty of the walk.

It renewed her hope that Tomyator might defeat her as it had defeated the diamond miners and the oilmen and the way it threatened to defeat her on difficult days. Perhaps this would be one of the many things in life that did not go to plan. The idea gave her a burst of energy that carried her more readily to the top of the slope.

The chain link fence of the Weather Station was stark against the snow and threw its sharp honeycomb pattern towards them. How small and inconsequential the enclosure looked compared to how large it loomed in her life and her fears.

'Ground zero,' said the engineer arriving beside her. And then, throwing an arm around Irina's shoulders, 'we made it,' and her voice sounded eager so that Irina could hear she was smiling underneath her scarf.

Gregor had driven the snowmobile inside the enclosure

and piled up the equipment in an untidy heap as if he had simply tipped up the sled and driven away.

Irina led the way, bumping through the low gate. The engineer followed closely behind and bent over the piles of boxes and tubing to check that everything had been unloaded. She pulled out a blue canvas bag from the heap. It was pulled tight at one end with a drawstring.

'Here. Help me cover it,' she said, opening the bag and unfurling a large plastic ground sheet that crackled and fluttered in the wind.

Irina took the other end and they stepped back, pulling it taut between them as if they were making a bed, in the practised way that women do the world over, and pulled it down over the pile.

The engineer wedged the sheet under and around the equipment and then stood, turning slowly to view the entire panorama with her hands on her hips.

'I know this is your territory Irina. It must be painful to see me marching in and commandeering it like this. Will you miss your trips up here?'

Irina didn't know. Would she? She had liked the idea of purpose and, although she hardly admitted it to herself, the sense of importance it gave her in the town. But it was tough going and she had already begun to wonder how she would manage if her ankle became any worse.

'A little, perhaps,' she said.

The engineer pulled down her scarf and pushed her lips out into a circular pout, considering, before looking up at the sky again and then stamping out a spot on the ground.

'I'll set up the solar panels here and the thermometer and

gauges next to them.'

'But it's usually misty here,' said Irina. She hesitated, afraid to be thought foolish. 'Will you need a battery or something to power it?'

'The equipment only needs a tiny amount of power and I'll set the panels up so that they track the arc of the sun. Fun fact: the efficiency of these solar panels increases in lower temperatures.'

'What if they're covered by snow?' said Irina.

'Good question,' said the engineer. 'Go to the top of the class.' She reached to hug Irina again but her gesture was clumsy and her hand banged heavily on Irina's shoulder and she looked at it oddly, as if it belonged to someone else.

'Part of the energy generated keeps the panels warmer than the air temperature and they're coated with a substance that melts the snow too. Also, they'll be angled like this,' she held up her hand to show the slant, 'so any snow should just slide off. That's the theory anyway. Let's see.'

She had pulled down the scarf from over her mouth and she smiled at the covered equipment. Her face was animated and her eyes, which seemed overly bright and brittle, skipped from one place to another without settling long enough to really take in what she saw.

She bent over the thermometer in a stiff way, like a much older person suddenly.

'Minus 40' she said. 'Wow.'

She began to stamp out a larger space in the snow to one side of the spot she had chosen for her panels. Her boot caught in a drift so that she staggered, but she managed to save herself and did not fall.

'I'll set up my tent here. I've got a little...' she struggled to think of the word and shook her head in confusion. 'It's gone,' she said, and a flicker of irritation rippled over her face.

'A heater! That's it. So I can take off my gloves inside to do the fiddly work and then dash outside in mad bursts to brave the weather. Cosy would be an exaggeration, but it should be tolerable.'

The 's' in every word stretched out too far and her tongue, which moved slowly like a lizard in deep shade, rounded the sharp edges from each word. She blinked sleepily.

Irina saw that the beginning of a filminess had formed on her eyes as the water on their surfaces thickened and became viscous from the freezing temperatures. The engineer had been in the open for much longer than Irina, organising and loading the sled. It would be too much for anyone, let alone an outsider.

Meanwhile, the wind was gathering pace. It had a harsher edge as it raced up the small slope and struck them sharply at the peak where they stood. Irina could always judge the wind speed by the sound the weather vane made as it spun and today it was high pitched and whining.

She was more expertly wrapped than the engineer. She was thankful for the thick outer covering of reindeer skin.

A few years back, when the bar was still open, a visitor had become disorientated in the fog. Not used to drinking strong spirits and blasé about the warnings from the bar owner, he had wandered in a wide circle around the swing and the slide, tracking his own footprints and making a deep channel. His coat was found in front of the café. A little further on was a trail of a hat, a red sweater, a shirt and finally a thick vest. And then the man, sitting in the snow, cross-legged and white chested with the pinkest nipples Irina had ever seen, with his hands neatly on his knees and his chin on his chest.

He was no more than twenty metres from the door of the old guest house.

The men had picked him up under his arms and taken him to Doctor Nevsky. Where else would they take him? He did look comical frozen in that position. 'He's a big fat Budha', said Zeena, covering her mouth with her hand and giggling for a long time.

People had exchanged looks that said 'she's not right in the head that one' and resolved to keep a closer eye on the children.

Later someone thought to pick up the clothes and they were frozen solid too. They reminded Irina of the cut-out-and-keep blue-jeans and maxi dresses and scoop necked t-shirts she had collected from the cereal boxes when she'd been a child. They came with tiny tabs you could fold to wrap around your cardboard lady who lived on the other side of the box.

They put the dead man on a jeep later that day, or the next, she didn't remember, and took him to Yakultsk, Irina supposed. People made small, dark jokes about it at the time. They understood that humour allows you to sidle up to a difficult subject and give it a kick, to show that you

105

will not be defeated by it. But then, after a while, they stopped mentioning it altogether, as is best in a small community where tragedies are too near the surface of everyday life.

The engineer's face was pale beneath her hat and her jaw was clenched to keep her teeth from chattering. Her blood was retreating from the existential threat of the wind and hiding to thrum, anxiously, around her heart and lungs. These were her vital organs after all. Her nose and fingers and toes were dispensable and would be sacrificed in this battle if her body were to win the war.

The tip of her nose and the small hoops of her nostrils already had a bright, waxy sheen so that they did not look quite as flesh should look any more. Her eyebrows and eyelashes were thickly loaded with ice but she did not brush it away.

Why not? Thought Irina. I could just go home. She pressed her lips together and pushed up her chin. She remembered the unfairness of her situation, stoking it purposely, to make herself resolute.

If she was bitter then she had every right. Besides, it wouldn't be her fault. Everyone in the town had seen how determined the engineer was to get out here. Irina couldn't stand here all day either. Even Moscow wouldn't expect her to drop dead of the cold on their say so. It was too much. Irina wasn't a young woman anymore.

She thought of Zeena mouthing, 'any new bookings?' in her fragile, desperate way through the condensation of the café window and her heart gave a thump. That damned café would have shut down years ago if Irina had not been in charge of reporting from the Weather Station. She had 'kept Tomyator on the map'. That was what Tanja from Moscow had said. Why must she be responsible for everything in this place?

She was angry with the engineer too suddenly. Dragging Irina out here. Bullying her into finding a sled. She felt a fool. Outwitted. If it wasn't for the engineer's insistence that she help her today, the ugly thought of leaving her here alone wouldn't even have entered Irina's head.

Irina wasn't *like* that. She stamped her feet. It wasn't her fault.

Irina looked back towards the town and the grey smear across the sky that was the smoke from the little chimneys. Her motel rooms were chilled and unoccupied except for the engineer's. A couple from Germany were booked in for two nights next week, and that was it.

The elongated note of a wolf's howl rose and trembled in the air. It came from somewhere to the East – probably miles away. The packs were small, five or six as a rule and there was no threat to people in this area. But the mournful, raw sound tipped Irina into her decision.

'Can you find your own way back?' she said. 'It's just a straight route. Follow the tracks.' It was an experiment, to say it out loud.

Irina gave a sharp nod to herself. The engineer knew the risks when she came. She wasn't a child and Irina was not responsible for her.

The engineer frowned, trying to understand the question.

'Yes', she said but she looked up at the sky instead of towards the town.

'Right then,' said Irina and banged her thick-mittened hands together. She would set off in a moment. In a second she would start walking back to the town. On her own.

The engineer stretched out a hand to touch the tube that housed the thermometer and, finding it to be solid and not just in her imaginings, held onto it to steady herself against the gathering gusts of the wind.

'Irina,' she said waving her free hand languidly from side to side, 'I so appreciate your help you know.' She spoke slowly and with an effort. 'I admire you, truly. This life you have. I was thinking about you last night, about how much I hoped we could become friends.'

She smiled in her open mouthed way and her eyes squeezed themselves together between her frosted lashes.

'I'd like it very much if you felt the same way.'

She was swaying now and her shivering had passed so that she seemed tranquil. It was just the cold talking. Irina knew that. People often said things they didn't mean when they were outside for too long.

Her lips were lined with blue.

Irina took her arm.

'We'll come back tomorrow. You've had enough for today. I can see it.'

The movement had brought Irina to her senses.

She would never have left the woman here on her own. She was certain of it. It was one of those silly ideas that had a way of creeping into your head, when the wind had blown away the remembrances of hearth and domesticity to leave an echoing emptiness. She shook out her hands to set the blood moving. It was almost a joke with herself. She had never thought about it seriously.

She pulled at the engineer's arm, nodding towards the path they had already forged, and she had the sense of danger passing.

They would stop at a house on Libsky street for a warm tea. It was no more than a few minutes away. The owners were used to Irina stopping on bad days to open her coat in front of the fire to gather in the warmth before setting off again for home. You're always welcome, Irina they said. Folk did look out for you here. What other choice was there?

The engineer resisted, even pulling back against her arm a little, but yielded to Irina's firmness and good sense. Her trusting obedience made Irina feel tender towards her. Taking a last look around, they turned and made their way back, together, into town, before it was too late.

Eight

'Best days of my life,' said Oleg to the engineer, knocking a finger on the kitchen table to emphasise his point. 'No question about it. Freedom. Camaraderie. Away from my mother.'

Irina watched him pour himself another vodka. He was careful to scrape the neck of the bottle on the rim of the glass. God forbid a precious drop should be lost.

The first one had been a welcome drink. There was another as they'd settled around the table. So this must be his third.

'Someone's keeping count of Oleg's drinks,' he said to the engineer, nodding towards Irina with a wide-stretched alligator's smile. 'She already has the look.' When he said 'look' he screwed his lips together and tensed his shoulders, shuddering in a camp parody of spinsterly distaste.

Then he laughed to show it was only a joke. Just a bit of fun.

But his eyes held Irina's with a note of warning. Come on then. If she had a grievance then why not air it publically? Because he would happily discuss the appropriate amount to drink when they had company.

Here and now. If that was what she wanted. If she wanted to push him on it.

The lampshade in the kitchen was a large white cone that hung low over the table. Irina had ordered it from a magazine but it did not make the kitchen look more modern as she had hoped. It was too big in the small room and dropped its scoop of light down harshly so that brows and noses made hard black shadows on the faces of the people beneath it. The edges of the kitchen remained dim.

The light gave Oleg a stupidly villainous look.

Irina turned back to the stove.

She couldn't bear the sight of the careful, feminine way he held the glass and the bottle anyway. She'd rather not look.

He was proud of his hands even though they were nothing special. He cleaned and filed his nails into perfect, even curves, blowing the dust onto the arm of his chair.

In the old days, the half moons of black grease under his nails had been impossible to remove completely and it hadn't bothered him at all. He had more time to kill these days she supposed. Her bitterness at it, at his leisure time, rose in her throat and she gripped the kitchen counter and stared up at the silent extractor fan.

She had ordered the new filter months ago. Oleg had taken it out of the box and shrugged. He'd fit it another day. Not now. When he had a minute. Every day that she could not use it she seethed with resentment, and was wearied half to death by the terrible repetitiveness of their battle.

He dismissed her complaints saying, 'You love having

something to moan about Irina. Admit it.' And, in a way, he was right. A formless, swirling, unnameable discontent with her life would surely have overwhelmed her. This, instead, a broken extractor fan or too many vodkas, was quantifiable and easy to grasp. It gave shape to her unhappiness in a way that did not make her feel mad. She was justified in her feelings and that, at least, gave her some satisfaction.

Oleg swung his round head back to the engineer, and could not think, for a second, who this woman was and why she was here. The little blank delivered a jolt of fear. It seemed to be happening more often these days. Just age probably. Although Irina was bound to make some snide comment about recommended units of alcohol or some such shit she'd read in her magazines. Fuck she depressed him. The way she kept on.

He pressed his fingertips into his eyes. Of course he remembered the woman. He reassembled his smile.

'Listen, I may not have been your typical studious type, too busy chasing skirt, but,' and he tapped his temple, 'it appears I did have the brains to graduate in the top five per cent of my year.'

He leaned back in his chair, ready to absorb her admiration, but the engineer just gave a small nod. It knocked his mood. He had been prepared to give her a chance but if she was going to be a bitch about it he wouldn't tolerate it. Not in his own house.

He licked his top lip before sipping less from his glass than he would have liked. He was irritated by Irina's nagging. This engineer woman must have picked up on the shrewish tendencies of his dear wife by now. See! He raised the glass again. He could have just a small sip if he chose to. It was no problem for him.

Irina set down a plate of dumplings in the centre of the table, drawing herself in to avoid brushing against the engineer in the narrow space, and returned to the stove to ladle crimson puddles of borscht into their best bowls. She made sure to put the bowl with a chip on its rim aside so that she could use it for herself.

Oleg tore a fist of bread from the loaf and waved it, knocking his elbow on the handle of the drawer behind him. 'You bastard,' he said to the handle, rubbing his elbow. 'It's lucky we have company or you'd get what's coming to you.'

Then he laughed too loudly with his head thrown backwards, to show that he had a sense of humour. Unlike some people.

He would give her a chance he decided and he started again.

'No luck with the girls on my course, I'll hold my hands up to that. They were all the type who preferred swotting to fun, if you get my meaning. The Thick Ankle Brigade we called them. Inky fingers, bottle-end glasses. Had their fat little noses jammed into books all the time.'

He poked a finger gently into her arm. 'No offence.' His tone was wheedling. 'Looks like female engineers have improved since my time.'

The engineer sipped at her vodka before poking him back hard – hard enough to leave a bright white dimple in his forearm that did not immediately rise up again.

She winked at him. 'None taken.'

He laughed again, but uncertainly this time and looked at the white mark on his arm. He was still in the mood to be teased. Just.

Irina made herself small to slide up and down the narrow space between the back of the engineer's chair and the kitchen counter, arranging the plates and testing the readiness of the soup with a teaspoon.

'Eat,' she said to the engineer, pointing at the dumplings. 'Don't wait for me.'

She had folded out the extra leaf in the table for the engineer's visit and shaken out the white linen cloth, so that it hovered for a moment in the air before descending like sudden snowfall and turning the table into a pristine version of itself. It was a trick she wished she could perform on herself.

The everyday jars and dishes had been stacked in the cupboard over the sink and replaced with a matching set of bowls and she had decanted the sauces into them. Perhaps it would have been better to keep the table small and have more room to move around the kitchen but it was too late now and at least the dishes looked pretty at the centre.

She wanted, very much, for the engineer to notice her efforts.

They had a number of appliances that were foreign made; a shiny Dualit toaster with four slots and a Kenwood blender and she had cleared the counters of the bottles of oil and the overspill of tins to better display them.

Irina glanced at them now and then, hoping the

engineer would comment on them. If she had commented, Irina planned to say, 'Oh I know it seems extravagant but I love to cook and high quality appliances last longer anyway.' It was pitiful and she hated herself for it but there it was.

She had rehearsed a number of conversations.

'My favourite gallery? It has to be the Hermitage in St Petersberg. We went two days in a row didn't we Oleg? Impossible to see everything in a few hours. Unless you're one of these tourists who just tick sights off their list and gallop past everything without really looking.' Then she would laugh and shake her head at people like that.

'We have a famous physicist to boast about actually. Dr Yelenev Spatzy. You've probably heard of her. She's high up in the International Space Station programme. We try to follow her progress don't we Oleg? She went to our little school. Her parents only moved away a few years ago.'

She had seen the engineer's novels stacked up in her motel room and thought the conversation might turn to books.

'The only thing I really miss about Yakutsk is the library. I read a book a week when I was younger. I've thought about a distance learning course at Moscow University. Literature. Maybe in the Spring I'll apply.'

She had been looking forward to this evening so that she could show the engineer off to Oleg and maybe to spite him. See how she likes me Oleg? She hoped he would see them talking and laughing the way they had begun to do over drinks at the coffee shop. Perhaps he would step outside of himself and their claustrophobic, domestic sparring to take the opportunity to view Irina as another person might.

She felt Oleg's mood without having to turn to look at him; the sixth sense of a long marriage connecting her to him like a physical wire. It was vibrating.

He'd looked the engineer up and down when she'd arrived and smiled at her with his mouth turned up more on one side than the other in a way she recognised as an attempt at being flirtatious.

She knew he had judged the engineer to be attractive but not out of his league and she was filled with contempt for him. His big bald head was doltish. What must the engineer think about the way his shirt gaped around the buttons? At least, Irina thought, she had a realistic view of herself and she touched her neck with the tips of her fingers.

The engineer was younger than Oleg but not too young as far as he was concerned. He was offhand and curt with very attractive women, knowing it was not worth his while to try to be charming. After all, where was the gain? But here were the familiar stories, amplified and exaggerated each time she heard them about his grades and his conquests.

Soon he would tell her about the bicycle race from the University to the Boat Club that he had won, 'even though, the finish point was in sight and there's me, up on the pedals, pounding along, and I look over my shoulder and say 'yup, it's in the bag Oleg' and I can taste the victory and when I turn back around there's a dog sitting in the road. A bloody dog. Right in front of me, sitting there licking its balls. So I brake and swerve, the back wheel goes and I hear this gasp from the crowd as I flip up, somersault in the air and then KABOOM, straight down onto my head on the kerb. So what d'you think I did then? Well I said to myself, Oleg's no quitter. So I picked up my bike, which, incidentally, was wrecked, and ran the rest of the way and carried it over the line. I was drenched in blood, dripping, so that the guy waving the flag fainted and hit his head too.'

Irina urged him to tell the story. So that she could be right about him and she could feed her resentment.

He'll be holding his stomach in Irina thought. She glanced over her shoulder to check. Yes. Her small triumph feeding the ice chip of disdain that lodged in her chest.

She filled a glass with iced tea and placed it in front of him. He did not look at her but pushed it deliberately with his finger to a spot slightly to the right.

She saw the engineer notice the movement. You see? This is how it is here Irina thought. Look what I have to put up with. She hoped she would understand Irina's serenity in the face of Oleg's ingratitude and think her noble and somehow see that this domesticity was not enough for her and that she was better than this life but bore it because it was her duty.

But what if she thought she was spineless and weak? Or just empty headed?

All of the conversations she had prepared had flown out of her head.

Irina, twisted the dishcloth over the sink with a sharp movement – that was how her grandmother had cracked a chicken's neck — and watched the water trickling away down the plughole. Plughole. What a stupid word. Plughole.

It was stuck in her head. She feared she would say it aloud and she bared her teeth, a gate to hold in an unpleasant word.

If only she could think of a film she had seen and some clever remarks to make about it but her head was fuzzy. It was too hot in here and her eyes were stinging from the spices in the soup. She cursed the lack of the extractor fan.

She put down the plates on the kitchen counter and looked, from the side of her eyes, at the engineer's profile with its long, straight nose. She was examining Oleg with an unaffected curiosity. Her small smile was friendly. Oleg's features were beginning to sag and his head leaned forward as if the weight were too much for his neck to bear.

Now the engineer would see what he was like. What Irina's life was like. She set out the plates on the table, pushing Oleg's plate with difficulty between his heavily planted elbows, saying excuse me please Oleg in a small voice, knowing that he would not move to make her task any easier. She was parading the indignity in a bid for sympathy and it made her hate herself. But what alternative did she have?

This woman's pity would be something at least, better than nothing, she needed so very little and it was desperate to her how easily pleased she would be. With some crumbs. She despaired of herself standing over this sink again and her inward-looking life of dumplings and dishcloths.

It's not fair she thought and wished suddenly to be blind drunk and oblivious to it all.

Soon Oleg would tip over from his quiet befuddlement into sharp remarks. And then, a little later, his eyes would narrow and dart around looking for reasons to find fault with the room and his food – too salty, too greasy, too hot, too predictable, too this, too that – on and on – and how he had wasted his life. He would end the evening running his white palms over his scalp and spitting nasty insults at her.

Irina checked the roasted venison, flapping away the heat from the oven with her apron. The quicker it was ready the sooner the meal could be over and the engineer could leave before that happened.

She had been looking forward to the evening and the hope that for once, for once, her pleasure would not be spoiled. She stabbed at the meat with a skewer and thought, pressing her lips together, that if it must be spoiled, she'd rather it would be in a spectacular fashion.

The engineer turned completely around in her chair to talk to Irina. Oleg's reactions were slowing and Irina saw the gradual thickening of indignation that descended over his face, at the realisation of the slight implied by a woman's turned back.

She reached across to touch Irina's forearm lightly. Irina looked at the spot. When had she been touched in kindness recently? She couldn't think.

'You must show me how to make these,' she said. 'The cooking gene skipped a generation with me and I am an absolute disgrace to my entire family in the kitchen. If I could go home with just one edible dish to offer I think they'd throw a party.'

'It's easy enough,' said Irina.

'You make everything look easy,' said the engineer. 'That's your superpower.'

Oleg filled his glass with vodka, drank it back, and refilled it. He gazed down into it with a frown as if trying to identify the liquid and then, with a bleak resignation and a choking sound like a sob, drank it down again.

'Hi.' Vasily slid into the doorway. He had taken a big gulp of breath as if he had been standing out of sight for a few moments, screwing up the courage to make his appearance. Irina felt a rush of warmth for him and the sudden realisation that he was shy and not just difficult. He was like her she realised with surprise.

She often entertained the Russian motel visitors at home and most left a large tip at the end of their stay that more than covered the cost. Vasily refused to eat with them but usually agreed to introduce himself at least.

Irina smiled at him, encouraging him, grateful for the effort and knowing how much it cost him.

'Hey,' said the engineer. 'You must be Vasily. Cool hair.'

'Thanks,' said Vasily. 'They don't think so.'

'If your parents thought your hair was cool then, let me tell you, it wouldn't be cool.'

'Ha! Do you know what I think would be cool? Studying for a degree or working. Not laying around in bed wanking half the day,' said Oleg and he curled his fist and gestured to his groin.

'Yeah, nice one dad,' said Vasily. His face was a mask.

Irina could not have guessed if the remark hurt him.

'I didn't know what I wanted to do until I was twenty-five,' said the engineer. If she had registered Oleg's comment she didn't bother to show it and she sided with Vasily, in the way that people who don't have their own children always do.

'My God Vasily, when I was your age I came home with a Mohawk. The drama! My mother didn't speak a word to me, not one word, for almost a month and she covered all of the photographs of me in the house with black cloths until it had grown out.'

She picked up a tea towel and draped it over her head, dabbing at her eyes mournfully with a paper napkin.

'One of the neighbours came round to borrow some salt, saw the photos decked in their miniature shrouds, and rushed out and told everyone in the block I'd died. I thought it was hilarious. My mother, not so much.'

Vasily's smile creased up into his eyes and Irina, not remembering the last time she had seen him show pleasure, was warmed and filled with delight by her friend and her son. Oh. This is what happiness feels like, she thought.

'That can't be true,' said Oleg. 'It's a stupid story.' His voice had slowed and thickened.

The engineer ignored his comment and grinned at Vasily. She was not merely pretending to be unconcerned as Irina would have been. She really doesn't give a damn, thought Irina and she felt an intoxicating burst of something fizzy rising in her chest, like hilarity.

She had not smoked for twenty years but suddenly longed for a cigarette to celebrate with.

The engineer reached across and touched Vasily's arm.

'When I was a teenager I thought I'd be so free when I grew up. I'd travel the world. Stay up all night partying with wild people in crazy places. The reality is Vasily, I woke up at four am a few weeks ago and I couldn't get back to sleep because I was trying to figure out which complete rotter keeps stealing my Tupperware from the office fridge. It was driving me insane.'

She remembered the tea towel and removed it from her head, smiling.

'My point being, don't be in too much of a rush to settle for the inevitable, boring bits of adult life.'

Irina placed the bowls on the table and dropped a fat blob of cream into the centre of each one.

'You are traveling the world though. You're here aren't you?'

And she sat at the end of the small table covered with a linen cloth her mother had given her. She dipped her spoon into the blue patterned bowl with its chipped rim and sipped at the sweet soup with her eyes on the engineer.

The woman had pushed up the sleeves of her sweater to show a slender wrist and the ends of golden forearms. A tattoo, blue and pink, Irina couldn't see what it was, perhaps a bird or a flower, peeped out from under her sleeve.

The engineer scooped up a spoonful, gathering a little cream at the same time, and blew on it gently. She shimmered slightly through the haze of the steam. She sipped at it, swallowed and widened her eyes at Irina.

'This too! I'm not going home until I've extracted every

single one of your secrets.' She turned back to her soup and knitted her eyebrows into a theatrical glare and took another sip. 'Under torture if necessary.'

Nine

rina had a flask of proper coffee pushed into one deep pocket and a slice of the Medovik in a zip-loc plastic bag in another. The custard had made a slick mess on the inside of the bag already. She made a mental note: bring Tupperware next time. She hummed to herself, in happy anticipation of next time.

She had added lots of extra milk to the coffee, because that was how the engineer preferred it and remembered, just at the last second, not to load it with sugar.

She had caught sight of herself smiling, distorted but recognisable, in the reflection of the metallic flask as she filled it at the café table and she glanced up to see Zeena looking at her oddly from behind the glass display case. Was smiling so out of character for her these days?

The flask bumped against her thigh as she walked across the square but it did not irritate her as something of that sort almost certainly would on a normal day. In fact, she liked the rhythm of the soft knocks. Good, Deed, Good, Deed, they seemed to say. She knew the engineer would be pleased to see her and the thought of the other woman's pleasure warmed her.

It was a still day. Tomyator's location, in a shallow dip like the scoop in the bottom of a dinner plate, meant the low fog that streamed into the square overnight often hung about all day; rebellious and obdurate.

A visitor to the town would not have dared to venture out, but Irina liked stepping into the absence of light and the way that the sounds were muted so that her own footsteps sounded distant and otherworldly.

This deaf blind state was soothing to her. If she could not see the row of black, unlit windows of the motel rooms she did not have to think about the mortgage repayments or the mould that crept around the shower trays. If she could not see the store she did not worry about the price of her shopping that seemed to rise, just a little, every month. Instead she could lose herself in dreams that she was back in Yakutsk, pushing Vasily to the park again, and walking towards all the excitement and promise of her future. On days like these she could summon the remembrance of that feeling again. She could entertain the possibility of hope returning.

From the gloom a person materialised suddenly, directly in front of her, so that they almost collided and both Irina and the man held up their palms in alarm and wore startled expressions, a mirror image, and then smiled at each other's surprise.

'Nikki,' she said. He was a neighbour from the apartment block and because it was too cold to stop and chat he simply nodded and patted Irina's arm, twice, in a friendly way.

It was a gesture that said 'that was a close call', and 'good morning to you' and 'I hope all's well at home' and 'take good care of yourself in this tricky weather Irina,' as he continued on his way.

It wasn't so bad here. They weren't a bad community she thought.

And she dived onwards into the peace and anonymity of the fog. Irina imagined the square to be stuffed with souls like herself, thinking themselves to be alone but no more than an arm's stretch from a similarly dreaming traveller.

There was a solitary kind of camaraderie to it.

At the edge of the square, where the buildings parted and the thousands of miles of emptiness began to unfurl, she stepped out of the bank of fog, just like that, and into a clear blue day.

She looked back at the grey wall and wished the engineer was here to see this. It was a clearly defined barrier, seemingly as solid as a wall of timber or bricks, but a wall through which she could float at will.

She leaned back and passed her hand through it and felt herself at the intersection of two worlds. It was a peculiar, light sensation and reminded her of joy. This was one of those days when she loved Tomyator.

It was possible to move faster now, more confidently, and the journey passed quickly. Later, at home, she could not remember her walk along Libsky Street and beyond the edge of the town at all.

She did remember feeling light on her feet, muscular and musical, and she remembered feeling eager to arrive.

The slight pull against her calves as she leaned into the incline on the final approach to the Weather Station was welcome, because that meant she was nearly there. She saw the sloped peak of the utility tent and halted for a moment, unexpectedly breathless.

Irina had made this trip thousands of times and she was unprepared for the bump of surprise that seeing the familiar landscape so changed had delivered.

The tent was much larger than she had expected.

Just a few poles and some canvas, that was all, but its physical shape interrupting the scene she had come to almost not notice was jarring. So the work was fully underway. It was really happening. Of course it was, and she felt foolish to have been so eager to arrive.

The engineer, or perhaps it had been a couple of the lads who'd come out to help, had made a high wall of snow around the tent, almost to its full height and with banked sides to bounce the wind that swept across the plains safely up and over its canvas roof.

They had left a gap, of perhaps twenty centimetres, between the snow and the canvas so that the air could flow around the structure. It was precisely done and Irina knew at once that the engineer had directed proceedings. It gave the tent a permanence and heft and she clenched her fists, anxiously, inside her mittens.

Whilst she had never considered the Weather Station to be especially pretty, it had been pristine and untouched. Now the snow inside the enclosure was trampled and dirty. Trails of oil spotted the pathway, a large, red plastic bin with a clipped-down lid stood at the entrance and a pile of thin steel rods had been stacked next to the gate. It gave her an uncomfortable sensation to see her Weather Station so changed by the engineer's arrival.

She tucked her head down and trudged the last fifty metres to the edge of the chain link fence.

All of her lightness and energy had seeped away. Irina's ankle throbbed and her thigh, in the spot where the flask had bumped, felt tender and bruised.

She wondered why she had come and hesitated by the gate, deciding whether to turn and make her way back home when the engineer appeared from behind the tent. She was carrying a wire cylinder the size and shape of an elongated bucket.

'Irina. You've come,' she called and she dropped the cylinder and put her hands on her hips. 'About bloody time too! I've been absolutely dying to give you the tour.'

She hurried over to open the gate for Irina, inviting her inside in a proprietorial way and Irina felt put out by her change of status. It was true, she was the visitor now, and she felt shy and tongue-tied.

The engineer led the way, along the short, stamped down path, to the tent.

It had an outer flap with a thick zip that the engineer undid, before stepping inside a small entrance chamber and beckoning Irina to follow. It was quieter out of the wind.

She closed it behind them, bending all the way down to the floor with a swooping movement that reminded Irina of that first night in the motel room, before unzipping the entrance to the main body of the tent.

'The whole tent is double-skinned,' said the engineer. 'Practically tropical in here don't you think?'

Irina nodded. It was almost warm, certainly bearable. The engineer removed her thick gloves and replaced them with fingerless woollen ones instead.

'See?' she said, wiggling her fingers. 'It goes up to around three or four degrees. Warm enough for me to be able to work at my table without losing a finger to frostbite at any rate.'

Inside it was tall enough for Irina to stand upright whilst the engineer had to tip her head a fraction to duck beneath the metal pole that ran along the centre of the structure.

The trestle table stood to one side and a canvas chair, placed on top of a thick rubber mat, marked out her work space.

On top of the table, small metal and plastic components and wires were laid out in neat rows. Next to them were pliers, wire strippers and a succession of small screwdrivers.

It was clear that the engineer wanted her to be impressed with her work and with this space that she'd built and Irina was flattered by it. She listened carefully, nodding in the right places, as the heater, that had an extractor pipe running out of the back of the tent, was demonstrated.

The smells were of canvas and metal and of wet rubber.

All around were the precisely arranged signs of her industry and Irina's admiration for her fought with her dread at the thought of how much had already been achieved.

She searched for something to say, looking around to avoid the engineer's clear eyes and landed on a briefcase that was open on the floor. Inside it were a series of small metal implements within precisely cut foam shapes.

'I love all these gadgets,' the engineer said, seeing her notice them. 'I can't wait to get these out there and start working. Do you think I'm an insufferable nerd?'

Irina nodded.

'Yes' she said, smiling, despite herself, at the woman's bubbling enthusiasm. 'Insufferable.'

'I know, I know. I sometimes think they're like my babies,' said the engineer. 'I can pour all my love into them.'

'Easier than real babies. Or teenagers.' said Irina raising her eyebrows. Vasily had been personable and friendly enough at dinner and Irina hoped to steer the conversation towards him and the evening they had spent together.

'Aren't all teenagers a challenge though?' said the engineer, ducking under the metal cross brace. 'I know I was. I suppose I'd feel differently if it happened to be one I'd produced.'

'Do you think you might like a child one day?'

Irina asked the question casually, running her fingers over the instruments on the trestle table, but she really was burning to know more about this woman and her life.

'I wouldn't be a good parent. I'd probably leave it on a tram by mistake. Like an umbrella. I'm sure it's very satisfying though.'

Her half-smile and cocked eyebrows said, if you like that sort of thing.

'Rubbish. You're patronising me,' said Irina. 'You don't think it's satisfying at all do you?'

The engineer grimaced.

'Oh Irina, I'm sorry but it looks like such a gargantuan

task for minimal reward. Is that too transactional of me?' She flipped up her palms in surrender. 'I don't care even if it is. I honestly can't think why you do it.'

She sat on the canvas chair, balanced an ankle on her knee and knotted her fingers behind her head.

'Did you know there are 15,000 babies born every hour in the world? I imagine them being fired out of prone women – in rows – like some monstrous factory conveyor belt. The worst of it is that every parent seems to think you're going to be fascinated by their little mewling creature in particular. And smelly nappies. Ugh!.'

She grinned and wrinkled her nose.

'Good God why?' No offence Irina but one kid is much like another as far as I'm concerned.'

She stood up, having delivered her opinion on the matter, and ready to get on with her work. She retrieved another case and lifted it up onto the table.

'You, at least, had the very good sense to stop at one.'

Irina picked out a small metal implement with a roughened sphere at the end and examined it.

'I did have another, a girl, but she was stillborn.'

The engineer turned, sharply, and put her hand to her mouth.

'Irina. Forgive me. I never think. I'm so sorry.'

'No, I'm sorry I mentioned it. I don't think about it that much these days and you weren't to know.'

Irina smiled and waved her hand at the engineer. It's of no consequence her gesture seemed to say. Managing other people's feelings about her own suffering had become her habit these days. It was easier that way.

'What happened?'

'What?' Irina looked up at her. She gave a laugh at the bluntness of the question and surprised herself with the harshness of the sound.

The women of Tomyator had heard the news of the stillbirth and hugged her when they saw her, averting their eyes as they did it to protect her privacy in her grief, and offered their gentle condolences. They placed their feet quietly when they were near, careful not to move suddenly or talk too loudly. They had agreed with each other that she would have trouble with her nerves. It was natural. They were sincere, Irina was sure, and she had felt properly part of the community then.

Some had made meals and delivered them to the apartment in plates covered with tin foil for a while and a neighbour had taken over the cleaning of the motel for two weeks and refused, point-blank, to accept any payment for it.

Vasily was scooped up by other mothers who insisted it would be no trouble to take him to their homes to play for the afternoon. Of course they would make him something tasty for his dinner too. One more mouth would make no difference.

These were gestures that mattered and Irina had appreciated it as much as she was able in her raw, skinned-alive state. But no one had ever asked her what happened. Not outright like that. So what happened Irina? Frankly and unflinchingly.

It was an odd sensation to be so firmly at the centre of an important conversation and Irina had a dizzying sense of the ground shifting under her feet; of the whole wide world performing a swooping about face and directing its attention at her.

She blushed, more from a kind of pleasure than embarrassment and it felt illicit, dirty almost, and she was ashamed to be so thrilled by the focus on her. 'You want to be the centre of attention' was a reprimand for bad children. But Irina did want it. When had someone asked her a question and genuinely cared about her answer?

She tried to make herself available for other people's troubles but was not able to offer her whole self back to anyone in return. Her eyes filled with tears, not at the remembrance of her pain, but in appreciation at being noticed.

The engineer did not avert her eyes.

'Look, you don't have to tell me if you don't want to, obviously, but I would like to know.'

Irina's arms hung straight down by her sides. They felt very heavy. She could feel their weight tugging on her shoulders as if she had carried a whole week's worth of shopping home from the store.

'What is there to tell? I felt like something was wrong inside – a few days before I was due. There was a kind of extra weight. She seemed to stop moving. When my waters broke it wasn't like with Vasily. There was no warning at all. It just happened. There was a terrible smell.'

She looked up at the engineer quickly, as if to catch her out, to see if she was disgusted with her.

Oleg had been disgusted. She remembered his reflexive grimace with squeezed together eyes and his intake of

133

breath. Had he put his hand to his nose? Perhaps she had imagined that. Anyway, she clearly remembered his clumsy attempts to mask his revulsion so that she would not be frightened. That was what frightened her most.

The liquid had not seeped, as it had with Vasily, but gushed in a shocking whoosh that had slopped down her thighs and pooled inside her pale pink slippers.

Well, they're ruined, she thought.

The plan had been to have the baby at home. Vasily had been delivered in the hospital in just two hours and although the pain had been white hot and searing it was not more than she could bear and she had forgotten it quickly afterwards.

The nurses had praised her and she had been smug. She was one of those women who kept quiet and just got on with it they said. She hadn't made the fuss that some of them did. You should hear them swearing and screeching the place down like they were the first woman in the world to have a baby. Some of them made a terrible scene apparently Irina told Oleg. They held hands and shook their heads scornfully at that type of woman.

They had talked about going back to Yakutsk a few weeks before the birth of this baby but decided, in the end, it would be easy enough to manage at home.

So when her waters broke, Oleg ran flat footed and wild eyed around the apartment, banging clumsily into the door frames. He dragged a blanket from the bed to wrap around her before helping her across the square, running ahead at the last minute, to bang on Dr Nevsky's door.

His wife had answered and brought them inside making

cooing, clucking noises of reassurance. If she thought there was anything wrong she did not betray it on her face. She had put her big, meaty arms around Irina and drawn her inside, away from Oleg and his frightened white face.

'Dr Nevsky delivered the baby, she came very quickly, and she was dead.' And when Irina said 'dead' a sob rose painfully like a flat pebble up into her throat and lay on her tongue, pressing it down in her mouth so that she found herself unable to speak.

Stillborn was the word everyone preferred to use. She understood why.

Stillborn sounded so peaceful. The baby was still, unmoving and untroubled. She was a beautiful doll. No blood moved through her tiny body. Irina's baby girl had not cried out in fear or pain even once.

Who could say that about their life?

Irina's baby did not complain and she would never suffer the unbearable trials of living. She would never have to worry about not having a proper best friend at school. She would never be disappointed by her husband or fight bitterly with him about his drinking and his temper. Irina's baby would not lie awake in her cold marriage bed with bleak thoughts of washing machine repayments.

Irina had considered it a silver lining of sorts; the thought of the peace and the purity of her baby's short existence.

The engineer did not apologise again or look away. She was listening, really listening, with her eyebrows squashed and bumpy with concern. She bit on her bottom lip. Irina could see the thoughts turning behind her eyes as she tried to understand.

Irina had never said the word 'dead' aloud about her baby before but there it was. It was sad, terribly sad, to say it but she had not been completely undone by it. It was a truth and she had faced it and been equal to it.

'But why did she die?' said the engineer.

'Seriously?' said Irina, jerked out of her thoughts and not sure if she had misheard. 'It happens.'

'But you must have needed to know the reason. If it was me, I'd torture myself with questions about why.'

Dr Nevsky had shaken his head and held her hand very kindly. His hands were large and the palms were soft, not like Oleg's narrow palms that were roughened and dry from his work. She was afraid when he unclasped his fingers from hers. She felt she might float up in the air and out of the window into the white sky without his hand to hold on to.

He explained that it was difficult to be sure but sometimes in cases like these the placenta detached from the womb which meant that the baby had not received the oxygen she needed.

'Do you understand?' he said.

His wife was chopping vegetables in the kitchen and the knife made a soft 'tuk tuk' sound when it met the wooden board. Irina knew she was chopping as softly as she could. That was very kind of her. Dr Nevsky must have discussed tackling this difficult conversation with his wife, in whispers, as Irina lay silently on the examination couch.

Waking, gasping in the night Irina imagined the baby opening and closing her mouth desperately inside her belly in a sac of fluid, flailing her chubby arms in panic.

She was drowning.

After it all happened, Irina had found herself faced with an unexpected and unwelcome stretch of empty time. Time she had thought would be filled with caring for the new baby now yawned like an accusation.

So she threw herself into cleaning, even though the apartment had already been rendered spotless in preparation for their new arrival, until Oleg complained about the smells of bleach and disinfectant.

'It smells like a hosp...' He remembered himself just in time. He was still being careful then.

One morning Irina had been in the bathroom, kneeling on the bath mat, which she had folded twice to make a cushion for her knees on the hard tile floor, when she noticed a movement, a pale suggestion of a shadow, in the water of the toilet pan.

One of Vasily's toys most likely. It wouldn't be the first time.

She leaned closer, pushing her hair behind her ears. There was a curious, smooth undulation beneath the surface, like a large bubble rising slowly.

It was dim in the bathroom so she stretched up to pull the light cord and when she leaned back over the bowl her baby's perfectly oval doll's face was rising up and her eyes, which Irina had never seen until now, unfolded their soft seams and showed brilliantly round and blue.

Her face broke the surface of the water and she spluttered and called 'mama', her first word, and Irina slammed down the lid and then screamed and lifted it again so that she could escape and be born but her baby was gone and Irina's legs had slipped crazily in every direction and she had fallen onto the bathroom floor.

'What is it?' yelled Oleg, dragging open the door and he became angry that it was nothing except Irina sitting in a heap and slammed it shut, furious that he'd been frightened.

Irina could not say whether her derangement – that was what she felt it was – had lasted a day, a month or a year. Time became slippery and elastic. Each night stretched to become never ending as the big red numbers on the clock moved forwards and backwards so that she was sure it must be broken.

She had seen her baby girl's face again, rising from a pot of water she was boiling for potatoes. She was not burned by the heat and did not speak this time but she smiled and had just the same dimples as her little cousin Alessia had when she was small. Irina could not risk cooking on the stove after that.

She saw her beneath the surface of the washing up water in the blue plastic bowl. Her hair floated out around her head. Irina had reached down, as gently as she could to feel her baby's face but the water dissipated into ripples that were lacquered in greens and blues with the grease from the dishes. She stood with her hands in the water, waiting for her baby to return, until it was cold and still. Then she left the dirty dishes on the table or piled them up on the draining board, even after Oleg lost his temper about the mess.

She could not tell him why she could not wash up, just

that she didn't feel like it these days.

In her half asleep state at home with Vasily banging his trucks against the furniture in the living room, Irina had imagined the baby as a mermaid, twisting and turning in the fluid, able to survive in water and in the air and how that would have been wonderful.

Time would shrink and grow until Vasily's whining for his snacks could not be ignored and she would wonder how long she had sat there.

Oleg had been fearful of her sorrow at first. He made her tea and flicked through the television channels until he found a drama or a comedy show she might like. He watched her from the corner of his eye to see whether she was getting better yet.

He tried to occupy Vasily for a month or so but soon he began to leave for work earlier than necessary to escape her blank face and the thick fog of despair that permeated the apartment. Then, Irina could not say how much later, he became irritated with her, slamming the cupboard doors in the kitchen when there was no dinner prepared for him.

'Mum can't be bothered with us son,' he said as he made rough sandwiches for them to eat together in a huddle, away from her. And his words were punches against her useless, failed body.

The engineer took the little metal implement from Irina's hands and put it into the case, slotting it into a piece of foam that was cut to the perfect shape and size. Irina liked the way it fitted in perfectly.

Then she took her hands and pulled her up to her feet and wrapped her arms around her. She was taller than Irina and Irina pressed her face into her neck, smelling her freshly washed hair that carried the aroma of the shampoo she decanted into the little plastic bottles in the bathroom. Irina was pleased the engineer was using them now. So it was familiar but strange.

'It must have been devastating,' said the engineer. 'Shattering. How did you survive it Irina?' And she held her tightly. 'No more work for today. This is more important. I want you to tell me everything.'

Ten

That night Irina could not sleep. She turned her pillow again and lay her cheek against its cool, smooth surface and exhaled a long flute of air. If she could mimic the sensation of relaxation then perhaps it would become real. But there was no comfort to be found in it.

She snapped her eyes tightly shut, and they felt dry and gritty behind her eyelids.

She rubbed at the two vertical lines between her eyebrows. She could feel the creases even when she wasn't frowning nowadays.

Oleg lay still in the furrow of the mattress; still as a corpse, but groaning sometimes or snorting in his dreams. How she envied him his dead-to-the-world sleep. And the way he plunged into it, suddenly and precipitously, like a man falling into a deep hole.

It was infuriating and she clenched her fists at the unfairness of it. Of all of it.

He would consider himself blameless of course. Even if she could find the courage to tell him what she'd done. To explain that her white lies had been for them. For the motel. So what would be the use of it?

Her pile of notebooks in the drawer in the living room were evidence of her deceit she supposed and she picked at the idea of the lie. She felt it very much to be one lie, repeated, and not a series of different lies and in that way it seemed less consequential. Keeping it secret from Oleg had originally been to protect him. He had been so wrapped up in his new job, it didn't seem fair to worry him.

Then, as is the way with a lie, the passing of time made it more difficult to revisit. So Irina had put it out of her mind.

She turned onto her back and placed her arms, stiffly, by her side, remembering the strange sensation of the engineer's arms around her and the chemical smell of the woman's hair. Thoughts of her baby girl and the Weather Station tumbled together in her mind. She turned over her truthfulness about one and not the other.

Oleg would never understand. But she longed to shake him awake and tell him that she was suffering and to beg him for help. She could not bear the weight of the family and everything it needed to survive, alone, any longer.

But he would bring her no comfort.

She held her clenched fists over the covers and they felt feminine and inconsequential. Her anger had no real heft or consequence in the world. Its only function was to burn at her from the inside.

He lay mute; a thick carcass of dense indifference. It seemed a rebuke. Even if she had knelt up in bed and pummelled him on his chest he could have pushed her arms away with a mutter and turned on his side and slept on.

Irina held herself tight and contained in the shut-up stuffy room in the black night and her mind began to spin with barely realised snatches of thoughts of the Weather Station and the engineer. What would she think of her when she found out? Her mind was cotton wool and scratchy like a warning of flu, and she hated Oleg, hated him for his useless, witless, oblivion.

Perhaps she was ill, or becoming ill. She did have a headache but it was no worse than usual. These stuffy rooms gave her headaches all the time.

She thought about the way her mother had shaken her awake in the night when she was a child, kneeling on the bed and digging her fingers into Irina's shoulders with her hair wild and flopping forward so that it brushed against her face.

It smelled of smoke and babies so that Irina knew it must be Wednesday. Bath night was Sunday but on a Wednesday her mother dropped thick white lines of talcum powder along her centre parting and combed it in to 'see her through.'

The light was on and she remembered the way the front of her night dress gaped so that her breasts drooped down, swaying in her agitation, in full view inside it. Her breath had been stale and urgent.

'You're ill. Christ. How are you so hot? Go and fetch some water Irina. Right now.'

She had been angry with Irina. And Irina had lowered her eyes and agreed that she was hot, shocked by the cold tiles on her soft pink soles. She gulped down freezing water from the kitchen tap until her stomach hurt, afraid to turn on the light, shivering in her shock and tiredness.

She understood now that she had not been ill at all. Her mother had been lonely and needed another person to be awake in the apartment. It was just too hard to be the only one who could not sleep.

It was an agony to Irina when Oleg grunted and rolled heavily to face her so that the cool slab of his belly flopped onto her hip. She pushed against him, her hands sinking into him, but he did not move and she felt his hot breath begin to condense into a moistness on her neck. She threw herself onto her side and away from him with a sharp movement, dragging at the covers.

She wished violently for him to be awake and to be tormented as she was but knew she would be furious at his befuddled questions about the time. What the hell did it matter? He would turn and paw at the light switch, missing it at first, and then blunder to the bathroom and urinate loudly, not bothering to close the door and saying 'ahhhhh' in that stupid way he did and then thumping back into bed, and that was unbearable to her too.

There was no air. Or at least no air that had not been filtered through the lungs of the family a hundred thousand times.

She thought she would throw off the covers and rush to the window and pull open the curtains and fling the windows wide to gulp in some fresh new air. But they were iced shut. Even if she had been able to open them the wind would have crashed into the room to tear around the walls, coating everything it touched with frost in minutes.

But she longed for air. Sweet air, scented with gardenia,

wafting from pots in sunny corners that would revive her. Cool air filtered through fields of tall grass still damp at its tips from early morning mists. Five o'clock in July air in Yakutsk. Irina thought of that exact moment, at the turning of a summer's day, when she had pushed Vasily home from the little park. She would shiver and pull her sweater over the newly tender skin of her shoulders.

Any damned air for God's sake. She pushed off the covers. A sticky sheen of sweat had formed between her breasts and she wiped it away with the tips of her fingers and onto the sheets.

Oh God. How could she survive the night in this hot room? She lay on her side and listened to the wind rushing around the square. It had a riotous, unpredictable sound and she gripped the edge of the mattress, feeling the raised seam through the sheet pressed into her palm, with a rising dread.

This was not a new feeling and she tried to reason with herself. Stop it Irina. Be sensible. She wished intently for sleep to wipe it all away.

'Sleep,' she whispered, as if calling out to a friend.

If she thought about it, if she was sensible, she knew the wind was no worse than usual. No worse, she told herself. But the swooping, cawing sound of it seemed more insistent than usual and full of whispering insinuations.

It was madness to consider that there were words behind those sounds. She would not give in to it. Mad people never knew they were mad did they? Of course not. She felt a bright tick of reassuring rationality. This wasn't like before with her baby. Then, she had not realised she was mad until it had passed.

Because what would a mad person do? Mad people rushed to the window and threw it open but she had not. Mad people heard voices telling them to run around the square without their clothes, or jabbered nonsense in public places, embarrassing their families. She was not mad but just afraid all of a sudden. She was deathly afraid of the wind.

It was lonely being so full of fear.

If only she had someone to say, Oh Irina, it's silly to be afraid of the wind and they would talk about something else, like a television programme, something normal, to take her mind off it. And she was horribly sorry for herself in this hot room with no one to talk to about inconsequential things.

Who's there? That's what the wind seemed to say. And then there was the soft, breathy tone of her damned cassettes.

Te gusta tu habitacion? Te gusta? The wind whispered. Te gusta?

No, she did not like her room, not at all, and she thought, with a start, how thin the protective walls were between their claustrophobic, too hot apartment and the gaping emptiness outside. It all seemed, suddenly, a bad joke to be crammed together in this little box, perched on the surface of an endless frozen plain.

Why had they come?

The walls could not be much thicker than the length of her hand. She held up her hand in front of her face but it was too black in the room to see it and then she caught her

146

breath in a kind of choke at the buried alive feeling the blindness gave her.

No she could not bear it another moment. She felt urgently along the bedside table for the lamp but when her finger found the raised round nub of the switch she hesitated. She could not bring herself to press it. If she turned on the light she would see the wardrobe with a missing handle, the red curtains, the glass of water beside the bed and she thought the scene too desolate to face.

So she stayed in the dark and she kept thinking of things and she wondered if the thoughts came from inside her or were being driven in by the wind. Unpleasant things. If only she could think of nice things. She thought of the empty shirts and skirts hanging still and silent inside the wardrobe and it was horrifying to her, the way they waited inside there, brushing against each other.

On the left were her clothes and on the right were Oleg's. They pressed against each other, empty of bodies to animate them and she thought of her and Oleg lying together in that bed and felt herself to be as empty as the clothes.

She thought of Vasily lying next door and she thought that he might be awake, lying with his eyes open staring into the same blackness. He had become cold and strange to her. It was frightening to have a stranger lying next door, no more than an arm's stretch away from where she lay. She thought of his high white forehead and his eyes staring up to the ceiling and the slow, shallow rise and fall of his narrow chest in the silence. Was he thinking about her? It was awful to her, not knowing what he was thinking.

She thought of the light, encouraging remarks she made to him at breakfast and the heart-clench of the disdainful silence she earned for her efforts. She received NO CREDIT.

She thought about Zeena's girls, grey-skinned, shrinking away from her and the way their eyes slipped back and forth between themselves and the useless torn vacuum cleaner bag that would have to be replaced and she could smell the dust and feel its gritty dryness on her cheeks and she thought about the coins in her purse and the penny pinching snap of the clasp closing.

She heard the ceiling creaking and groaning, felt the air in the room rise and fall like breathing, and she thought of a black and white photograph she had seen once in a newspaper of a little girl in an iron lung, her head turned towards the camera and smiling. Like it was the most normal thing in the world. Never mind, her expression said.

She hated to think of that picture.

Irina put her hands on her chest, the fingers splayed out as wide as they could go, and she felt them rise and fall with her own quick, sharp breaths and the pressure of the air in the room weighing down on her.

The hot, heavy air was crushing her to death and she thought that if she moved her hands away the full weight of it would descend and push down on her chest and force her down and down into the soft mattress so far that the thick spongy material would close over her body, and then her face, filling her mouth so that she could not cry out for help and then there would be no sign left that she had been there at all.

What would Oleg think in the morning when he could not find her?

No worse, no worse she thought. She had endured nights like these before. This was no worse.

But as she listened with a sickly fear to the shouts of the wind and to the groaning of the ceiling a new sound came. The sharp cracking of wood and plaster, close to, made her blink, blink, blink into the black room and itchy tears sprang into her eyes.

The cracking came again, louder and more consequential this time until there was a deep whoosh, a feeling more than a sound, that gathered itself from under the bed and swept all of the air upwards so that the ceiling separated from the walls, in one great piece, with a crack like a back breaking, and was fired up and away into the black sky.

She watched it ascend.

It was a white rectangle and it went up and up and up becoming smaller and smaller and smaller. At first the ceiling was the size of a bed sheet, then her best linen table cloth, a bath towel from the motel, a tea towel, a handkerchief, a letter from a friend that never arrived, the postage stamp on the letter and then too small to see.

She stared up at the wide sky that was crammed full with stars. Why did people always go on about stars? As if they were romantic or something? She found the stars supercilious, remote. They had light but no warmth and that was her idea of hell.

'No one cares about you,' they said as they passed overhead and she pushed her fingers into her ears.

The walls swayed in time with the wind, they were not resolute, not now that they had seen what had happened to the ceiling.

The first brick, a brick from the very top of the wall where it had met the ceiling, cracked from its mortar and was plucked by the wind from its precarious, newly exposed, position, to be sent spinning out into darkness.

Another, from the opposite wall, creaked before being flung, tumbling, into the black night. Then time speeded up and all the bricks began to peel off, in rows, hurling themselves out into the night so that the walls became shorter and shorter, unravelling like unpicked knitting, until the wall was no higher than the window.

These windows were triple glazed. They were A1 quality. Surely they would resist the wind.

The woman from the agency had shown them a cut away model of a section of window and explained how each layer would reduce heat loss by some percentage or other. Numbers bored Irina, she would rely on Oleg to explain it to her later, and as the woman had talked, Irina had looked through the three panes of glass at a man calling across the square to an acquaintance. He was animated, gesturing. His mouth was opening and closing but no sound penetrated the apartment and she had looked away because it gave her an uneasy feeling to be so shut in.

The window was no match for the wind in the end though, triple glazed or not, and it was blown outwards and away with the bricks.

All the walls had vanished now but the wardrobe with the broken handle stood firm. Irina turned her head to the left, slowly because she was filled with dread, to see that Vasily was awake and that his eyes, glittering, black against his white face, were on her. His look was knowing and full of disdain. He twisted his lips in a small way, as if he were thinking of the worst thing he could say to her. His eyes held hers for a while, and then he turned away, pointing his white, narrow back towards her.

Irina had a new view of the Square now. She strained into the black spaces between the dark grey outlines of the buildings towards the far reaches of the land, beyond which she imagined she could drop off the ends of the earth.

The only light came from the motel. The engineer's light was on and Irina could see a suggestion of a shadow as she moved about inside the room. Those curtains were so thin and cheap. She had always hated those curtains.

She called out to her, again and again, but the wind took her cries and tossed them uselessly up and into the air.

So Irina lay back on her pillow, pulling the blanket to her chin, with round, frightened eyes, as Oleg snored beside her and the wind raged and screamed and dragged at her hair.

Eleven

'I blame you entirely Irina,' said the engineer. 'How much longer?' She flicked at the stiff motel curtains in her impatience before flopping onto the bed and putting a pillow over her face.

'It'll pass,' said Irina. 'Tomorrow. Thursday at the latest. And mind my mattress.'

It was the third straight day of filthy weather in Tomyator and Irina rejoiced at the delay to the engineer's work. She looked out of the window at the snow, thrashing in fist-sized clumps in the air, holding down her smile, and urged it on. She wished it would continue its pounding progress forever.

A dull suggestion of yellow light came from the direction of the apartment block but she could not quite make out the shape of the building itself. Alexi's sign was invisible too. The store would be open by now but his customers would be at home, weighing up how badly they really needed cigarettes or toilet paper.

He would be leaning his elbows on the counter and rubbing his bony hands over his scalp, fretting about the delivery truck she was sure. Monday was the usual delivery day but here they were on Tuesday, still watching and waiting. It had probably parked up somewhere on the road to wait, with its engine rumbling, for a break in the weather.

At times like these it seemed a foolishness to try to exist here at all. The weather was pitiless.

The engineer sat up, swung her long legs off the edge of the bed and huffed. She shuffled her large, thickly socked feet on the nylon carpet. There was a sharp crackle of static.

'How are you so outrageously robust? Honestly. How do you do it? You must be made of stronger stuff than me.'

'Now you're whining,' said Irina. 'It makes you sound like a townie.'

In truth, the engineer had complained very little. Not about the limited hot water that spat out from the shower nozzle with a faint smell of sulphur. Or the diet of noodles and chocolate. Not once about the lumpy bed in the uncomfortable room. And Irina noticed her good grace and admired her for it.

'Be grateful. At least I've organised a distraction,' Irina said.

She took the engineer's coat from the back of the door and held it up; an instruction to action.

'Let's go,' she said, shaking it. 'We mustn't be late.'

It was wonderful to her to say 'let's' and 'we' and 'us' and 'our' and all of the other warm, connecting words to the engineer. They rebounded softly between them, colouring conversations with rich, unexpected hues so that everything, formerly familiar, felt foreign on her tongue. It was like learning a new language to Irina.

She reflected that she had never liked the sound of her own name. It was so ordinary and unremarkable. But when the engineer said her name, 'Irina' in that eager, forthright way of hers, 'Irina', as if she had just thought of something she must tell her and could not possibly hold it inside, it sounded so surprising and full of possibilities that she felt she could really be a new person in that moment.

The distraction had not been Irina's idea but she had leapt upon it nonetheless.

The suggestion that the engineer give a talk to the schoolchildren during her visit had come from Moscow.

Tanja had written in a breathless, jargon-filled manner of the importance of engaging with young people. There was mention of mentoring, outreach, and role models in a dashed off email that had arrived late on Friday afternoon. Irina had puzzled, briefly, over the notion that their little school could be a 'launch pad of aspiration', but she was becoming used to Tanja by now and didn't spend too much time worrying about hidden meanings.

The engineer had seemed keen on the idea and Irina had organised it, obediently, with the teacher. Now that the Weather Station was out of bounds, she was even more pleased to have something productive to do.

The school was a small timber building, faced with horizontals of tough cedar and striped with green seams of moss that had been wedged between the logs, to keep out insects and to stop the water from seeping between them.

The water was a bigger concern than the insects.

A summer raindrop, surely the most moderate and modest manifestation of the Tomyator weather, would land gently and trace its silent course downwards and around the swelling roundness of the log, seeking the lowest point on its quiet journey back to the ocean. Finding a hole, the droplet would slide inside and discover it had not been the first to take this path. Whilst not the sea it might have hoped for, the drop fell – grateful – into a tiny dark pool.

When winter returned, the water would freeze and expand. A chip of ice, no larger than an acorn, could break a log apart. The lesson being, if anyone cared to learn it, that it was the accumulation of small things that made the difference out here.

The two windows, one to the right and the other to the left of the door were flanked with carved shutters that could be closed and latched shut in the event of bad weather.

They were open and Irina smiled under her scarf. Today's conditions clearly did not count as being especially bad and she allowed herself a quick surge of admiration at the stoic, bloody mindedness of the town.

It was a well-kept building. The town's people contributed their labour to keep it in good condition without discussion. They thought it the neighbourly thing to do. If they had bothered to talk about why they gave up their time for this building in particular, they would have agreed that they had a reverence for education as a means of escape from the town.

As they scrambled on the roof checking for rotted planks, or hammered down the flashing around the metal chimney pipe, they stopped to catch their breath and to look around from this new view point. They shielded their eyes with their hands and imagined how far away their children might travel, and then picked apart their own mixed feelings about the matter.

The shutters were sanded and painted a fresh, garden pea green every summer. A neat wooden portico sheltered the door and its two walls and pitched roof protected Irina and the engineer from the worst of the snow at least.

The two women had crammed themselves into it, standing shoulder to shoulder and were buffeted by the blasts of wind that felt like dull kicks against their backs.

The noise of the wind whistling, two high tones, was such that even if they had shouted directly into the other's ear, their voices would not have been audible.

The engineer tried the door but it was locked. She pressed the bell and leaned her ear towards it, scrunching her face as she strained to hear, but it was impossible to tell whether it had sounded inside.

Just as they began to suspect they would have to peer into the windows to attract someone's attention, the ancient supervisor appeared and opened the door a crack to look at the two women with suspicion.

She had a face entirely typical of a Siberian elder; a face that the visitors itched to photograph with its deep walnut ridges of wrinkles and monumental, wide-bridged nose. But the woman's round jaw was set as hard as a horseshoe and her expression was so stonily forbidding that they rarely dared to ask.

She frowned and her black eyes, already deep set, seemed to shrink further back and away from the cold wind, sheltering beneath the shelf of her brow. She ran her heavy, wrinkled hand across her hair which was pulled back severely. The woman was mostly grey but there was an undercurrent of nicotine that showed she had once been blonde.

As far as Irina was aware, the woman had spent her life in a classroom and not toiling in a field and she guessed that Siberian genes, rather that a harsh, outdoor life, were responsible for her ferocious, wind hardened appearance.

Perhaps she knew that she didn't look much like a teacher, because she wore a striking pair of sharply angled glasses with pale blue frames and bold orange arms. They had a jaunty, Mediterranean flavour, and were so startlingly at odds with her face that it looked as if she had put them on for a joke.

The woman flicked her coal eyes quickly from one to the other, alert to a trick, and pulled the door closed a little to repel them.

'What is it?' she said through the crack.

'It's me, Irina' said Irina. 'This is the engineer I was telling you about from Moscow. She's giving a talk to the children. Remember?'

'Of course,' said the woman, affronted. She took off her glasses and looked at the lenses crossly as if they had tried to deceive her.

'Come in then.'

She held open the door and made a flapping gesture, as if they were late and she had been inconvenienced by waiting, but she did not step out of the way and it was difficult to squeeze past.

Irina and the engineer pushed forwards together, elbow to padded elbow, engaging in a small, determined battle, shoving the other a little and giggling, like schoolgirls, in an effort to cross the threshold first. The engineer was stronger and Irina staggered sideways and stepped on the teacher's foot so that the woman shrieked, 'my bunion' and Irina did not dare meet the engineer's eye for a while.

Hissing, the teacher closed the door behind them and locked it with a key which she removed and dropped into a pocket in her skirt, giving them both a disapproving look, before pushing past and leading them into the short hallway.

She was a solid bodied person whose small, quick, steps, beneath her floor-length black skirts, leant her the impression of processing on wheels.

The hallway was lined with occupied coat pegs, to the height of Irina's hip to the left and her shoulder on the right. The coats had dripped to form a viscous line of sludge under each row.

The teacher rolled, regally, along the hallway and led them to the door on the right, listening at it for a moment with a slyly excited look before throwing it open and looking around the room quickly to catch any wrongdoers in the act.

There were around twenty children in the classroom and they turned to look at the new arrivals, hopeful of some entertainment at least. They were interested enough but took care not to show it too obviously, as is the way with all teenagers.

They were confined behind wooden desks with flip up

lids which were set in four rows of five facing the desk of the teacher, upon which was an open packet of biscuits, and a selection of pens all savagely mangled with teeth marks. On the blackboard was a single word: Carbohydrates.

It was a horribly uninspiring room and Irina's spirits sank a little at the sight of it. The walls, the floor and the ceiling were painted the same, dull camouflage green. It reeked of the children's boredom and Irina felt sorry for them trapped in its stultifying confines.

No wonder Vasily had been reluctant to attend. There was so little to look at. A large map on the wall had been stuck with so many pins over the years that there was little more than a ragged hole where Tomyator should be.

A small free standing bookshelf contained age stained books with spines wrinkled from repeated reading. The titles and the authors' names were so fractured as to be almost illegible.

A chart showing plants of the region had curled up from the bottom, where the blue tack had become brittle from the cold, and given up on being sticky. Irina pressed the corners back down again and it held, for now.

She looked around. Other than that the walls were plain.

She had remembered the room as being more colourful but perhaps she was thinking of the class for the younger children. She and Oleg had sat on the tiny plastic chairs and leafed through Vasily's exercise books with his teacher as she pointed out his progress. They had stared hard at his untidy writing and his flat drawings and glossed over his shortcomings as they focussed all of their fervent hopes upon him.

Her eye was caught by a girl with fingernails splodged unevenly in peeling black varnish, leaning back in her chair with her legs sprawled into the aisle in an attitude of worldly insouciance. Irina smiled a greeting and the girl began to smile back, before remembering herself and turning her face away to yawn extravagantly. She curled herself away from Irina, examining her nails, embarrassed to have let down her guard.

She looked to be fourteen or fifteen. Irina's daughter should be that age now and Irina's heart bumped at the girl's gauche posturing. She wondered if Vasily ever thought about what it would be like to have a sister and if he found it hard to be an only child. Irina removed her hat and tucked her hair behind her ears and felt bleak. Why on earth had she never thought to ask him?

There were five computers on a shelf at the back of the room. They were covered with greasy plastic covers as if to preserve them for a special occasion. The plastic was sepia with age.

A hot air heater wafted a smell of burning dust and plastic around the room and although her cheeks tingled with it, a chill seeped upwards through the floor.

The youngest of the children was perhaps eleven and the eldest sixteen and Irina knew most of them by name.

'They're really good kids mostly,' she whispered to the engineer. She wanted to be encouraging. Not that the engineer seemed in need of it. She had planted her hands on her hips and looked confidently around the room, trying to catch their eyes and smiling at the children who responded.

She looks forward to everything thought Irina. She charges at it all.

At the front young Ivan was hard at work outlining an already carved set of initials with his pen. Gouging the groove a little deeper, humming, with his tongue out. He had unusually low set ears that curled over at the top and a purple complexion.

Irina slid around the outside of the room in the bashful, creeping manner that visiting adults always assume in children's classrooms and stood at the back with her hands clasped in front of her. She suppressed a small smile of pride in her friend and felt a pleasurable twinge of anticipation in her tummy.

The engineer bounced to the front of the class and waved a two-handed greeting.

'Thank you so much for having me,' she said and heaved her case of instruments onto the teacher's desk.

'I'm a meteorological engineer and my specialism is measuring localised weather systems and analysing their significance in wider patterns of climate.'

She held up her palms.

'I know. A terrible mouthful. Don't be put off. I promise you it will all make perfect sense by the time I've finished.'

She had told Irina that she often gave talks to schoolchildren and it was clear she saw no reason why this one would be any more difficult than usual.

She plucked off her hat and threw it, like a frisbee, into the middle of the classroom where it was caught by a girl who smiled and blushed. The children murmured and sat up a little straighter in their seats.

'Quick reflexes,' the engineer said, pointing at her. 'A vastly underrated life skill in my opinion.'

She shrugged off her coat and hung it on the back of a chair before hopping up to sit on the teacher's desk, gripping the edge with her hands and kicking her feet back and forth. She looked around the room.

'Maybe you've heard that I'm visiting from Moscow.'

The children were still and silent, unexcited by her news and Irina felt a pull of allegiance to them. She had grown to be like them and understood the mask of indifference assumed for incomers; they always expected you to be impressed at their otherness to you.

All of the children would have known of her arrival and their parents must have discussed her, at length, over the meal table. But, like Irina, their natural instinct was to give as little away as possible to a stranger.

The engineer, sensing the mood, tried another approach.

'Who can guess the best part about my job?'

'The money?' suggested Ivan.

The engineer burst into a loud laugh, startling the front row, and then, realising the boy had not been joking, laughed again at herself this time, shaking her head at her mistake and grimacing goofily at Irina who covered her own laugh with her hand.

Her unselfconsciousness was miraculous to Irina. She had not been thrown off track one bit.

'No, not the money. Good guess though. No, the best part of my job is meeting young people like you.'

There was a long silence as the children considered the likelihood of this statement being true. Outside the snow flew past the windows sideways and the wooden schoolroom creaked its resistance to the wind.

The engineer jumped off the desk and began to pace up and down in front of the children. She had a chalk smudge on the backs of her thighs.

'It's a special privilege to meet you guys in particular. You're incredible,' said the engineer.

Irina looked at the backs of their heads. Most had hair inexpertly cut by their mothers that stuck out at angles but was flattened into greasy whorls where their heads had met the pillow.

Bath night was not a simple affair in homes with no hot water on tap. She felt a keen jolt of tenderness at the sight of their innocent heads turned towards the engineer and at the back of their pink and purple rimmed ears.

'You survive in one of the planet's most extreme climates and people from all around the world would be amazed to hear about your lives. Can you imagine that?'

She was paler than when she had arrived, with smudges of grey beneath her eyes which remained, nonetheless, bright blue skies unclouded with self doubt. Traces of red wind burn spread like a rash across her forehead. Her hair, pulled back into a loose ponytail had dulled and was dry at the tips.

The harsh strip lighting showed where the faint lines on her forehead would set into wrinkles in a few years.

But she was lit from the inside with her pleasure in the moment and Irina thought her uniquely beautiful.

She wasn't thirty-five as Irina had guessed but forty. Only five years younger than Irina and yet somehow she had not yet outgrown the indomitable optimism of the very young.

Irina searched her memories of her younger self to recall if she had ever been like that. She didn't know.

She could not have stopped looking, watching her talking and walking back and forth, even if she had wanted to. And she did not want to.

What was it? There was nothing childish or naïve about her but she was unafraid of displaying her own happiness. Like a young person who had enjoyed only sunny days and could not imagine that they would ever come to an end.

The engineer believed she deserved her happiness. That's your superpower thought Irina.

She was a burst of colour in this dingy room. She was brightness and energy and warmth.

The supervisor had taken a seat at the back of the room, nearest the heater and her head had already begun to nod forward onto her chest. But the children were looking up and paying attention.

'I'm going to show you some of my equipment and explain how it works. It's super high tech stuff. Any questions so far?'

A girl on the back row, Nadia wasn't it, raised her hand.

'Are you married?'

The engineer, spotting the chalk dust began to brush at it vigorously.

'No. I nearly was once but in the end I was travelling so much that we agreed it probably wouldn't work out for us in the long term.'

She flipped the catches of her case and flicked open the lid.

'Now, before I start, who can tell me the difference between weather and climate?'

The children looked at their fingers or fiddled with their pens. Irina knew that they would know the answer but there was an unwillingness to give of themselves without understanding what would be received in return. It was built in to the children of Tomyator. It looked like stupidity or belligerence to an outsider but it was just the guardedness that small communities develop to protect themselves.

'Have you heard of Global Warming?' she said, and her pale eyebrows were scrunched together in concern, and the faint lines showed across her forehead.

'Duh,' said a boy at the back.

'Amazing. Then you'll know the impact it will have on your lives unless we get off our backsides and do something about it now.'

A boy on the front row said, 'What's it like living in Moscow?'

The engineer stopped and considered for a moment. She ran her hand across her forehead.

'In what way?' I mean, it's just what I'm used to. You need to be more specific. Remember that I'm an engineer so I like precise questions.'

She hadn't patronised the boy or tried to steer him away from his question. She had listened and the children sat up straighter because this was something new for them. At last, they seemed to say.

The engineer pulled the teacher's chair from behind the desk and placed it in front of the row of children. She sat, crossing one ankle over onto her knee and showed her palms. She was ready to answer the questions they really wanted to ask.

'My dad says Moscow is full of junkies and pervs,' said the boy, to sniggers from the older children. He turned round crossly to his classmates. 'It's true.'

She nodded, careful not to embarrass the boy and Irina was warmed by her sensitivity.

'I'm not sure about the perverts but there is a problem with drugs and drug related crimes in Moscow. Although I've travelled to other big cities in other countries and I think it happens almost everywhere.'

'Do you take drugs?' said Ivan, looking up from his carving.

'Ugh! No! And I've never tried any of the really nasty ones. I smoked cannabis for a while when I was at university but only because all my friends did it. Pretty dumb choice. It just made me feel sick.'

The engineer sat answering the children's questions with a directness and an honesty that made Irina's heart soar.

As the hour wore on, the engineer began to steer the conversation, expertly, towards her work and how much she loved what she did and why it was important to her to share her knowledge.

By this time the children were entirely rapt and focused on her and she concluded with a demonstration of the various instruments and measuring devices she had brought along to show them.

It had been an effortless performance and she smiled and performed a comical 'phew' at its success, pretending to wipe her brow towards Irina as the children passed around the instruments and examined them.

Then Irina imagined herself as a teacher standing at the front of the class like that. She imagined the pleasure of all the young faces turned towards her as she imparted her knowledge. But on what? She knew nothing except cleaning and scraping a living from the motel.

The engineer's accomplishments seemed so far distant from her own. Oh how she admired her for them. She felt her to be a wonderful person.

Irina looked out of the window; the snowstorm still raged. She wondered how she would be able to bear it when this heat and light was gone.

Twelve

Behind the five motel rooms ran a narrow corridor and at the end of it was the utility room containing the boiler, the ancient vacuum cleaner, a deep stone sink, Irina's store of soaps, shampoos and the washer dryer.

It was an industrial sized machine, a robust Guoxin monster that could swallow up a 25kg load with ease. The vibrations from the spin cycle could be felt all the way along the corridor. Over the years it had walked almost a metre towards the door and neither she nor Oleg were strong enough to push it back into place.

It had taken four men to deliver it. They slid it out of the truck on rollers and onto a flatbed trolley that they maneuvered across the square and to the entrance. The trolley definitely would not fit through the doorway and it was a few centimetres wider than the corridor itself. The men whistled and gave each other knowing looks. Here we go, lads – those looks seemed to say,

Oleg should have notified the office that there would be difficulties at his end they said. They couldn't be blamed for this particular problem. They'd done everything they could. That was for sure.

The oldest man leaned on the handle of the trolley and rubbed his mole-spotted neck. He wore the brown coat of a warehouseman as a symbol of his experience in these matters. Either they left it here or they could load it back on the lorry and take it back with them and Oleg could have it out with the company. It was up to him.

The other men looked unhappily around at the square. A teenager on the swing stared across at them, smoking his cigarette and blowing rings into the air, hoping the men would notice and think him rakish and unusual. Despite their long, uncomfortable journey they began edging towards the lorry, desperate to start back for home.

Irina had wrung her hands and begged them to at least try, and after some sighing and grumbling they eventually relented. They fetched a canvas sheet from the lorry and laid it on the floor in the corridor. The idea being that they would maneuver the machine onto it and drag it along to the utility room.

It was a smooth shiny metal cube and the men positioned themselves at the corners, spreading their feet and puffing out their cheeks in anticipation.

'There's nothing to get hold of,' they complained, but they pushed it off the trolley anyway and, as it tipped over the raised lip, they were taken by surprise by its weight and it lurched forward so that one of the men trapped his finger between the wall and a sharp corner.

'Son of a whore,' he said to the machine.

His finger was very red and had a clear mark where the edge of the machine had pressed into it but it didn't look that serious and the men told him to stop complaining and get this damned job over with so they could get back to town. He said that workplace injuries were no laughing matter and he was sure the union rep would back him up. Who the hell's laughing they said? But he went back to the lorry and sat in the cab to sulk anyway.

Sweating and red faced, and with Oleg's help, the remaining men managed to drag and push the monstrous machine into place in the utility room and they were pleased with their success in the end. They knew they'd sort it out one way or another they agreed. They weren't the types to let a washing machine get the better of them.

Irina was very grateful and, as a thank you, Oleg gave them five thousand Roubles to share. The oldest man tucked it into his pocket with his lips pressed together and exchanged looks with the other men, thinking, with a grim satisfaction, that it would go further three ways than four.

The men were supposed to install it for them but the instructions, taped to the lid, were in Chinese, so Irina had to send away for the Russian manual and Oleg set it up himself when it arrived.

He had crawled inside the giant drum to show her how enormous it was so that just his bottom and the soles of his pink socks poked out and she had pretended to close the door and turn it on. They were delighted with it and with their life in that moment. Everything seemed new and about the future.

But they had taken out a loan they couldn't afford to buy it. It was a miscalculation and Oleg thought that, perhaps, it had been Irina who made the mistake. Although he'd pointed it out quite gently.

The terms and conditions seemed to suggest it was a sort of lease and they wouldn't ever own it outright. Instead they'd have the chance to upgrade to a newer model at the end of the term.

They had thought they would be washing towels, bedding and clothes all day but in the end a small one would have done just as well and every time she ran it, and thought about the monthly payments, it was with a sense of loss, sometimes rage and always with a nauseous regret.

Most people only stayed one or two nights and didn't require a service wash and the towels were small and infrequently used.

Irina crouched to unload the engineer's small load of washing, mixed with hers, into the pink plastic wash basket, while the engineer sat in the canvas camping chair and watched her. She didn't offer to help as most women would.

The weather had not improved but the engineer seemed resigned to the interruption to her work now.

The smell of washing powder and fumes were soporific and she yawned loudly, in a way that showed she was comfortable rather than bored.

Irina separated their clothes into two piles. The engineer had five pairs of pants in the same style and in assorted colours from pink to green. They all looked new as if they'd been bought in a pack for the trip.

Irina folded them briskly before picking out some thick, white cotton vests with long sleeves. The long johns were bristling with static and had to be unwound from the other underwear. There was a single shirt that would need ironing. She held the clothes against her chest as she folded them before stacking everything neatly in the basket. She patted them down and liked the soft feel of the cotton on her palm.

'At home I send my laundry out,' said the engineer. 'Is that awfully bourgeois of me? Probably is. But laundry seems such a pointless waste of life.'

'Thanks,' said Irina, straightening up.

The engineer knotted her fingers behind her head and stretched out a toe to poke Irina's calf.

'I won't take it back.'

Irina opened up the ironing board and set it so that she was facing the woman.

She liked looking at her long face, with its anarchic eyebrows, and the way she squinted when she smiled.

'Tell me all about your life at home,' said Irina, 'while I do your ironing.'

The engineer scooted her legs up so that her feet were on the seat and wrapped her arms around her knees.

'My flat is adorable, so cosy. It's in Kitay-Gorod in an old print works. I'm on the second floor. It's miniature but there's just me so it's perfect. I have a living room, a galley kitchen, a bathroom of course and one bedroom. When it rains for a long time there's a smell of ink that seeps out from the walls.'

She touched her nose, remembering, and Irina realised, with a lurch, that she was looking forward to finishing her work in Tomyator and getting back home.

'It has the most gorgeous antique oak floorboards in every room. That's what hooked me. I love their imperfections. They're pock marked with square dents where the print machinery was and there are old trails, where the varnish has worn thin, from people's feet.

The partitions for the rooms were put in when the building was converted into flats but there's a pathway worn into the wood that runs from the window in my living room to an interior wall and then appears again on the other side in my bedroom. It's as if a ghost has walked right through it.'

She pulled the neck of her jumper up and over her head and made a ghostly 'whooo' sound. Emerging, smiling and tousled, she said, 'People in the other flats have sanded them out but I like seeing the reminders of how things used to be before me.'

The engineer closed her eyes for a moment, and turned a little to her right, orienting herself and determined to be accurate in her description.

'The window of my living room looks out onto a courtyard. It would be gloomy except one of the residents has claimed it for herself – that's a whole other story – and filled it with planters full of lavender and poppies. In the summer, at midday when the sun is overhead, it's a solid column of gold light and everyone opens their windows to catch the scent of the lavender.

'My favourite piece of furniture is a table I rescued from a building that was about to be demolished. It has a solid oak top but the legs are all different and mismatched. They've obviously been added from various other tables over the years – nailed on to keep it in use. It's an ugly thing really but I like that idea of reinventing yourself, adapting and hobbling onwards, not caring what you look like. I sit at it to eat, to work, to read. And I like to do jigsaw puzzles like an old lady.'

She smiled her big, slant eyed, smile.

'Are you disappointed? Did you think I would be more exciting?'

Irina held up the iron and raised her eyebrows.

'I may not be the best judge of what is or isn't exciting. For what it's worth, it sounds wonderful to me.'

The engineer laughed.

'I suppose it is wonderful. Although frankly it's a desperate squash, furniture wise. As well as my ugly table I have a sofa bed in a shade of lime green that I somehow imagined would be stylish and avant garde but turned out to be a mistake. However, that sofa cost a month's wages so I'm determined to learn to love it.' She made a fierce face.

'And there's an armchair my grandmother had in her flat for as long as I can remember. She died three years ago. I so wish you could have met her Irina.

I don't sit in it much. I prefer to look at it and imagine her perching in it, cutting out the obituaries of people she hated from the newspaper and sticking them in her Scrapbook of Death. She held a grudge but I adored her.'

She turned sideways and ran her finger along the bridge of her long nose, 'I inherited this from her, as well as the chair.'

It was warm in the laundry room and the domestic smells lay comfortably around everything like a freshly washed blanket.

'A friend made me a rug as a moving in present. It has

stripes ranging from the palest yellow to deep orange, but it's too pretty to walk on so I've hung it on the wall in my living room. It looks like every day of summer in one place. It makes me happy every time I look at it.'

She looked up at Irina as if only just remembering she was there. 'Do tell me to shut up, immediately, if I'm being boring.' But Irina shook her head, wanting her to continue. The flat was taking shape in her mind and she did not want to be returned to this grey breeze blocked room, for a few minutes anyway.

'The kitchen is narrow with one wooden counter running the full length. Two people can hardly pass in it.

Downstairs, right under my bedroom, there's a bar that fills up with students that has terrible Indie type bands. It's impossible to sleep through so when I'm at home I usually work from midnight until about three and then sleep late.

The only thing missing is a pet. But I'm away too much so I'm forever trying to bribe my neighbour's cat into loving me by proffering saucers of tuna and of milk in the corridor. It's extremely undignified behaviour I know.'

It had been a quick description but Irina could smell the warm lavender and feel the warmth of the orange rug and she longed to see it.

Irina had plugged in the iron. She licked the tip of her finger and touched it on the flat metal foot to hear the hiss even though she knew it would be hot. It was an old fashioned gesture, like tapping a cigarette on the box before lighting it, that had no real purpose these days. It was another habit, a rut.

'So what else do you do in your apartment? I'd like to be

able to imagine you there.'

Irina had meant to say 'when you're gone' but her throat tightened and she swallowed the words back down again and they made a painful lump in her throat.

She looked back down at her ironing so that the engineer would not see her eyes shining.

The engineer shrugged.

'Whatever I bloody well feel like. Invite friends to sample my disastrous cooking. Read. Stay in bed all day. Work. Or stay up all night. Listen to the radio. What everyone does I suppose. What do you do?'

Irina nodded at the iron.

'This. And trying to make something for dinner that Vasily will eat without complaining. Cleaning up after them.'

'But they're home all day right? Neither of them are working at the moment. Why can't they clean? Especially Oleg.'

Irina couldn't explain why but she knew he wouldn't. He had recently started smoking again, another expense, and he let the tip of his ash fall onto the carpet and then rubbed the mark in with his foot.

He read the newspapers, furrowing his brow in self-importance but with his mouth hanging open. They came three days late in a bundle from Yakutsk and he left the disordered pages to be kicked around on the floor. He made a virtue of his self sufficiency in making snacks himself when Irina was too busy, but left a trail of stickiness and crumbs and discarded every dirty plate on the floor to be trodden on later.

He dropped his clothes on the floor and kicked the covers of the bed into a heap so that Irina couldn't help but think it a deliberate effort to make an impression on every space he was in. To remind her that he was important and that he was angry with his life and how it had turned out. Each dirty cup and abandoned sock was a flash of spite and disappointment that she could not escape.

She had tried, tentatively, to ask whether he would mind being a little tidier and he had been injured as if she had attacked him. And really it was all so banal and pointless that she hated herself for having to ask and for the nagging tone that he had forced her to adopt. The situation was so entrenched in their way of living and seemed so impossible to change that she did not have the energy to try.

It was a common complaint of women; a husband who would not help around the house and the mundane nature of it bored her beyond what was bearable.

To be criticised for it by the engineer, on top of everything, struck her as terribly unfair and she blinked away the start of tears.

'He's old fashioned. It's just not the way he is.'

There was a defiance to her tone that wasn't about Oleg, but about her own choices. After all, she had chosen him. She had chosen this life. Others had it worse.

'I'd revolt,' said the engineer airily. 'I'd refuse to wash his clothes or cook until he picked up his own mess.'

'It's not for everyone maybe but that's just the way we live our lives.'

The engineer clasped her hands behind her head and raised her eyebrows.

'Oh come on. If you could choose any life, don't tell me you'd choose one where your primary daily activity involves picking up after someone who makes no effort to show that they even appreciate it. I don't believe it. What's the point?'

Irina put down the iron. She was stung by the criticism. Was her life pointless? Her tone was sharp in retaliation.

'You're very certain about things aren't you. There's more to it. You're being too simplistic.'

'Well then explain it to me. Tell me why you do it.'

Irina frowned, angry at being asked to justify a life she was able to tolerate but did not love.

'Because it's my duty. Haven't you ever felt that something is your destiny – mapped out for you – and nothing you can do or say will shift you off that path. We're married and he is struggling so I have to support him. What other option do I have that wouldn't destroy everyone's life? Because we have a son to look after. To prove to my mother that he's not a deadbeat.'

She took her small, pink jug of water from the sink and refilled the iron.

'My mother hated Oleg and I think that was probably one of the things that attracted me to him. She thought he was too wild. He had this old wreck of a car with two exhausts and when she heard him outside the house my mother would sort of...' Irina mimed dabbing her eyes with her sleeve, '...as if the thought of him made her ill. I loved that. We'd laugh about it. He always tooted his horn all along the street when we drove off, purposely to annoy her.'

She smiled to herself, remembering how she would hang on to his arm to try to stop him sounding the horn and how he would laugh and overpower her.

'I just wanted to be out of there. To be free. He was part of that I suppose.'

She picked a shirt from the pile of clean laundry.

'No comment from you required.'

'Us engineers are renowned for our wild, freewheeling ways,' said the engineer.

'It wasn't that. I didn't want to be wild, just not the same as everyone else. My sister went to University to do a business degree. When she graduated she got a job at Gazprombank behind the counter. She was always showing off about her silly uniform. She thought I was jealous but I pitied her for it.

It was a white shirt with a yellow and blue neckerchief and a stupidly tight red pencil skirt. She said all the girls had their zips undone behind the counter – it was impossible to sit down otherwise. And fur boots because it was freezing in the bank. The shirt had short sleeves so that no one could sneak off with any bank notes.

She's married now. Two girls. Still behind the counter and happy with it I suppose.'

Her story tailed off. She wasn't sure what point she was trying to make.

'I was probably brighter than her but I didn't do well at school. So what was there for me? I could have worked in a shop. Trained to be a hairdresser maybe. I wanted something different.'

'You are an adventurer Irina. I knew it.'

'Well maybe adventure is not all it's cut out to be in that case.'

Irina folded the shirt she'd finished ironing and put it on top of the washing pile.

Thirteen

Irina had dreamed she was in a gulag. It was so vivid. Finding a hole in the chain link fence, she had fumbled with frozen fingers wrapped in rags, bloodied scarlet, to pull and scratch away at it to escape.

The wider the hole gaped the more urgent her scrabbling and dragging became. The only sound, in her dream, was of her own frantic panting.

Suddenly, the wires melted away. She was ready to scramble away and out into the wild with her arms spread as if to grasp at freedom and with a glorious expectation of relief at last. It had an erotic quality; a swelling, frantic urgency that must be sated, come what may. Irina crouched and crawled forward through the hole she had created.

But, on her knees and finding only a gathering terror at the vastness of the spaces that echoed endlessly in every direction, she had crept back inside again, choosing confinement.

She had woken with her eyes wet, although she couldn't remember crying, and she was flooded with the empty, spent sensation that often followed tears.

Oleg was silent at breakfast, holding his head, and she was glad, for once, of the lack of conversation. He had made himself a tea without calling into the bedroom to her and he stared down into it, at a morose angle, with his chin drooping close to the mug.

She cleared away his teaspoon from the draining board, wiping the smear of brown water it left behind and putting it into the sink, gently, so as not to make a noise that would irritate him.

The back of his neck curved forward, leaving a gap between his skin and his shirt collar. The shirt was not dirty but the years of grease leant the material a shiny quality that refused to clear completely, no matter how often it was washed.

He looked vulnerable, like a little boy. Once she would have slipped her fingers into that space and stroked his neck, instinctively, in passing.

It was unthinkable now. When had that changed?

He scratched his thumbnail back and forth across the stubble on his jaw. It made a dry, penetrating sound and she closed her eyes for a moment, cooling her fingers against the rim of the sink, to compose herself. It was unreasonable to be so irritated by a sound like that after all.

His silence was expectant.

She knew he was waiting for her to ask what was the matter so that he could sigh and say he didn't feel so good, not that she gave a shit about him – and she could not tolerate that conversation this morning.

She took a jar of soup from the door of the fridge, left over from last night's dinner, and she poured it into a pan to warm through.

It was a venison soup, dark red and thickly meaty. The potatoes were in a canvas sack, in the cupboard next to the sink, and she picked one that fitted neatly in her palm, peeled it and chopped it into small yellow cubes and dropped them in to fortify it further.

There was a pleasure to domesticity, properly attended to. It had its own rhythms.

The familiar rituals of peeling, chopping, stirring, and whatever other movements that were demanded, required no mental effort after all this time. So she could lose herself in the feel of the butter sliding across her fingertips and the thick, wet, scents billowing from under the lifted lid of a pan.

She enjoyed the feel of her implements. She felt proficient. The knife with its smooth metal handle was weighted more at one end so that she felt its firm pressure on the heel of her hand when she pushed the blade smoothly through meat.

When she held the wooden spoon between her thumb and forefinger it created a gentler, more organic connection with the food that it stirred. The tip of the spoon had been worn flat over the years but she was reluctant to replace it. She was thankful for its service and would not be disloyal.

At the end of it all, to her surprise and satisfaction, she had created a stew or a pie or a plate of dumplings.

'Well, I'm glad to see you approve,' she said, smiling at Oleg and Vasily and with a question in her tone, as she cleared away their scraped clean plates. 'It's a relief more than anything. It was a new recipe. I tore it out of one of Zeena's magazine. I know that's an awful thing to do but at least it was one of the old ones. I had to substitute a few ingredients but I think it turned out well, don't you?'

She would run the water into the sink, looking back at her family as she waited for it to fill. 'I might not have bothered if I'd known how complicated it would be. I reckon it took me twice as long to prepare as it said.'

She paused.

'It was a lot of effort.'

Oleg unfolded his newspaper on the kitchen table.

'I thought you said you liked cooking,' he said.

She had taken the leftovers to the Weather Station.

'Divine,' said the engineer, sipping at the soup. 'Literally divine Irina – not figuratively. I've burnt my tongue horribly but I don't care. It's a price I'm prepared to pay.'

She put down the cup on the trestle table and hugged Irina hard, lifting her off her feet, making her laugh, before returning to the soup.

'It's amazing. You're amazing. I do appreciate it you know.'

Irina shrugged, pleased. 'It's nothing.'

'It's not nothing,' said the engineer. 'I appreciate it.'

Her spare boots were drying on top of the heater and there was a wet, cabbagey smell, stronger than the smell of the soup. Irina sat on the canvas chair. She took off her hat and balanced it on her knees.

'This smell reminds me of The Young Pioneers and the awful summer camps. You're probably too young to have gone. They stopped them in the Eighties I think.'

She wrinkled her nose and pulled off her mittens and dropped them in her lap.

'I am too young,' said the engineer. 'Just. But I would have adored it all. I was always making my own little camps. My mother had to threaten me with violence to make me come inside in the summer.'

Irina said, 'I was one of those kids who didn't join in. I kept a piece of paper as a calendar stuffed in my shoe and I marked off the days until I could go home. Although I hated it at home too.'

She gave a small laugh as if that were an amusing thought – to be unhappy at home – and the engineer paused between sips, with her pale eyebrows raised in expectation, to encourage her to continue.

Her mother had been exasperated, Irina remembered, by her refusal to jump on the bus with the other, normal, whooping children.

How old had she been? She had still sucked her thumb, she remembered that. The weeks running up to the trip had been spent in a sick, anxiety about it. What would the other girls think of her?

She could manage during the day but the night times seemed impossible. Every time she vowed not to give in, her thumb would slip into her mouth, the pad of her thumb, soft and swollen from the spit, stroking the roof of her mouth and her index finger curled up to caress the bridge of her small unformed nose. She could not suck her thumb in the dormitory.

She had tried falling asleep with her hands under the pillow but had woken, disappointed, to find they did not obey her when she was not awake. In the end she had worn her mittens in bed to break the habit. But she took care to hide them away before her mother saw them. The mittens were shameful to her in a way she could not quite explain.

That day, the day of the trip, she was waist height to her mother who wore a skirt that flared out above her knee with brown and yellow diamonds connected by thin lines in a mustard colour. She could feel the roughness of the material on her cheek as she hovered close to her mother in the crowd. Her mother's hand with the cigarette, red tipped and dangerous, drifted around close to Irina's head.

Irina could tell she was irritated by the scene, the crowd and the waiting around by the way she took hard, frequent pulls on her cigarette. When she blew out the smoke she put her hand on her hip and tipped up her chin sharply to point the plumes into the air.

She wore tan tights that were bobbly at the knees and, close to, showed lines in them like the veins on a leaf. Her shoes had high heels and the plastic around the tip of the heel had peeled up to show the white stuff underneath. Irina kept her eyes on them; the thought of that little spike descending and spearing through her shoes and into her toes — surely it would go all the way through — was terrifying. Not that her mother had ever trodden on her before but Irina was programmed for vigilance and she was sure that she was safe only because she was careful to stay out from under her feet.

'Thank Christ for that,' her mother said when the engine of the bus started up.

She unpeeled Irina's fingers from her sleeve and held her

hand at arm's length, as if holding the lead of a small dog. The girl's tears made her feel hot and impatient and, knowing that anger was inappropriate, she blamed Irina for her awkwardness in causing it. She made her feel like a bad mother. The kid did it on purpose. She was always difficult like this after all.

She dug her fingernails into Irina's hand and said, 'The other children won't want to know you if they think you're a cry baby.'

Her mother had a clear, loud voice and this statement seemed to be intended as an announcement for everyone to hear. Lest they imagine that she was indulging the whiney child.

She leant close to Irina's ear, with an icy smile, a mirror image of the other mothers who bent low to press kisses on the cheeks of their darlings and hissed, 'Don't you dare get it into your head I'm being mean Irina. Don't give me that look. As if it's me who's the nasty one. You need to understand that I'm teaching you how to make the best of things.'

Her breath was sour from the cigarette and sweet underneath from the vodka.

Irina had finally stepped up on the dimpled metal steps of the coach and crept into a seat. The rough cloth cover was scratchy against her bare thighs; she was wearing a summer dress from last year that was too short that her mother had said would have to do. God knows, she had enough to contend with without running around shopping for new dresses and besides she was not a State Worker so the trip to camp had not been free. Did Irina think she was made of money? Irina folded the tops of her socks to cover a hole she had made with her finger when she was pulling them up this morning.

Her socks never seemed to stay up as well as the other children's and they were much less white.

Her suitcase was pale blue and had rounded corners and the colour had scuffed off them to show the toughened cardboard underneath. It had a hard plastic handle with four smooth indents on the underside of it to slide your fingers into. Irina had slipped her fingers into the slots at home to practice carrying the case. She felt it would be one less thing to worry about on the trip.

She pushed the suitcase under the seat as far as it would go and then, anxious that she might forget to take it with her at the other end, she pulled it out again and set it up on its side on the seat next to her.

None of the other girls had sat beside her so there was room.

Irina sat very still and stared at the two blond plaits of the girl in front. They bobbed and swayed in a carefree way as the girl settled herself excitedly. They were plump and shiny. They strained against the confines of the girl's ribbons. That's how healthy and full of life those plaits were.

Irina's hair was cut short, to a level just below her ears, and she had a fringe that lurched up into an arch in the centre. 'You moved,' her mother said, clattering the scissors down onto the table and lighting a cigarette. 'It serves you right.'

As the engine rumbled and the other children broke into

an excited cheer, Irina rubbed the dust from the window to see a glimpse of her mother's brown and yellow checked skirt as she moved away through the crowd. She had not bothered to stop and wait with the other women who all strained on tiptoes, scanning the windows, eager to catch a last precious glimpse of their child.

Irina had knelt up on her seat, pulling the skirt down behind her to check it covered her bottom. She waved along wildly with the rest of the children as the bus began to pull away, not wanting to be left out. She stared straight ahead with a wide smile and hoped no one would ask which one was her mother.

The bus crawled away, along the main road of the town and past her school. It was a Saturday and without the throng of children, it seemed desolate to Irina; as if it had been closed and abandoned for years.

A little further along, two old women in headscarves knelt on the steps of the municipal buildings, scrubbing at them with brushes dipped into their shared bucket of water.

Near the edge of town, the bus began to pick up speed. A group of boys had drawn a goal, in chalk, on the wall of the new swimming baths and kicked a ball, listlessly, towards it. One of the boys turned to watch the bus roll past, shading his eyes and following its progress until Irina could not see him anymore.

She pulled at the hem of her dress and tried not to worry about the way it showed so much of her legs. She thought they might be thinner than the other children's legs but she wasn't sure.

The Young Pioneer uniforms would be provided for them when they arrived. It had said so clearly in the letter that confirmed her attendance, and the time and place of departure. Her mother had skimmed over it too quickly though and Irina wished she had the letter with her to check the details properly.

She remembered that each child would receive three white shirts, two pairs of blue shorts and a red neckerchief. The letter had said that the children must take care of their uniforms and any loss or damage would have to be paid for on their return.

Irina would be careful but she worried that one of the other children might damage her uniform. They might spill something on her shirt or pick up her neckerchief in the morning by mistake, thinking it was theirs.

She decided that she would wear her uniform under her nightclothes to be safe. Her mother did not have the money to pay for damaged or lost uniforms.

Other children were already counting out their coins and talking about the chocolate they would buy – they would certainly share it around because they were fair like that – if there were a trip into a village.

She was almost certain the letter had said that food would be provided for free but, now that she was here on the bus, she began to feel doubtful. She would be away for four weeks and she thought, perhaps, she could go without food for a week but any longer than that would be impossible. Her stomach rumbled. Irina sat rigidly, with her hands knotted in her lap, listening hard, so that she would catch it if anyone mentioned the cost of the food.

The bus soon filled with hot, oily engine fumes and the smell of onion and salami sandwiches and the sweat from the children. Two girls sitting opposite Irina knelt up in their seats to talk to their friends in the row behind. The bolder ones strolled up and down the aisles and then crouched down next to a girl they liked the look of to find out which school they were from and where their mother and father worked.

A girl with pig tails and a honking voice stood in the aisle, placed her hands on the metal bars that looped over the headrests, and began to swing her legs backwards and forwards, in higher and higher swings.

'Oi! Olga Korbut! Get your skinny arse on the seat where it belongs,' shouted the driver, spotting her in his mirror, and the children hooted with laughter.

The girl poked out her tongue and plonked down in the seat next to Irina. She looked at her scuffed blue suitcase and her too short dress.

'Are those your school shoes?' she said to Irina.

'No,' said Irina, although they were.

The girl looked doubtful and swung her own feet up onto the seat.

'These are called tennis shoes,' she said. 'I've got two brand new pairs exactly the same.'

Having got the measure of Irina, she stood up abruptly and scooted across the aisle to sit next to another little girl with her blond hair tied back prettily with a bright pink ribbon. They put their arms across each other's shoulders, whispering and throwing arch looks at Irina.

The road was rougher now and the driver, making no

concessions to the conditions, bounced the bus ruthlessly onwards.

It was hot and Irina did not want to draw attention to herself by trying to open the window. She took her handkerchief from her pocket and bent over, pretending she was retrieving something from the floor, so that she could be sick into it as quietly as she could, before wrapping the mess up in a ball and pushing it under the seat as far as it would go.

She was relieved that nobody had noticed but her mother would be so cross that she had come home without her handkerchief. She hoped she would not be sick again or need to go to the toilet. She did not know how long the journey would last and was too shy to ask if anyone else knew.

A decade later, Irina was astonished to learn that the Young Pioneers Camp she had visited as a child was less than 40km from the outskirts of Yakutsk.

She had remembered the journey as lasting more than a day with the view from the window changing from day to night and then a bright, headachy morning again. She was certain she had slept for a time. Perhaps her mother had been right to dismiss her complaints about it.

'Oh you loved it,' she said to the teenage Irina. 'Don't be difficult on purpose. You had the time of your life.'

She did not trust herself and it made her feel shaky and uncertain about her own reality.

Irina watched the engineer bending over the trestle table, still listening intently as she worked.

'I can picture you in one of those uniforms,' said Irina.

'Marching around collecting firewood. Leading the songs.'
She felt resentful of her for a moment and her untroubled childhood because surely it had been so easy for her.

She thought about the pretty, popular girls who had been her tormentors. Not that they had pushed her around or called her nasty names. It wasn't like that. Her torment came from their confidence and the way their eyes slid over her, unseeing, in the dormitory. They sat on each other's beds and shared secrets in earshot without bothering to lower their voices, because they didn't care whether Irina heard or not.

'Can you?' said the engineer, straightening up. 'I doubt it. I was already this height by the time I was twelve. My feet were the same size as my father's.'

She pointed to her right eye and raised the eyebrow above it in a high arch.

'Before that I had a patch for my amblyopia. The whole family had to learn to say am-bly-o-pia. My mother made an enormous scene in the clinic when the doctor called it lazy eye. She threatened to report him, scared him half to death. Her daughter's eye? Lazy? How dare he?'

The engineer laughed and Irina saw that she loved her mother very much.

'It's quite a common condition. The sight doesn't develop properly in one eye because it relies on the good eye to do all the work. They put a patch over the industrious one so the freeloading, slacker eye has to step up. Over time it improves.'

She rubbed at it with her knuckle.

'My mother insists all stories must have a moral so there

was a lot of earnest talk about effort trumping natural ability and how encouraging the weakest to fulfil their potential benefits the collective.

When I complained about wearing the stupid patch my mother said it was a sign I was special and if other people couldn't recognise that then it was their loss. So of course I was an insufferable prig.

Here's a picture for you Irina: pre-adolescent me, a beanstalk, lolloping about on my giant clown's feet, with an eye patch and my nose permanently stuck in the air. But it protected me from pig tailed little girls showing off about their bloody shoes. I suppose it gives you a kind of shell.'

She drained the last of the venison soup from her cup, before running her finger around the inside and licking it.

'Think of this as our revenge Irina. We have our own camp now. Our rules. And we're best friends for ever so everyone else can go jump in a lake.'

Irina, smiled. 'You survived your childhood unscathed then.'

'Not quite.'

The engineer pulled down her rubber over trousers, the waistband of her elasticated trousers and woolly long johns to expose her hip bone that was stamped with a vivid red scar.

'My brother pushed me out of a tree house – he still swears I fell – when I was twelve. I had to have a pin fitted. I set off all the metal detectors at airports.'

Irina looked at the raised mark that ran around her hip and the two red puncture dots, a colon, followed by a curved red bracket. Like the email from Tanja. Ha Ha!

The reminder of Moscow made her wince. It was a small, fleeting tightening around her mouth and eyes that she quickly brought under control but the engineer noticed it nonetheless.

'It's ugly I know.'

Irina shook her head. She did not think it was ugly. She would have liked to touch it, to run her fingertips lightly over the bumps.

'I heard you on the phone to the university today,' she said, as casually as she could muster. 'What did they want?'

'The usual.' said the engineer. 'Definitely not a social call. They didn't ask after my health or if the food was good.'

She smiled and pointed at the flask. 'Obviously the food is incredible and if they'd asked I would have name checked you. They want to know how much longer I'll be here because time, Irina, especially in academia, is money.'

Irina nodded and looked around at the work to try to gauge how much longer it would take to complete. She did not dare to ask.

Fourteen

The engineer had six paperbacks on the bedside table, stacked up with their spines neatly aligned. Irina turned her head to one side to read the titles but she wasn't especially interested to know what they were. That was just something you were expected to do when you saw someone else's books. She could not have recalled them a second later.

She was much more interested in the personal effects.

On the matching table, on the other side of the bed were a box of herbal tea bags, some tissues in a plastic packet and a small red leather wash bag that was zipped closed.

Irina was stirred by the thought of opening the little case and turning over all of the items in her hands. In the way children poke through the drawers of their mother's dressing table, stealthily, searching for clues about what goes on in their heart. The comb perhaps? Tweezers? Silly things of no consequence to anyone but personal to the engineer. They would be precious to Irina.

Next to the case was a blister pack of pain killers. Six of the tablets were missing. Irina wondered if her back was still causing problems. She hadn't complained about it.

Then again, she never complained.

A pink, rolled up tube propped in the corner was a yoga mat. Irina knew this because the engineer had used it to show her some poses called things like 'side plank' and 'down dog' that she said stopped her seizing up.

She was no expert, Irina had said, cocking an eyebrow, but it seemed to her that the engineer was very bad at yoga. She wobbled inelegantly, poking out her tongue and grimacing as she tried to tuck her long legs into impractical positions. Until Irina had laughed and the engineer gave up, laughing too.

The room was beginning to smell of the engineer a little. Not in an unpleasant way but just with the scent of occupation. Irina breathed it in consciously as if trying to make a memory.

Most guests only stayed a day or two and even though the windows were frozen shut, the outer door could be thrown open for a few minutes before the new arrival turned up. This room had been sealed for almost three weeks now.

The engineer had a steaming cup of spiced noodles and an open packet of biscuits on her desk. They were chocolate coated with a thin vein of sickly marshmallow, one of Alexi's most popular brands.

Her laptop was open.

'I'm going to carry on working,' she said, poking out her tongue from the side of her mouth and wiggling her fingers in a typing motion. 'You don't mind do you?'

Irina didn't. It was nice to be in company without the expectation of having to say anything or meet another's needs.

The engineer sat and rolled her head from side to side, as if she had been working for a long time.

'Is it peculiar of me to enjoy writing reports?' she said. 'Don't answer. I know it's odd. Sometimes I wonder if I'm the last person on earth to ever read them. I think, what if I slipped in a couple of jokes? Or a recipe for risotto? Who would even notice?'

Irina sat on the edge of the bed neatly, with her knees pressed together and her hands in her lap. She examined the long tendon at the back of the woman's neck. The engineer had tied up her hair and the few strands that had escaped tickled her so that she brushed them away every now and then. Her neck's white smoothness made her look very young. Irina watched the muscles dancing, left right, left right as she typed.

'Is it a report about your progress?'

'Yep.'

'About wrapping it all up?'

'Uh huh.'

She would have liked to read the report. Irina had not noted down the temperature for three weeks. She wondered how quickly Moscow would realise she had been misstating the figures. Perhaps they would think her stupid rather than deceitful.

She twisted her fingers together in her lap. The idea of whispering out a confession now, pulled the knot in her stomach tighter.

Irina took off her boots and lay down on the bed. She was exhausted suddenly and her arms, which lay by her side, were heavy and stiff like metal pipes. She would have liked to climb under the blanket, pull it to her chin, and curl up. But it seemed an eccentric idea so she didn't.

I never do what I feel like, she thought.

The pillow smelled of the motel shampoo. Irina frowned at the dark yellow shadow on the ceiling made by visitors who had smoked in bed. When she considered the effort involved in fetching stepladders and paint and moving the bed and covering the carpet with a dustsheet she felt the deadening heaviness increasing in her limbs and thought she would rather die than do it.

She hated this room and surely the engineer must loathe it too. She was typing very quickly now and it sounded like someone's footsteps running away.

She propped herself up on her elbows and said, 'Please come to dinner with us tomorrow. I don't like to think of you here on your own, existing on packet noodles and chocolate. It's not good for you. You'll get fat. And spotty.'

The engineer twisted to face her. The glued together chair creaked.

'Is that an invitation from you, or from you and Oleg?'

'Oh he won't care whether you're there or not. He's always like that with guests. Don't flatter yourself that it was a particular reaction to you, the great Muscovite engineer.'

The engineer raised an eyebrow.

'Remember when we were at the school? I told that kid I nearly got married but I was working away too often so we agreed it wouldn't work out?'

Irina nodded.

'That was the abridged version.' She pushed her knees

against the edge of the desk and leaned the chair back, balancing on two of its legs.

'Maksim his name was, is, – I love that name don't you? He was dark and dashing and it suited him beautifully. Anyway, it wasn't us being apart that he couldn't hack, it was the fact that every trip I went on meant more experience or more exposure, so it was good for my career.'

The chair creaked again and the engineer, noticing, settled all four of its legs back on the floor.

'Even early on I found myself playing down the trips. Saying they were an awful bore and pretending I'd really rather not go.' She rubbed her eyes. 'A climate conference in New York? Yeah, a chore but, you know, my boss is insisting…I made excuses to myself that if a white lie saved his feelings it didn't count. Really, Irina, it was a betrayal of myself. I'm not sure who was stupider – me for the lie, or him for believing it.'

The engineer rubbed at a mark on the back of the chair with her thumb.

'I couldn't figure out the difference between compromise and sacrifice. In terms of love that is. In the end, neither option appealed.

He was, still is, a geologist. Our work overlapped to a degree. But I was better known, more senior definitely. In the end, when I honestly picked apart my feelings about it, I realised he didn't want me to be more successful than him.'

She gave a small, firm nod, as if to persuade a wavering version of herself that she had made the right decision.

'I wrote a paper – one that people actually did read! It

was submitted to a climate committee at the UN and everyone was calling to congratulate me. It was a big deal, you know? To have my work reported in the international press and not just in arcane, specialist journals with miniscule readerships.'

The engineer knotted her fingers behind her head and smiled her wide, sloping-eyed smile at Irina.

'I may have been rather full of myself for a while. Almost impossible for you to imagine I'm sure Irina. Anyway, I was basking, luxuriantly, in the warm sea of approval and congratulations when one, slightly less than positive review of my piece appeared in some minor publication. The author queried one of the references I'd cited. It was nothing really, so small and inconsequential but Maksim couldn't wait to email it to me. 'I thought you'd want to know' he said.'

The engineer shrugged.

'Pompous bastard. So fuck that. And fuck you, I said to myself.

He still believes I left him because my ego was bruised. Look. It was bruised. I was mortified. It was an error, and who likes to have their mistakes leapt upon so eagerly?

The truth is Irina, I ended it with him because I got lucky. I had a glimpse into a future relationship with him that would always be defined by a kind of schadenfreude. The luck being that I saw it before it was too late.'

She was animated now, energised by the retelling of the unfairness and by the remaking of the story – from one of misfortune and lost love to a lucky escape. It was positive thinking. Just like they recommended in the magazines.

Irina understood that this was a story she had chewed over and explored many times before.

'I thought he was amazing. I loved showing off about him. He was gorgeous, film star handsome. He made cantankerous old women with moustaches laugh. He was a ridiculously clever guy. I mean astonishingly bright.'

She was counting out his virtues on her fingers and she looked into the air, smiling and remembering.

'Maksim was the first man I'd ever met who properly cooked. He brought me home made bread on our second date. Can you imagine? I practically swooned. Once he ran a half marathon, and I waited at the end in the rain for an hour so I could take a photo of him crossing the finish line. I was so bloody proud. I was impressed by him. I admired him. I felt his accomplishments reflected on me for choosing him and having been chosen by him. I thought we were a team.'

She untied her hair, gathered it together again behind her head and wrapped the elastic tie around the ponytail twice, pulling together the loose ends more neatly. It was a firm, practical gesture. That's that, it seemed to say.

'But it didn't work the other way around.'

She laid one hand on top of the other on the back of her chair and propped her chin on them to look at Irina.

'Oleg is the same with you. He wants you to be less than him, just so that he can believe himself superior. He'd rather be right than happy. He's miserable – not a crime even in Tomyator – but he's dragging you down with him from pure spite.'

She paused, 'And you're letting him get away with it.'

She turned back to her work. Her point made and damn the consequences. Irina felt horribly insulted and wounded in a way that she struggled to codify.

'You're exaggerating,' she said flatly. Then, 'you've only met him once.'

'I'm a good judge of character,' the engineer said.

She turned around again.

'Look Irina, the first time I met you I was so bloody impressed. Maybe it was because my brain was half mushed from the road trip but you appeared out of the mist in the middle of the night, an icy vision, trailing vapour, and dispensing towels and keys with all of your composure and self-possession. It was extraordinary.'

'I had my pyjamas on under my clothes,' said Irina.

'You see?' said the engineer. 'You simply have no idea how bloody brilliant you are. You're a strong woman running her own business in the middle of this mad town, managing her family in the most testing, the most extreme circumstances and being entirely uncomplaining about it.'

'Oh I do complain,' said Irina.

'Stop it,' said the engineer. 'Honestly. You're tough. You're a prize fighter. I think you're...' she stood up and paced around before putting one foot on the seat of the chair, '...formidable.'

She gripped the back of the chair, her eyes bright with an idea.

'You can choose to be happy you know Irina. There's no glory in misery. Why don't you come back to Moscow with me? I'll be finished in less than two weeks. I have a sofa bed. You can stay with me.'

Her voice was eager and urgent.

'The hotel business is booming in Moscow. They must be crying out for decent people with the right skills. You've run your own hotel. You'll easily find a position, probably with accommodation. It would be perfect.'

Irina closed her eyes and lay her head back down. It's a motel not a hotel she thought. Her head felt larger and heavier than usual. She wondered how her hair looked fanned out on the pillow.

'It's a ridiculous idea. I'm married. I have a child. I can't just pack up and leave on a whim. And what makes you think I want to leave Oleg? He's not the monster you think.'

Oleg was spiteful and self-centred. He was vain. He was a drunk. He took her for granted and hated her for her willingness to tolerate it. But she did not hate him back. It would be too hard to bear this life if she allowed herself to hate him, because there was no escape from him, so she made a conscious effort not to. She took a deep breath and looked on the bright side. She whispered 'never mind' to herself and considered how other people had it worse.

'You may not want to leave him I didn't want to leave Maksim; I adored him most of the time. My friends all thought I was completely crazy to dump him.'

Irina heard the chair creak and then the ebb and flow of the engineer's voice as she walked up and down the small room.

'But it's better for you. You're formidable remember. You'd manage. And Vasily is a grown man for God's sake, not a child. He's almost twenty-two isn't he? You're making excuses Irina.'

The engineer's voice sounded close to Irina's ear.

'If you don't want to go because you're too timid, then be honest and say so.'

It was a silly, outlandish idea. Irina could see the glare of the bulb through her eyelids. She tried to imagine herself on the green sofa bed in the little flat that smelled of printer's ink when it rained and the sound of music drifting up through the oak floorboards.

She was astonished to find that she could imagine it. Quite easily and quite vividly.

She saw the rug on the wall that was orange and felt its warmth tingling on her skin.

The engineer would be working at her laptop, humming. Or maybe cooking for them both. Perhaps Irina should cook. The engineer had already admitted how awful she was at it. She could teach her. They would be hip to hip in the narrow kitchen and they would be comfortable and easy, even as they brushed against each other. They would pass each other pans and ingredients without having to name them. Their movements would be in harmony. Cooking would be a nice way to pay her back for her kindness in letting her stay.

Irina had read about the markets in Moscow. They were famous. There would be delicatessens where she could pick up exotic ingredients to put together something really special. No more relying on endless tinned beans and jars of frankfurters from Alexi.

They'd talk in the evenings, over herbal tea, about inconsequential things or about life long secrets. Nothing would be out of bounds between them. They would be intimates.

If the engineer invited her colleagues or her friends around for a dinner party or drinks, Irina could help her to prepare, tidy up the flat. She wouldn't mind tidying up for the engineer.

They would all drink wine together and gradually she could meet some new people of her own, make new friends. She would get a bold new haircut. Wear something because she liked it and not give a damn what anyone said. Be a different person. Leave her mistakes behind and start afresh. Be free.

It was a delicious, warm dream and she relaxed back into the soft mattress and luxuriated in it.

'Well?'

Irina opened her eyes.

The engineer slurped a mouthful of the noodles, dripping the juice across the desk. She wiped her chin with the back of her hand.

'Think about it,' she said.

Fifteen

Irina let herself in to the apartment and closed the door gently behind her. It wasn't late, not yet nine, but Oleg would already be in bed and it was better not to disturb him.

It was dim in the hall. She raised her hand to the light switch, hesitated, and let it fall again. She did not need the light to carry out this most automatic of tasks; the peeling off of her outdoor layers to hang behind the door.

Besides, there were no bright punches of colours on the walls to see, or warmly worn oak boards to reflect the rich orange light back at her. So what would be the point?

She felt restless, dissatisfied and confined. She was not yet ready for bed but there was nothing else to do. What would she do if she were in Moscow?

She longed for entertainment suddenly. Anything.

To the right, her bedroom was in darkness and she could hear the soft rumble of Oleg's snore, but a muted light leaked from under Vasily's door, at the end of the short corridor.

She crept to his door and tapped, pushing it open a crack, to peer inside.

Vasily was lying on his stomach, propped on his elbows with his eyes fixed on his console. He didn't speak or look over at her, but thumped his head down onto the mattress and pulled a pillow over his head to block her out.

Irina twisted her fist tightly on the doorknob, hesitating at the threshold, before stepping quietly inside and closing the door behind her.

The room was gloomy and had the musky, masculine scent of hibernation. Vasily had made a den of his discarded clothes and dropped towels. His shoes were scattered, kicked off in corners. The edges of his sheets had come untucked and the grey slab of mattress was exposed. The room reeked of the numbing boredom that is uniquely and exquisitely painful to the young and she felt deeply regretful that this was her son's life and that she had brought him here in the first place.

Another smell, a medicinal tang, drifted from an open bottle on the floor next to his bed. Irina recognised it as the face scrub she'd ordered for his acne. There was a slick stain on the carpet that showed where it had been spilled before. She rubbed it with her toe and tried not to be irritated by the mark that she knew she would have to try to remove.

'We could be going to the cinema if we were in the city,' said Irina. She had intended her voice to be casual, conversational, but her tone was high and bright and she felt foolish.

She sat on the edge of his bed, gently, so as not to startle him with her nearness. He lay, still and rigid, with his head still under the pillow. The ends of his black hair protruded. He had used too much dye she thought. Or left it on for too long. His hair had a crackling, synthetic quality. She had seen the snapped off ends in the sink in the bathroom.

She examined his back. The muscles that ran from his shoulder blades were taut.

'I say 'we,' she gave a laugh. 'I'm sure you'd prefer to go with your friends.'

Irina couldn't think of a current film. There didn't seem much point in keeping up with the new releases. She stood up and pulled at the edge of the bottom sheet to see if she could tuck it in and Vasily flinched at the movement.

'How many cinemas do you think there are in Moscow?' she said. 'I bet there must be twenty at least. You could probably see a different film every day of the week if you wanted to.'

She wondered if there was a cinema near the engineer's apartment.

The crumpled top sheet was pulled down exposing his spotty back. The skin was red and angry across the glockenspiel of his narrow ribcage. When he had been a baby she had loved to feel his smooth skin under her palms as she dressed him and she had squeezed his chubby buttocks and pulled strands of his fine hair through her fingertips.

He had luxuriated in it. Squirming against her.

'Leave him alone for Christ's sake,' Oleg said. So she had done it when he wasn't around. Feeling guilty at the sensuous feeling of the skin under her fingertips and at his delight in it.

She had no desire to touch him now. She was a little repulsed by the idea of laying her hands on his grey, greasy skin and she was washed over by a panic at that loss of intimacy. Where had little Vasily disappeared to? She could never have imagined that time was so fragile. His skin, his smell, these ugly spots and protruding bones were alien to her now. She held out her hand and tried to imagine herself laying it on his back and stroking it and she could not.

From this new angle, sitting on the edge of the bed, Irina could see that he had pushed a pile of dirty plates and bowls under his desk. A knot of his scrumpled socks and t-shirts lay frosted with old dust.

There were some torn football posters on the wall, players and teams she didn't recognise, but they were old now. Vasily had put up nothing new for five years at least.

The books on his shelf were children's books. She didn't think he was nostalgic, just too lazy, or indifferent, to clear them away.

She stood up to look at the certificate she had put in a frame. 'Vasily Petruchevsky; awarded in recognition of helpfulness to others at all times' from school.

Only the video games were current.

'You'd tell me if something was worrying you wouldn't you,' she said. 'Anything. I wouldn't be shocked. You could just say it – anything – and I might be able to help.'

Had he ever had sex? Or even kissed a girl. She didn't think it was drugs. She would know if there was a problem like that in the town.

'He flounces about like a fucking queer,' Oleg had said after some argument or other, but Irina didn't think it was that. She had found some magazines under his mattress when she had been making his bed and all of the pictures inside them were of women with their legs spread and their labia held open by their own long red nailed fingers for better viewing.

She had been surprised. She didn't think young people bought pornographic magazines these days.

'I know there's not much to do here Vasily. It must be hard for you. When I was your age I was always out with my friends at bars, going out with boys.'

She touched the back of his calf through the sheet. He didn't recoil.

'I was pretty cool in my time.'

She hadn't been cool. Not by a long way. Not even by the standards of Yakutsk. But she had yearned for excitement and to be rebellious. She had no interest in radical politics or underground music, so, Irina had made sex her cause. At fifteen, or so, she took it upon herself to begin to have sex with a succession of boys and men she met in the coffee shop, in the shopping mall near her house, and in the university bar.

It was ridiculously easy to pick up boys, even grown men, simply being willing was enough it seemed, and she was pleased to find something she was so good at.

As she'd performed oral sex, bending over their eager laps in the back row of the cinema and fucked them in doorways in alleys that smelt of urine she'd thought, yes, look at me now. Like the motel guests who looked at the map of the region and marvelled at the distance they had travelled, Irina rejoiced as each jolt propelled her further from her anxious and stultifying childhood.

She felt herself to be daring although she never

considered it dangerous. She kept it a secret, not because she felt it was wrong, but because it was powerful to have a life that her handful of school friends knew nothing about.

How scornful she felt about their babyish crushes on the music teacher and the way they giggled at boys who glanced at them at the bus stop. It made her seem haughty to them at times and a coldness grew between them. Sensing her disdain, they began to leave her out of their plans.

It was lonely in a way. So Irina tried her hardest to immerse herself in her secret life, to be consumed by it. Sometimes, and especially when she was more used to it, she found her mind wandering. Irina imagined her mother happening upon the scene, and the thought made Irina shiver with pleasure.

It wasn't a sad story. She'd liked it well enough most of the time. It was exciting. She'd imagined herself transported and not sweaty and uncomfortable in the toilet of the bar with her knees lifted so her feet couldn't be seen from under the door of the cubicle.

None of the boys stood out particularly. Afterwards they were contemptuous, grateful, afraid or cocky. Occasionally an inexperienced boy would expect her to become his girlfriend and become cross when she laughed at his mooning expressions.

She had drunk too much and danced at the weekend discos with anyone who asked her in a determined search for gaiety and oblivion that seemed a fraction too far away to ever quite be grasped.

She told her mother nothing of course. She supposed Vasily was just as secretive as her. But he was stuck here in Tomyator, in his bedroom that reeked of dull Sundays and old socks and, unlike her, he never went anywhere to develop a clandestine life.

'If there's something you'd like to do, training for a career or something, you could go to Yakutsk. It doesn't have to be that far away. If that's what you're worried about. What do you think? You can't spend the rest of your life hiding in your room.'

His silence began to irritate her. She eyed the dry hank of hair and imagined how it would feel to pull it. To shock him. Hurt him. Once when he was a toddler and crying in the night she had lost her temper with him and bitten him on his cheek and it had terrified her; the animalistic rage that a crying child could cause. She could still feel that moment when the plump cheek gave between her teeth and she had pulled back from the act panting and horrified.

'You must want to do something.'

She clapped her hands together, brightly.

'What's your ambition?'

It was childish of him. Staying silent like his. What was he trying to punish her for? She'd always put him first.

'There must be something that inspires you. Or someone? A famous person you admire. Like a pop star.'

She saw a shudder ripple across his back when she said 'pop star' and was hurt. It wasn't fair of him. She hadn't meant to patronise him and it struck her that he was no longer a child but they spoke so little that they had not developed the language to talk together as adults might.

Perhaps Vasily felt the same way. She felt in need of a new vocabulary and she didn't know where to start.

'D'you think we've got into bad habits Vasily? With each other I mean. We never really say how we feel about things do we?'

He shifted under the sheet and loosened his grip on the pillow so it just rested on his head and was not pulled down tight around his ears. She sat, carefully, on the edge of the bed again.

'It hurts me to think of you being fed up, depressed even, but I can't help you if you don't tell me what's bothering you. Honestly Vasily, I do know it's not easy to open up to your mother. Look at me and Grandma – we never managed it and it's too late for us now.'

She tucked her hair behind her ears and gave a small, rueful, laugh.

'Maybe it's my age, who knows, but I can't get this idea out of my head, that there must be more to life than Tomyator and watching television. There must be. You're young and you've got bags of time and opportunity but still, it's a terrible shame to waste your twenties.'

He had been a bright little boy and despite everything, she didn't doubt his cleverness, or his capacity for kindness. Oleg's sarcastic remarks about the paintings he had brought home from school, or the face he made when he bothered to look at his report card probably hurt her more than Vasily, but she leapt to his defence nonetheless. She truly believed he could be anything that he chose to be. If only he would listen to her encouragement and let her help him.

She wanted, viscerally, for him to be happy.

'You don't want to end up like dad, Vasily, do you? He's disappointed with his life. He's unhappy that he doesn't have a job. Working gave him a sense of purpose and I bet you'd be the same. There are more openings in big cities. I've tried to suggest moving but you know how he gets.'

She laid her hand on the small of his back. The sheet remained a barrier between them; she would not have touched his bare skin, but this felt like a new intimacy for them and she felt encouraged.

'We do our best to keep him cheerful, but it's not much of a life for us is it? Having to tiptoe around his moods. Then there's the drinking.'

She thought about the engineer's blithe observations about her life here with Oleg.

'It might be too late for dad but perhaps we could talk about what we could change? For you and me. We could make some plans couldn't we?'

Vasily curled upwards, snakelike, twisting towards her with his lips stretched wide across his teeth in an expression of disgust. The sheet slipped down and the thrust of his white chest, clearly striped with protruding ribs, was violence and vulnerability at the same time. Irina recoiled and put her hand to her mouth. She was afraid he might strike her.

'You're an utter bitch,' he said. His voice was even and it was all the more shocking to her, this cold, controlled tone coming from his contorted face. 'I literally can't stand you. You came here because *you* wanted to. You got the motel because *you* wanted it. If dad's miserable it's because of you

215

and your complaining. We like it here. So why don't you leave me and him out of your pity party. In fact just leave us. You know what would make me happy – you ridiculous, sour, pathetic old woman? If you'd hurry up and fucking die and leave us alone.'

Irina jerked up and away from the bed, catching her heel in a pile of clothes and almost falling as she stumbled backwards to the door. One hand covered her mouth and with the other she felt behind her back, desperately for the handle.

She scrabbled at it, scraping the skin from her knuckles before pushing open the door with a sob and half falling over the threshold, away from him and his words, as if escaping from a fire.

Sixteen

'Gregor is off to Kazan, aren't you Gregor,' said Alexi. 'Tell Irina all about it.'

'I'm going to Kazan,' he said, not looking up from his console.

'He's never been one to toot his own horn – eh, my little Pushkin here, my young Brecht – but listen to this – he's been accepted on the Russian Literature course at the university,' said Alexi. He leaned across the counter, grabbed his son's fat cheek and squeezed it. He left a clear white imprint of his thumb. 'I'll miss my boy but it's for the best.'

'Brecht was German,' said Gregor.

'Rubbish' said Alexi. He considered for a moment. 'What does it matter? It's all the same. It's still literature isn't it.'

He grinned at Irina, rolling his eyes to the stained ceiling.

'I can expect more of that once he's got all of his certificates. If he's not too clever to talk to his old dad, that is.'

Ivan, from the petrol store, dropped an armful of tins

onto the counter with a clatter. He grabbed uselessly, his reactions slowed by drink and age, at a stray tin of kidney beans that rolled away from his thick fingers and onto the floor with a thud.

He wiped his fleshy, purple mouth on his sleeve, to clear the cloudy spittle that had gathered at its corners, preparing for a pronouncement.

'I was a vivacious reader in my youth Gregor. Tolstoy, of course…' He looked mistily at the shelf of sundries for a long moment, unable to summon up another name, '…and the other good ones.'

Ivan lived alone and his eagerness to be included in a conversation often exceeded his ability to contribute anything meaningful to it. He planted his filthy paw on the counter, feeling himself to be centre stage.

'Literature,' he said, and nodded his shaggy head thoughtfully. After a moment or two he touched his nose with a blackened finger and winked at Gregor. 'Literature,' he said again.

'Should I be taking notes?' said Gregor and Alexi flicked his eyes at him sharply. He recognised the frailties and the loneliness of the people who used the store and understood its importance as the hub of the community. Alexi did not like unkindness in the store. Not just because of the money people spent there as Gregor imagined.

Irina had never seen Gregor read a book or show the slightest interest in anything except working through the giant bags of chips his father stocked, and playing with his games.

He had spent so many years, seemingly glued to the

stool in the store, that when he did venture into the square, the townsfolk greeted him in an exaggerated, overly cheerful manner, as if he had just returned from a long foreign trip.

When Gregor moved he was like a walrus; slow to get going but then seemingly borne along by his own momentum. He looked to contain only liquid and sloshed through Tomyator like an overfilled paddling pool.

She tried to imagine him sitting in a bar with a group of friends. Or waddling to lectures across a busy campus, and could not.

'Very impressive Gregor,' she said brightly. 'When are you off?'

'September,' he said, rolling his large buttocks from side to side on the small seat of the high stool.

'He has a reading list as long as your arm before he even gets there. I've never heard of most of the books,' Alexi said happily.

'There are five books,' said Gregor.

'I have short arms,' said Alexi, wiggling his bony fingers.

'The thing to remember Gregor is to maintain a laser-like focus,' said Ivan, leaning across Irina to insert himself back into the conversation, trailing a waft of tomato soup and diesel fumes. The skin of his face was textured like the surface of a cauliflower.

'Don't get distracted by drinking too much with your buddies or by spending all your time with beautiful young ladies.'

He slid his hand under his sweater and scratched vigorously at his armpit, closing his filmy eyes in concentration and then sniffed his fingers absentmindedly.

'They'll suck you in with their come-to-bed eyes and their voluminous breasts and before you know where you are…' He coughed, bringing up a considerable amount of phlegm into his mouth and, realising he couldn't spit it out in the store, swallowing it down again noisily. 'Be like me. Keep them at arm's length. I always have, that's my advice. Commit yourself to your studies. It's a noble pursuit. Anchovies! Alexi. I knew there was something else. Where have you hidden them?'

Alexi lifted the hinged lid of the counter and disappeared into the deepest corner of the shop, knelt down and began rummaging at the back of the lowest shelf.

Irina squeezed Gregor's thick forearm. It gave a little under her fingers like a ham.

'Well done Gregor. You kept it so quiet. I didn't know you were a literature buff.'

'I'm not. It was the easiest course to get on,' he said.

'Where will you stay?' she said. 'Do you have family in Kazan?'

'No. Luckily. A room in a student flat.'

There he was, in her mind's eye, lowering himself solemnly from the train onto the platform, probably covered in crumbs and with greasy fingers from some salami he'd been stuffing, carrying his old fashioned suitcase, knowing no one and starting his new life.

She had allowed herself to feel disdainful of him and his slovenly ways. He was certainly no better than Vasily she'd thought. Now that he was leaving to make something of his life she burned with jealousy. Not for her son but for herself.

Irina imagined herself disembarking from the train at Moscow and in her imaginings it was summer, July perhaps, and she had no luggage to worry about, not even a handbag.

She would be wearing a summer dress, white and silky and wrapped around her waist and flaring out prettily, spotted with daisies with fresh yellow centres and it would flow, coolly, in the warm railway station breeze around her bare legs.

The light would be golden arrows, dropping softly through high, arched windows and landing directly in front of each foot a moment before it met the ground. The splashes of light would track her confident, leisurely, elegant progress alongside the gleaming silver body of the resting train.

Had she slept on the journey? She certainly felt refreshed, younger almost.

Somehow she would know the way to the exit. She wouldn't have to ask a guard or double back past the newspaper kiosk and find herself, cross and dusty and back where she started.

Yes, there was the exit.

Irina had not been to Moscow railway station but imagined it would have many platforms flowing together like the tributaries of a river to meet at the base of the wide, shallow stairs in the shape of a pool formed at the base of a waterfall.

She would ascend, all grace, into a well-to-do, tree lined

street, busy with handsome men hurrying to work, but not too busy to notice her and smile. She would turn confidently and walk, in the centre of the pavement, at her own pace.

She would float along the broad streets and she would be wearing high heeled shoes but they would not pinch her toes and she would be free of the ache in her ankle. She would glance into the shop windows filled with artful displays of scarves, or of hand made chocolates arranged on delicately tiered glass shelves with the chocolatier leaning into the window to arrange his wares.

The door to a shop selling rare musical instruments would be open and the sound of someone tinkling the keys of a, of a what? She didn't know what instrument exactly but it sounded very beautiful. Ethereal. Was that the word?

Ah, here was a dusty bookshop, what a find, with the name reproduced in faded gold paint, in an arc, on the glass. Inside an old man with a neatly trimmed white beard in a waistcoat and a red bow tie stood behind the counter and waved.

There were hard backed books with rust coloured leather spines, crammed untidily into boxes at the front of the shop on a collection of charming old tables, and she would pick one up, blow away the dust and stand a while to flick through the pages – she noticed her nails were beautifully shaped and painted an elegant blue grey colour – as the people flowed easily around her.

A woman's perfume, an expensive one probably, the smell of coffee carried by a person too busy to sit around in a café (they were always on the go in Moscow) and the buttery scent of croissants baking would flow over and around her.

Irina preferred magazines usually but she felt she might get to like books more if there were other readers around her. The engineer probably had bookshelves full of them that she could recommend and she would definitely make sure she read them from cover to cover.

A church bell ringing would interrupt her and she would look up at the sound and spy the gleaming gold turrets that dotted the Moscow skyline. She would replace the book, waving an apologetic 'not this time' to the shopkeeper and continue on her way to the little flat that smelled of ink and lavender.

Alexi appeared with a dusty jar of anchovies and cracked them down on the counter.

'I have triumphed,' he said, clasping together his hands and raising them over his head, waving them back and forth in a victory celebration and making a noise like the roar of a crowd.

Gregor wedged a yellow finger and thumb into the packet of corn puffs and shoved a handful of the fat pupae into his slack mouth.

'Brilliant,' he said, indistinctly through crumbs.

Alexi began to tally up the cost of Ivan's tins of stewed meat, jars of frankfurters, tinned peaches and mayonnaise.

'What about Vasily?' he said to Irina. 'What's the lad up to? I could do with some help here if he's planning on sticking around. Mention it to him if you think he'd be interested.'

Gregor lifted his eyes to hers and looked away again

quickly. He and Vasily didn't seem to get together anymore. Perhaps they didn't have much in common these days.

'I'll ask him,' she said. She was hot and bitter with shame at her son's lack of ambition and angry with Alexi for pointing it out in front of everyone. She was disappointed in her own child, a sickening feeling, and she felt ashamed of herself and of her envy.

She knew she wouldn't even mention it to Vasily though. He would think it beneath him to be humping boxes in the store. It would only cause a fight, and she was losing her appetite for it.

Seventeen

Maia knew two styles; a bob and a pixie cut.

Irina wondered if either of those cuts would be thought chic in Moscow. The pictures in the coffee shop magazines weren't of ordinary women, she knew that, but it seemed to her that longer hair was more fashionable these days. Even for women her age.

Maia unravelled her black cloth pouch, flamboyantly, onto Irina's kitchen table. Inside it were her scissors, a set of combs and a series of metal clips for pinning one hank of hair out of the way whilst she worked on another one.

She wore her brush in a holster at her hip. Every time she reached for it Oleg yelled 'don't shoot' and ducked his head under the kitchen table.

She pursed her narrow lips and tutted in pretend annoyance but her eyes flicked across to him often and she tossed her own hair, which was long and red and backcombed, and then sprayed into hard waves like rolls of copper.

'I'm not saying it's not a lot of work because it is a lot of work,' she said, touching her curls, 'but it's marketing isn't it, when you think about it? An investment in my business.'

The rolls were so fixed that they sprang out from her head, fully formed and seemingly indestructible, when she removed her fur hat.

'Blow drying is an under-rated art,' she said snipping at Irina's wet hair fussily and peering at the results from different angles. 'I always say that cutting hair is one art but blow-drying is another art. People have told me I'm a very artistic person.'

She inserted a red tipped finger into one of her own curls.

'I wouldn't trust anyone else to put direct heat anywhere near these for example. 'A,' because my hair is naturally unruly and, two, I have a hyper sensitive scalp.'

Maia admired herself in the black glass of Irina's kitchen window. Her hardened features resembled a metallic face, embossed on the front of a coin.

Irina sat, silent and with her wet hair slicked in strands, in the black nylon gown that Maia brought with her. Maia had fastened it too tightly and the thin material dug into her neck. Irina's reflection in the kitchen window was sour and unpleasant to look at. The frown lines between her eyebrows showed as black shadows, and she wished she had pulled down the blind.

The cut was almost finished but she did not want the blow dry. Irina was screwing up her determination in order to refuse it.

Maia charged 500 Roubles extra for a blow dry and besides, Irina wasn't going anywhere to show it off. She wondered how much blow dries cost in Moscow. It would look the same as usual in the morning when she got up anyway.

Then there was the fact that the hairs were blown around the kitchen and she'd feel them between her teeth, later, when she was drinking tea. Or they'd find their way into the butter if she had not remembered to cover it.

It seemed a luxury to have someone cut your hair when you could do it yourself or tie it up and it was mainly hidden under a hat. But Maia was struggling with her bills like everyone else and when she asked Irina, in the queue in the store, whether it would suit her to come over this week or next for a cut, Irina was caught off guard. She didn't have the heart to refuse in front of everyone.

This was definitely a haircut she couldn't afford and she frowned at her reflection. She was a pushover; forever being blown into blind corners by the stronger will of others.

She sighed. It was important to look half human for the guests she supposed. She would definitely refuse the blow dry so at least it would not be too expensive.

'Hah. You're going really grey now,' said Oleg.

Maia had pinned up a section of hair at her temple.

'Some people might be pleased to have any hair at all,' said Maia. 'Not looking at anyone in particular.'

Oleg rubbed his head roughly, grinning.

'Everyone knows baldness is a sign of virility.'

Maia put her hand on her plump hip and arched an eyebrow.

'Says you.'

Her banal coquetry was intended as a joke, she took care to include Irina in her look, but the round hip was produced nonetheless.

Irina wondered if perhaps they would have an affair and, if so, whether she would care at all.

Maia's husband suffered from a chronic lung condition, Irina was unclear what condition exactly and didn't care to ask, and he was rarely seen these days. He occasionally drifted out to the square in the summer months, less substantial than the thin silver rays that pierced weakly through the clouds.

Since her husband was out of the picture, Maia had developed a reputation in the town as a man-eater. It was undeserved. Irina thought her to be brassy on the surface but essentially lonely. She had the kind of eager desperation for affection and admiration that men were attracted to initially but found frightening close up.

They had no children and lived on the small pension her husband received from the oil company and Maia's hairdressing. Irina couldn't help but admire her determination to survive.

She and Oleg would probably be well-suited. She thought Maia would wait until her husband died before trying anything with Oleg.

She was more than welcome to deal with Oleg's grey, skid-marked pants and the way he blew his nose in the sink and left the snot dotting the enamel for her to clean up. Perhaps it was better than a husband with a chronic lung condition. Maybe that's all anyone wanted – a situation marginally better than the one they were faced with today.

What would the affair matter to Irina if she went to Moscow? If anything it would be preferable to know that Oleg was happy and she would not have to feel guilty. Or even to think about him. She didn't quite hate him after all.

Perhaps she should suggest that they got to know each other. She glanced at herself in the reflection in the black window and saw that her mouth had turned upwards in a twisted, sardonic sort of way. It was the type of smile you saw creep up onto the faces of unhappy people and it reminded her of her mother.

'That engineer woman is the talk of the town,' said Maia. 'How's she getting on? She certainly marches around the place like she owns it.'

She fussed with the hair over Irina's ear, ruffling it now and then with her fingers to create 'volume' which was something Irina's hair did not seem to have.

'The technical details go over my head,' said Irina, 'but she's making progress I think. Most of the equipment is installed and she's going to be finishing off and testing for another week or so. Then she'll be gone.'

Gone. Irina looked around at the cupboards and the tiles and thought how tired they had become. The second hand of the white kitchen clock ticked around self-importantly and she was washed with a sudden bleak misery.

Oleg was staring glassily at Maia's breasts that jiggled in time with her snipping. The tips of her small nipples jabbed against the cloth of her t-shirt. She had a soft fold over the waistband of her jeans that ebbed and flowed with her movements. Oleg had forgotten to hold in his own stomach.

'That's a shame,' said Maia. 'That was a nice long booking for you.'

'Too right', said Oleg, nodding his head but keeping his eyes fixed on her breasts. 'All courtesy of the Meteorological Department of Moscow University. With extra for meals and washing. It was a lot of extra trouble – a lot – but we haven't held back on the bill if you know what I mean.'

He smirked at Maia to show off his cunning. But it had been no extra work for him and Irina had not charged any more than normal for the laundry and extra food. Irina disliked him intensely for that sly look.

'You should persuade her to have one of your artistic blow dries. She'll probably put that on their bill too. You should double your price. Triple it,' he said.

Maia had placed her hand on Irina's head to turn it but at the suggestion she stopped and rested it there instead. She thought for a moment, seeming to have forgotten Irina as she leaned on her like a bedpost or the end of a bannister.

Her hand was heavy and Irina knotted her fingers together, under the gown, in irritation. She wanted to push her hand away, violently, and to drag at the tight nylon noose around her neck.

'She's not the type. It wouldn't be her thing,' said Maia. She pointed the scissors at Oleg with her free hand.

'Do you know they have these celebrity stylists in Moscow with salons that have spas in them and the customers get a glass of champagne while they wait? Not that they make them wait long I expect. They wouldn't put up with waiting would they? Not those sorts of customers.'

'I'm sure she doesn't go to that type of salon,' said Irina,

230

jerking her head so that Maia noticed her again and removed her hand.

'Who knows?' said Maia. 'People surprise you. They'll have baskets of exotic fruit on tap. Mangos. Pineapples. I've seen photographs.'

'Whoah there,' said Oleg laughing. 'You've seen a photograph of someone having their hair cut and eating a pineapple?'

'Not exactly,' said Maia, flushing. 'But you don't know what goes on do you?'

She was cross with Oleg for laughing at her and she began to snip again, sharply and too close to Irina's ear.

'All I'm saying is that she's all teeth and good mornings but people like that can be a bit false. To your face they're friendly but they wouldn't lower themselves to get a haircut from someone ordinary like me. They'd rather get it done in Moscow. That's just my opinion.'

'She's definitely full of herself,' said Oleg, keen to ingratiate himself with her again.

'You should hear her banging on about the Weather Station. Irina laps it up.'

He shrugged. 'Admit it Irina, you do. I've caught her out a few times, chucking around technical terms she doesn't understand. I've called her out on it to her face.'

He tapped his finger on the table in time with his words.

'She does not like that one little bit.'

He looked at Irina with a contemptuous half smile, grimly pleased to be able to hurt her twice; once with an insult about her intelligence and then with a jabbing follow up by criticising her friend.

'Women like that with their hoity toity delusions of intellectual superiority really grind my gears.'

Maia brightened, now that Oleg was back on her side. She nodded eagerly, circling Irina, with her nose almost touching her head, to check on her work.

'I'm the same,' she said. 'It's stuck up in a way isn't it. Not to be nasty, but she has this way about her. She wanders around with a superior sort of look, as if she's breathing different air from the rest of us mere mortals.'

She snorted, flaring her nostrils.

'She's nothing special looks-wise by the way.'

Maia tossed her coppery curls defiantly, arching her neck and glancing at herself sideways in the window's reflection.

'Not that I'm claiming to be anything special.' She threw a quick, sideways look towards Oleg. 'But it's important to look after yourself if you think about it,' she said. 'Do the best with what you've got. Me, for example, I try to make the most of my assets. Put on a bit of lipstick. Do something with my eyes.'

She batted her eyelashes rapidly, as if attempting to dislodge an irritating foreign body and pouted. It was the face that women made in photographs these days. Visitors took pictures of themselves like that with the view in the background and Irina thought them ridiculous.

'I'd like to think that some people appreciate it,' she said and Oleg grinned back at her stupidly.

'She's not like that at all,' said Irina and it was louder and more forceful than she had expected and, Maia coloured a little. Perhaps she had gone too far with her flirting with Oleg. It was only in fun. She would never make a play for another woman's husband. Irina had just taken it the wrong way and she was embarrassed for her and this display of jealousy. She was making a fuss about nothing after all.

'Just my impression,' she said mildly. 'You know her better than us I suppose. She just looks offish. D'you know what I mean?'

'Not really,' said Irina.   She tore away the Velcro fastening of the gown at her neck, scattering hairs across the floor, with something like fury. 'I won't bother with the blow dry today thank you.'

Eighteen

'What if we went back to Yakutsk?' she said, brightly, as if the idea had occurred to her just that very minute. 'You know, if we just couldn't make the motel pay?'

'Don't start,' said Oleg.

She rubbed her palms on the seats of the sofa and thought how threadbare it had become. It had two worn patches where their bottoms sat. It was the sofa they had bought when they first moved to Tomyator.

They had chosen all of their furniture for the apartment on the same trip to the shopping centre in Yakutsk. The shop assistants had smiled at them indulgently, pleased to help the attractive young couple furnishing their new home together, and Irina and Oleg had been self-conscious about the attention.

Oleg had examined the underneath of the kitchen chairs with a serious expression to check that they were solidly built and Irina had shaken her head at the displays of fashionable cushions and rugs that the assistant had steered her towards. They had a baby to consider she told the woman. And they were moving house because her husband was taking up a management role. Irina looked much younger than twenty-three then and was sometimes still taken for a teenager. She felt these women in the shops were patronising her, so she had been standoffish and chosen deliberately grown up furniture and sensible sets of plates to show that they were mature.

When all of the furniture had been delivered and they arranged it in the apartment she felt disappointed. It was as if she were visiting someone else's home, and she couldn't think why she had selected it.

She looked around the room at the boxy sideboard faced with oak veneer and the two small, non-committal, occasional tables topped with matching lamps shaped like bulbous wine bottles. They were so familiar that she couldn't tell whether they were ugly or attractive anymore.

'It's worth thinking about at least,' she said, tucking her hair behind her ear. 'It gets harder every year doesn't it? I was talking to the travel agent on the phone last week. She was despairing.'

Irina stretched across the sofa and touched his thigh.

'She said it's the same everywhere. It's not just us. People are cutting way back on trips.'

'Despairing?' said Oleg. 'Don't believe it. She does all right.'

He did not move his eyes from the television. Irina examined his profile for clues to his mood.

He seemed peaceful. His hand was wrapped around the TV control and he stroked the side of the black plastic, up and down, with his thumb.

His feet were two, curled soft creatures tucked up beside

him on the sofa. He had undone the button of his trousers so that his round football of a belly could rest more easily on top of the half unfastened zip.

Only the two lamps were lit and the room was snug and they were companionable enough. Come on Irina, it's not so bad, she thought.

The suitcase hidden under the bed seemed foolish, now that they were almost contented.

Yesterday she had pulled it from the top of the wardrobe and wiped away the layer of dust with a damp cloth. Her heart had hammered as she unzipped it and flipped open the lid.

It was just a fantasy she told herself. If she were really going to Moscow, what would she take? How would it feel to start packing?

She had forced herself to smile. To reassure herself that it was a game she was playing with herself. But there was an illicit excitement to it that made her fingers tremble.

She squatted, with a crack of her ankle, next to the bedside cabinet and opened its door. It was a sturdy piece of furniture covered with wipe-clean, white melanin and, like everything else in the apartment, it reeked of practicality.

On the bottom shelf of the cabinet, in a plastic file, was her driving license, her marriage certificate, Vasily's birth certificate and her passport. Irina had never been abroad, or even been to Moscow. She opened it and flicked through the empty, unstamped pages before looking, hard, at her picture.

She hardly recognised the girl who looked back at her

although she thought she had not changed. It was a strange sensation. What was so different about it? Was it the softness in her expression? Perhaps it was the struggle to keep a straight face. Oleg had put his hand under the orange curtain of the photo booth to tickle her at the very moment the lights flashed.

They had both applied for their passports at the same time, soon after they had met. They were certain they would want to travel.

In a pile, pushed to the back of the cupboard was a short stack of photographs. They had become sticky, each picture bleeding into the back of the one on top of it. Irina sat on the bed and unpeeled the layers, excavating the geology of her own life.

She squinted at them, tilting them away from the glare of the too bright overhead light. She felt that these photographs might help her to make up her mind, one way or the other.

In the event, they were just bad photographs; where a heavy shadow had thrown the subject's face into darkness, or someone had their eyes closed or had their hand in front of another's face.

There was Irina at about eight, and her sister, both in scratchy-looking dresses in front of a wall at some occasion. Irina screwed up her eyes and held the photograph close but it was too blurred to be able to tell whether she had been happy or sad.

She had taken hundreds of photographs of Oleg when they first met, posing with his foot on the bumper of his car, lighting his cigarette or sitting with his elbows on the table at the bar and smiling at the camera. He looked carefree then and she wondered if it was her who had made him unhappy in the end.

There were pictures of Vasily as a baby in a swing with his head turned from the camera or disappearing from the side of the frame. In some of the photographs a flare of light had blotted out a section of the image and cast a sepia wash over the rest of the picture. She had thought them not good enough for the album but throwing them away seemed an act of violence so Irina had pushed them into the limbo of the back of the shelf instead.

They felt sticky and disappointing in her hands. If she were to go to Moscow, she would not take them with her.

'She said no one has the money for more than one holiday a year. When you think about it like that it makes sense doesn't it? If it's a choice between a week on the beach in Crimea or here, it's no surprise we can't compete.'

Oleg grunted.

'Egypt is popular now she says. Egypt! It's so cheap apparently. We'd never have even dreamed of anything so exotic when we were young would we? I can't imagine us on a camel can you?'

Oleg looked at his watch.

'Sounds like she has a lot to say.'

He was becoming irritated by Irina talking over his programme. And by unwelcome reminders of opinionated women.

'How much longer is your little pal going to be here?' he said shifting in his seat.

'A week she says,' said Irina. 'If everything goes to plan.'

Oleg sniffed. He did not like the woman. She was bolshie. Her independence unsettled him. He'd be glad when she had cleared off back to Moscow. The way Irina ran round after her got on his nerves.

They sat in silence for a while, both thinking about the engineer's departure.

Irina looked around at the walls and her dissatisfaction grew.

She had never felt fully at home here. They had not chosen the heavily patterned wallpaper favoured by the older residents or hung tapestries woven with complicated scenes, or displayed gilded icons in dark wooden frames. It was more modern to have plain walls – they agreed on that at least – and they had picked a soft peach colour. Twilight Blush. She still remembered the name.

Once they had their blank canvas they were embarrassed to realise that neither had the imagination or flair to make the best of it.

They had hung Oleg's three professional certificates behind the television in wooden frames. On another wall was a black and white print they'd felt to be artistic, of a cobbled street in Montmatre.

It was nearly night time in the picture and the street was winding and glistened blackly with old rain. Some couples sat outside a café at small tables. They all leaned towards each other, urgent and tense, like lovers. Next door there was a small store with a striped awning with the shopkeeper, in his long apron, standing in the doorway.

They had talked of visiting Paris when they first met and had thought this picture captured the city exactly as they imagined it.

But if it were not for the white dome of Sacre Couer poking from behind some houses at the top of the hill, this scene was not so different to their own square. A café and a store. People drinking coffee or buying bread. The thought depressed her. That life was essentially the same wherever you went.

The calendar they ordered every year from The Siberian Times provided a splash of colour in the room, depending on the month.

She sighed and dropped her hands down heavily onto the sofa so that Oleg shot a glance of irritation in her direction and increased the volume, by one notch, on the television. He angled himself away from her and stared, frowning, at his programme.

If she did pack her suitcase she would leave him a note on the kitchen table. Wasn't that what women did?

Dear Oleg,

I have devoted myself to accommodating you and your life. You have broken my heart with your indifference to me and crushed my spirit with your casual cruelty. I am a real person with hopes and dreams...

Oh, it was ridiculously melodramatic. Oleg's irritation was fading now and she saw the lines around his eyes soften as he began to smile, in a stupid, slack-mouthed way, at the scene on the television.

Oleg had never hit her after all. He did not have affairs.

Plenty of men were unfaithful, but not Oleg. She thought she might be more attracted to him if he had the energy, or the organisational ability, to be enjoying secret liaisons. Even if they were with brassy hairdressers.

She could not possibly leave Tomyator and her life here because her husband of more than twenty years did not pick up his own dirty vests and shirts from the bedroom floor. Or because he left stubble in the sink.

Dear Oleg,

I'm leaving you because I came upon the unflushed toilet for the umpteenth time and took it as a sign of your disrespect.

It wasn't just that of course. He didn't take his boots off. He drank too much vodka and became nasty with it. Irina had to remind him to shower and sometimes he had a musty smell.

It bored her to have to list the reasons.

None of them, on their own, would seem anything other that trivial and feminine grievances committed to paper. They didn't seem sufficient to justify leaving. Though to whom she should justify it she couldn't quite think.

The truth was, Irina wanted to make the best of things. She could tolerate almost anything if only she and Oleg could at least be a team and face this life together.

Dear Oleg,

I would have liked to talk about our little girl sometimes.

Oleg laughed and turned sideways to see if she found the programme funny too, but Irina's face was pulled tight with thoughts of the empty motel rooms and her eyes were shining with tears.

'Christ,' he said. 'What now?'

'We should think about the motel though shouldn't we? About what's best for all of us,' Irina said and a single tear spilled down her cheek.

Oleg switched off the television and threw down the remote control on the cushion between them. It bounced up in the air and they both froze, holding their breath, to see if it would hit her. If it did bang against her arm the conversation would go in one direction and if it dropped, in a more neutral way, between them, it would surely go in another.

It did not hit Irina and Oleg snorted, with relief and irritation.

'Us?' he said, baring his teeth. 'I never wanted the motel. I said it would be too much for you. I warned you Irina. You were the one who thought you were some great hotelier.'

He banged his palm down on the arm of the sofa.

'Irina Petruchevsky – the queen of hospitality, yapping on about fancy curtains and the best soaps and never listening to anyone because you always knew better. I went along with it to keep you happy as usual. If you've failed then at least admit it Irina. Don't pick a fight about it with me.'

'It doesn't have to be a fight.' She said, looking straight ahead with her hands folded in her lap. 'You're making it a fight.'

Oleg uncurled his legs from the sofa and planted both feet firmly on the floor in the direction of the television, and slapped his hands onto his thighs. Only his face turned towards her. It gave the impression of physical force held in check.

'I'm laying out the facts. Not playing along with your fantasy 'what if?' game,' he said. 'Facts! Remember them?' He spoke slowly and fixed his eyes on hers with something that looked to Irina, with a shock, like hatred.

'Fact. We have a loan to pay off. Fact. We're not making enough for anyone to want to buy it. That's the way it is here Irina. Unless you have a buyer with deep pockets you've forgotten to mention.'

That wasn't fair. Yes, it had been Irina's idea but Oleg had been happy to go along with it. Their marriage, Vasily's arrival, their excitement over Oleg's new job and then being offered this apartment were all events that had happened so smoothly that it was unthinkable to them that life would not be one successful decision after another. They were tricked into complacency by their run of good fortune and did not consider that anything in life could defeat them. They had each other after all.

Oleg had been encouraging, to a degree. He wasn't old fashioned about his wife like some men and he sat back, letting her take the lead when they sat in the old owner's cluttered living room, talking about the purchase and looking through the books.

She had been pleased her husband was modern like that. His confidence in her was encouraging. She flicked through the accounts, not fully understanding the numbers, but running her finger down the columns of figures, nodding now and then, as the man talked about rising occupancy rates, and of wealthy foreigners looking for experience holidays.

He had indicated the paperwork and winked.

'You won't find the tips in there my dear. However hard you look.'

He rolled up his sleeve and pointed at his heavy gold watch and smirked. Some of the thick, black hairs on his arm had become caught between the strap's metal links.

'Let's just say, in the motel trade, there's official income and unofficial income.'

Now she recognised Oleg's willingness to let her take charge had not been an indication of his confidence in her but a signal of his innate passivity. She had thought him agreeable and easy going when they had first met. Gradually she came to see that he was blown here and there by the stronger will of others and, having never firmly backed a course of action, could claim credit when it was a success, and be full of knowing scorn when it wasn't.

It hadn't mattered at first. Everything did go their way. They congratulated themselves on their good sense. It was true that her excitement about the motel and its potential had swayed him but now that occupancy was falling and the burden of the loan threatened to overwhelm them, Oleg had revised their history to show that he had been against it from the start.

'We could advertise it for sale and see what happens,' she said in an even voice. She knew her tears angered him and she set her jaw and became rigid and stiff-shouldered in her fight to keep them back.

'Even if we sold at a loss we could find work in Yakutsk and clear off the loan quicker than if we stayed here.'

'Ah, we could find work? We? We? So it's me not having a job that's put us in this position is it? Not you Irina. Not you insisting we take on a business that you can't make pay.'

He stood up, seeming old in the tentative way he curled out of the sofa, and went to the drawer and dragged it open. He jumbled the contents roughly. He had the excuse he needed to have a cigarette. His injured pride. Her nagging. Who could blame him?

She knew he would not go onto the balcony to smoke it but would light it here and drag on it, deliberately, daring her to comment.

'If we're trapped here it's because of your motel.'

He held the cigarette tightly between his front teeth.

'You can't see it can you? It's you. It's you and your dumb hoping for the best crap that's put us in this position. Get real for once Irina.'

His nostrils flared into a sneer and he leaned down towards her on the sofa, pressing his face close to hers so that she could see the grout of this evening's dinner between his teeth.

'As if a fucking website is going to make a difference. I mean Jesus. Who in their right mind would want to come to this shithole anyway?'

'Well you did for a start,' said Irina quickly, flaring with an anger that sent bright red spots to her cheeks. She was filled with contempt for him. 'I wanted to stay in Yakutsk.

I only came because you wanted to.'

She paused and looked at her hands that were knotted together in her lap.

'You said it would be good for your career.'

And when she said 'career' it had a sarcastic, taunting tone that she could not help and she held her breath for a second to listen for his response because she knew it would hurt him very much.

The silence was loaded up with history and bitter recriminations and unhappy remembrances.

'Fuck you Irina,' he said and went to the bathroom, pushing his zip down further as he walked and gripping the short remains of his cigarette between his teeth.

He slammed the door behind him. Along the corridor, there was a soft echo, as Vasily closed his door quietly against the fight. He would be putting on his headphones and turning up his music now.

'I can't do everything on my own Oleg,' called Irina and her voice sounded horribly weak and thin.

How could she tell him that the motel would close soon? Perhaps not for a few months until the new temperature readings became public. But it would be soon. They must make plans.

She stood quickly, too quickly, and felt dizzy and out of breath. Her heart was pounding and she tasted acid in her mouth.

Oleg would stay in the bathroom for a while she knew. She hurried into their bedroom and flipped open the small jewellery box she kept on her dressing table. Irina didn't have much jewellery, there was never an occasion to wear it, but she picked out her favourite piece, a silver brooch with an oily black stone, like a sucked liquorice, mounted in its centre. She held it again her chest. When she looked at herself in the mirror, she saw that her neck was mapped with red blotches.

She pulled out the suitcase from under the bed, flapped open its green vinyl mouth and put the brooch inside, an icon.

It looked a little ridiculous there, on its own. But it felt like a protest she had to make.

She would add something precious or useful or even frivolous to the suitcase whenever she felt she could not stand another day of this life.

And when the suitcase was full, she would have the courage, and the evidence, to leave. It felt like a plan, to create a checklist of her grievances. The uncomfortable feeling that she was over reacting would be evidenced by the proof of her full suitcase and she would have the courage to go.

When she did, she would be truthful in her note.

Dear Oleg,

I'm leaving you because a woman I admire has asked me to.

Nineteen

'Irina Petruchevsky,' said Alexi. 'You're here.'

He spread his arms wide, apparently delighted to see her.

It was an out-of-the-ordinary greeting and Irina, who had thought of nothing but the engineer's departure for days felt a different unease, plucking at her heart.

She was not equipped for a new alarm, so she cast about for an activity, any activity, to bat the uncomfortable moment away.

The list! That was something at least. Irina took off her mittens and stabbed her hands into her pockets to locate it. Damn it. She must have left it on the freshly scrubbed kitchen table.

Everything was freshly scrubbed.

At home, and unable to bear the thought of the engineer leaving and the emptiness ahead, she had thrown herself into her housework with a kind of mania. All of the kitchen cupboards had been emptied of their stained bottles and jars and the shelves washed with cloths sopping with bleach. Her fingers were white with it, like bones, so they seemed not to belong to her when she looked at them.

She swept and mopped the floor furiously. A tile, cracked God knows how long ago from a dropped pan, was scarred with a thin seam of black grease and Irina knelt there, running the point of a knife along it to try to gouge out the dirt.

When a shadow fell over her she knew that Oleg was standing in the doorway, assessing her. He sniffed sharply, the way he always did before a pronouncement, but he thought better of making a comment and went away, quietly, instead.

Irina realised she was panting.

She had taken down Vasily's curtains and washed them, wiping the curtain pole clean of grime with quick movements, and then removed the plastic rings that slid along them, scrubbing them in a sink of boiling water.

Vasily had remained on his bed, silent and with his eyes closed as she stretched over him, balanced awkwardly on a chair, to rehang them.

'Mental,' he said, and she felt, in that murderous moment, like she was.

Now, here in the store, she was not angry but worn out, expecting every surprise to be unpleasant. She did not have the strength for another unpleasant surprise from Alexi.

She tried to visualise the list.

Bleach. Oregano. Peppercorns. Milk. What was the other thing? She had five things to pick up. Come on Irina. What was the fifth thing? Bleach. Oregano. Peppercorns. Milk. She couldn't think.

It was impossible to imagine she could find the strength to return later. She had to remember.

The light was harsh inside the store; a headachy luminescence that seemed to throw no shadows, so that the rows of bottles and tins looked flattened and two dimensional, like a backdrop in a play.

It gave her an unsteady, frightened feeling.

The lights ran in long strips behind corrugated plastic covers and they made a high, buzzing sound.

The picture of the shelves swayed and Irina felt dizzy and put her hand to her face. Just tiredness. She was tired to death for God's sake. Her fingers traced the pouchy flesh under her eyes and she knew they had become as purple as bruises recently.

Irina's energy was already so depleted and now she felt whatever was left of it begin to drop away through the soles of her feet and into the floor and she put a hand to the shelf to steady herself.

It would be unthinkable to faint here. Sprawled on the sticky floor to be gawped at by open-mouthed locals who would crowd around her to get a better look at the spectacle.

Unthinkable. She focused on the shelf and took a deep breath.

She looked hard at a tin of green beans and could not fathom them. The label was a mass of muddy, shifting colours. The words on the tin made no sense to her. She was hot and cold at the same time as if she had a fever.

'Is something the matter?' she said in a light tone to Alexi, turning her head slowly along the shelf as if searching for something in amongst the incomprehensible jumble of words and colours.

'Nothing at all,' said Alexi, cracking his knuckles. 'Just extending a friendly welcome to a loyal customer.'

She turned to him and turned up the corners of her mouth, mechanically, into a half-dead facsimile of a smile. The tips of her fingers tingled with sweat.

'All of your customers are loyal,' she said.

It was an old joke and he laughed much more than the remark deserved. But his smile, when it settled, was nervous and he scratched at his chin and then shoved his hands in the pockets of his overall before it fell away altogether.

He cleared his throat.

'It must be almost twenty years we've known each other now. The boys were little together. Now look at them,' he said.

'Yes,' she murmured. 'A lot of change.'

It was a stupid reply. What had changed in twenty years? Certainly not the store or her daily routines. If she had changed at all, then it was that she had lost hope.

Alexi looked at the counter, running his brown, flat tipped fingers back and forth across it.

'All this time Irina, I've always thought a lot of you. Always. You're a hard worker like me. We soldier on don't we? We're alike like that.'

She could not identify the look on his face. His hard features had relaxed and softened so that there was a tentative, questioning, vulnerability around his eyes. It made him almost unrecognisable to her.

He smiled at her in the way that someone who is not used to children smiles at a toddler; well meaning and kind but self-conscious, half in trepidation at the unpredictability of the target of their affection.

'I think you're a great girl,' he said and his eyes moistened so that he blinked to clear them.

He seemed struck with an awareness of his own hands suddenly, so that he wrapped them around one another, and would not have to think about them. His awkward angularity was touching in a way. It gave her a glimpse of the boy he'd once been.

His wet eyes were startling to her and she forgot about her tiredness.

Alexi had seemed old to her when she'd arrived in Tomyator even though he couldn't have been more than forty. Younger than she was now. She had never considered him in terms of being a man and what a man was. But he had a son and had, presumably, had a wife too. Of course, he must feel the loss of that sometimes.

She wondered whether thoughts of Gregor's departure had made him sentimental. It happened when one's children flew the nest she supposed. It had never crossed her mind that a man like Alexi, perpetually surrounded by people, might be lonely.

She closed her eyes for a moment and then opened them suddenly, trying to suppose that this was the first time she had laid eyes on him.

He had an oval shaped face, burnt a reddish brown by the wind, that tapered into a narrow chin, like an acorn balanced on its point.

His features were unremarkable and sat in all the usual places. Perhaps they were undersized on a grown man. He had a smallish mouth that strained to contain his big, square, wide-set teeth. His pressed together lips over those large teeth gave him a pugnacious expression, when he was not smiling, that was at odds with his mild character.

He was spry and had a busy, good-natured, vitality and his hair was still dark in the main. It only showed flecks of grey at his temples. His brown, grocer's coat emphasised the boxy, squareness of his shoulders. He was straight-backed, in the deliberate way of men who are conscious of being short.

Alexi hadn't run to fat like a lot of men in middle age. She allowed herself a small smile. That was a change in itself; considering that a man of sixty was middle-aged and not just old.

'We see each other most days don't we Irina? It's hard not to care, at least a little, about someone you get to know over such a long time.'

She supposed she did care about him to a degree. She would be sad if he were to be taken ill or if he died. But Alexi was like a family member whose likeability, or not, you had never really considered. Your feelings were of no consequence; you were stuck with them anyway weren't you?

He was staring straight at her, wide-eyed, with his hands flat on the counter. His eyes were a dark green, and the whites were very bright and clear, like those of a younger man. She had never noticed them before.

He leaned towards her, blinking rapidly, preparing to say something urgent and unusual. He licked his narrow lips and cleared his throat again.

Oh, poor Alexi. She saw it now. How silly. She smiled and turned her head to one side. Her nervousness floated away.

Did he imagine that they might have an affair? Of course it was out of the question but she wasn't offended by the idea. There had been rumours about Alexi and a woman who lived on the floor below Irina at the apartment block but she had never been able to believe it was true. It was impossible to imagine Alexi naked. She and Oleg had agreed that he had probably been born wearing his brown coat, over his white shirt and with an already tightly-knotted tie.

She turned back to the shelves and picked out a jar of honey. It hadn't been on her list but her mouth watered suddenly at the thought of the sweetness and she couldn't resist it.

It was a pleasurable sensation and she felt a sudden return of her appetite. She had not bothered with breakfast that morning.

Who didn't enjoy being admired? But Alexi...Alexi. She'd never thought of him in that way.

Now, she wasn't some naïve kid. No need to get carried away. Irina knew full well it was just his loneliness that had made him reach out to her. There were probably ten other women in the town he might have chosen.

But for now it was her and it wasn't the worst thing in the world. God knows she felt lonely herself often enough. Oleg could hardly stand to look at her these days. Who could blame her for basking in a little flattery? It made her feel girlish and light-hearted so that she forgot her sore ankle and the stiffness in her neck.

Alexi exhaled noisily and shoved his hands into the pocket of his coat.

She did feel a warmth for him, a sympathy, but she could not lead him on. He was an unattractive little man, but, for the very first time, she considered him to be more than a shopkeeper. He was a person with feelings and she would not be unkind. He was a good man and he didn't deserve cruelty.

But, oh, to be the focus of admiration was wonderful. She stood straighter and raised her eyebrows into arcs of expectation.

She wouldn't mention any of this to Oleg. He wouldn't understand. What on earth should she say to Alexi? She felt an overwhelming urge to rescue the poor man from his own awkwardness. But not just yet. Not for a few more moments at least.

He was blushing and she held down her smile, amused to see a shopkeeper acting like a love struck schoolboy. He gathered some delivery notes that were scattered across the counter and arranged them into a pile.

'I'm sorry to be blurting it out like this. I had to say something.'

He was relieved now that he had begun his confession and she waited; she wouldn't interrupt him.

'It's nearly 95,000 Roubles Oleg's totted up. He swore me to secrecy. I was stupid to go along with it but enough's enough now.'

'What did you say?'

'I think a lot of you Irina. It wouldn't be too much to say

I care about you – I know you're like a slave to that motel – but I don't know what I was thinking, setting up a tab for him.'

A note of self-righteousness had crept into his tone now. He tapped a finger on the counter, eager for this scene to be done with now that he had taken the plunge.

Irina coloured suddenly, a fire in her cheeks and across her forehead that was quick and bitter.

'I don't understand,' she said. 'Oleg's spent 95,000 Roubles here? On what?'

Oleg never came home with extra shopping. Even if she sent him with a list, half of the items were missed off, or he made excuses about them not being in stock because he was too lazy to go back.

'Come on Irina,' said Alexi. He did not like her tone and especially the implication that there was nothing of value to buy in his store. These people seemed to forget that they relied on him and he was beginning to feel cross with her now. He wouldn't be taken for a mug by the whole family.

And then she knew full well on what because Alexi nodded towards the underside of the counter where he kept his vodka, away from prying eyes, as confirmation.

Alexi was not smiling now. She thought he was impatient to get this conversation over with and to get some resolution. He looked to her to provide it. As usual it fell on her shoulders and she was filled with an angry, burning self-pity at the unfairness of her predicament.

She clenched her small fists and turned to the window, twisting her face into a grimace that she couldn't help, but knew would have looked utterly mad, glaring out between the metal shelves at the square towards their apartment.

A woman, tightly wrapped and leaning at an acute angle that showed the precise strength of the wind, walked in front of the window. She glanced in, moving her head as little as possible, as everyone did, but did not stop or acknowledge Irina staring out at her.

Irina would have liked to throw open the door of the shop and run away, across the square, towards the flattened plain of the airfield, past the old hangar with its collapsed roof and along the runway, beyond into the flat bleakness of nothing and nowhere and to keep running until she could slip out of her own thin skin and leave herself entirely behind.

I could start to scream now thought Irina. She felt the physical shape of it gathering in her throat and she clamped her hand over her mouth.

She heard the squeak of the hinged counter lifting and tensed as she felt Alexi coming towards her. She twisted her face away from him as he stood beside her and his voice, sounding strange and not like the usual joking, jovial Alexi, was horribly close to her ear.

'We've talked off and on. We're old pals after all. I know he's been finding it hard not working. It gets you here,' and he touched his heart, 'not to be able to provide for your family. He said it was all getting on top of him. It was just the one bottle at first and he'd pay me back a few days later. And then it was four days, then five days.'

He leaned around her, peering nosily into her face to see how she was taking the news and he put his hand on Irina's arm to claim her attention.

'Listen. Maybe you should talk to him. Give the poor guy a chance to get things off his chest. It's not easy for him you know.'

'Do you think it's easy for me?'

She had spat it out and her eyes glittered and Alexi stepped back, surprised by the force of her anger. She was a hard woman in some ways. No wonder Oleg was driven to drink.

Still, he would have his money, come what may.

Twenty

Irina could see the whole apartment from the hall and as she hung her coat she looked through the living room and into the kitchen to see Oleg reach up to the kitchen cupboard where he kept his vodka, hesitate, and then put his hands in his pockets.

'Take it,' she thought. 'Take it.' She urged him to open the cupboard and take it down, and pour a tumbler and throw it down his throat and smack his lips and fill it again, and drink it down and drink and drink until he was oblivious and she would not have to talk to him for another day.

It would give her time to gather herself. Time to think how to tackle him about Alexi's impossible bill. About what he had done to them and she was filled with a white fury at her impotence and at his self-pitying recklessness and at the inevitability of her own failure to change him.

He turned and his eyes settled on Irina with a lazy disgust and he thought her dowdy. It was depressing. What the fuck was up with her now? She always looked so fucking sour. A fucking sour old woman.

He kicked at the leg of a chair.

'I've been at Jan's. In case you're interested. He's like this.'
He held out his hands in front of him and shook them
violently in the air, and then glared at her as if she were to
blame.

'He can't even hold a glass now. Vera has to help him
drink through a straw like a baby. Sitting in that chair all
day, shaking. What's the point of a life like that?'

He picked up the ketchup bottle, looked at the label
angrily, and put it down again.

Thinking about the scene made him shudder.

Jan's wife had bent down and grasped her husband's
ankles and heaved his swollen purple feet up onto a stool.
Oleg couldn't look away from them and at the bruised rim
of fat that spilled over the edge of his slippers. Jan had
looked at them too; bewildered and frightened as though
he didn't recognise them.

His wife bent over him to put a blanket over his lap. Her
face was set hard and she tucked it around his legs with a
rough, jabbing movement so that Jan's eyes flicked to her
with a cringing, apologetic look.

'He reeks,' Oleg said. 'Like sugary piss.'

The air in the small apartment had been thick with it
and Oleg pulled up the front of his shirt and held it to his
nose to see if he had brought the cloying sweetness back
with him on his clothes.

Oleg's own hand had the most minor of tremors
sometimes in the morning but not like that. Nowhere near.
And Oleg had never rolled around the town drunk and
causing trouble like Jan had before things got really bad.

Their situations weren't comparable at all. In fact it was

reassuring for Oleg that, despite Irina's nagging about it, compared to Jan at least, his drinking was on the minor scale of things. It was manageable. And that thought fuelled his resentment of Irina and the way she complained about his ordinary level of drinking so that he turned his mouth down in a contemptuous sneer.

What the fuck did she know about it? He wasn't stupid or a kid. Alcohol could be a slippery slope if you didn't watch out. But he knew what he was doing.

Oleg had eyed the half full vodka bottle on the side table. Jan's wife had shrugged at him, too worn down to be concerned about anyone else's view on the matter.

'He can't do without,' she said. 'So that's that.'

'She should leave him,' said Irina. 'Just get the hell away from him.' The remark had burst from her and Oleg looked up suddenly, surprised by this new tone.

'He's in nappies Irina!' he said. 'What? Do you think she's going to leave him sitting in his own shit?'

Irina walked into the kitchen briskly so that he had to step aside and she tugged at the cord to open the blind. It rolled up quickly and snapped to a halt and she was satisfied that the clacking, angry sound matched her mood.

The kitchen was spotless but she picked up a cloth from the side of the sink and began wiping the surfaces with quick, sharp movements.

'How do they afford it?' she said. 'I mean, where do they find the money to pay for all that alcohol?'

Oleg rolled his eyes.

'Christ Irina. I know what afford means.'

'Do you?' she said, turning to him sharply. She still held

the cloth in her hand and as she squeezed it she felt the water run between her fingers and begin to drip onto the floor.

Oleg looked down, warily, at the growing puddle and up again at his wife.

It was a mess she would have to clear up herself so there was no satisfaction in it for her. She turned to the sink and threw the cloth into it instead.

The women of Tomyator did not like Vera. She made them uneasy. She had not bothered to cover up her black eyes or the blue and green imprints of fingers and thumbs around her neck. She displayed them – daring people to judge her.

'At least there are no children to worry about,' Alexi had murmured once to Irina as Vera left the store. And that was as far as it went. Perhaps her life was better these days. Now that Jan was incapacitated at least.

The men who were unpleasant to their wives but did not beat them were grateful to be able to point to Jan as the worst of them. The men who did beat their wives, consoled themselves that they were not nearly as vicious as him. So in a way the town needed him. Everyone has their part to play, after all.

Oleg did not beat her. Should she be grateful? Could she be?

Irina could not trust herself to speak again and she turned, walking away with a rigid, juddering gait, and went into their bedroom, closing the door behind her.

It had taken all her strength not to slam it.

She slid out the suitcase from its hiding place under the

bed, flipped open the lid and looked inside at her folded underwear. She had packed five pairs of white pants, her newest ones, and two bras, one beige and the other white.

There was a summer dress she had never worn. The dress was more than five years old now and probably impossibly out of fashion for Moscow. It had a row of pale green buttons running down the front and a long strip of fabric in the same colour to tie around the waist. It looked meek and brow-beaten in the bottom of the suitcase. She stroked the material, sorry for the dress that had never been worn.

She imagined herself throwing the case into the back of the jeep for the ride to town and approaching the railway station. She thought about hauling it up onto the narrow metal steps of the train and stowing it under her seat.

It was an old suitcase and did not have the little plastic wheels that all suitcases, even the small ones, seemed to have these days.

The wheels were not practical in Tomyator. They became clogged with compacted snow that melted away to leave dark puddles on the carpets of the motel rooms.

If the square had been swept clean, the wheels caught in the gaps between the paving slabs and jolted the cases onto their sides.

Why couldn't people just carry their cases? What was wrong with everyone these days?

She had packed a small red-leather covered album filled with pictures of Vasily as a blond baby and then a smiling toddler. They were all pictures taken in Yakutsk. She had packed, and then unpacked a photograph of her mother in a small silver frame. Tucked into the fabric pocket were ten slim notebooks filled with her neatly inscribed columns of figures from the Weather Station.

They were all old things. She was preparing to leave everything from her current life behind.

She felt calmer now, in the quiet of the room with her thoughts. This was a fantasy of course, she knew that. She rested her back against the edge of the mattress. The open suitcase spoke of opportunity, if she were prepared to take it, and that made this confinement easier to bear. Like the imaginary letters she had hoped she would receive from guests who would become friends, it was the possibility of escape that comforted her.

Irina closed her eyes and was transported once again to Moscow railway station where she would step down from the train and into the warm, summer scented, air.

A porter appeared, tipped his hat and smiled, and took the suitcase from her.

He was friendly but not overly familiar. He had a deferential air and looked down and away from her eyes, and bent forward in a half bow, when he addressed her.

He called her Miss.

He led the way towards the swooping shallow steps, parting the crowds for her, so that they could glide effortlessly up and onto the street.

It was as busy as ever but the crowds were good-natured. A group of women on their lunch break passed in front of Irina. They strolled with their arms linked and they bent forwards together, like a chorus line acknowledging applause, as they laughed. Students with rucksacks and self-consciously eccentric haircuts sat on the edge of a fountain, showing each other their phones. A man, almost running, with an armful of pink roses checked his watch twice, before slowing to a walk with a smile. He had plenty of time. A wiry cyclist in bright lycra, hopped off his bike and hoisted it onto his shoulders, before leaping down the steps and into the station to catch his train.

All of the colours were brighter than was usual in real life and it reminded Irina of trips to the cinema when she had been a child.

The porter whistled once and a yellow taxi pulled up immediately. He held open the door for her to slide inside. As she waited there was a small bounce followed by a deep 'whumpf'. The porter had dropped her suitcase into the back and safely closed the boot. She had a warm sense that everything was taken care of.

Irina shifted. The tiles of the bedroom floor had a nasty chill and a numbness was beginning to seep into her backside. She was unwilling to return to Tomyator just yet. She ran her hand over her belly and felt it was still flat like a young woman's and she sat straight and lifted her chin so that the skin on her neck would be smooth and taut.

She closed her eyes and felt herself being carried smoothly along the well-made Moscow roads, watching the happy crowds of purposeful people thronging the pavements, from within the soothing comfort of the silent car.

The sun shone through the passenger window making a bright rectangle of light on the seat next to her, and the heat warmed it, so that a rich, earthy smell of leather filled the car.

Irina started as the bedroom door opened. Oleg filled the doorway, clenching his fists. She tilted her face up towards him, panicked in that moment, and then she flushed with a hot satisfaction at the thought of the confrontation that must follow.

The open suitcase was a chasm between them.

At last, she thought. She held her breath, waiting to see how this scene would unfold.

Finally he would see how far he had pushed her. It must change things between them. There was a cutting, nerve jangling brilliance to her sharp feeling that she would hurt him with this threat as much as he had hurt her. She jutted out her chin.

It would serve him right.

She glanced down at the suitcase and up at him, eager to see how frightened he would be.

But Oleg walked, heavily past her and around to his side of the bed where he pulled open the drawer of his bedside cabinet, rifled in the cluttered interior, and slammed it shut again.

'Where the fuck are my spare glasses?' he said. 'You must have moved them. The arm's hanging off these,' he wiggled it angrily. 'If I can't find them I'll have to put fucking tape on them. Like a tramp as usual. While you spend our money getting your hair done or sitting in that coffee shop.'

He sat heavily on the bed. 'It's depressing. You depress me.'

He put his head in his hands.

'Jan's dying. My oldest friend is fucking dying and you're

oblivious. You don't care. Not about him, and one hundred per cent not about me.'

Oleg fell backwards onto the bed with his arms outstretched and his pregnant belly trembling.

'Have you even thought about how something like this cuts me up? Seeing him like that. It's like a knife, twisting in my guts.'

He lay there for a while, looking at the ceiling and thinking about other ways to describe his pain. He sighed now and then.

His anger had flared briefly but had passed now and settled instead into a self-pitying melancholy. His tone, when he spoke, was flat.

'You've become so hard Irina. Like your mother in a lot of ways. No wonder your father didn't hang around. The poor bastard.'

It was just an observation so nothing for Irina to feel upset about he seemed to say. It was Irina who had complained about her mother after all. Oleg was just repeating it.

Irina's heart was knocking out of time. Her hands shook and she felt the heat rising on her neck and chest. The open suitcase sat, stupidly open mouthed.

Oleg sighed again and there was a crackling whistle behind it. He was smoking more these days. Another damned expense she thought and clenched her fists.

'This place is a dump. Vera makes an effort at least. It smells terrible, like rotting meat, but what can she do? With him in that state. But at least it's homely. She's got these plants on tables, and ornaments. Everything's sort of, arranged.' He waved his hand vaguely.

He heaved himself up again although he had nothing to do and nowhere to go and stood up from the bed, pressing hard on his thighs to lever himself onto his feet. He was irritated at the way she stared at him without speaking.

'You look at me with such disgust Irina. It's as if you despise me.'

He walked around the bed, stepped over the open suitcase and went out, slamming the door behind him.

He had not commented on it. He had not wondered, for a second, why his wife of almost a quarter of a century was sitting on their bedroom floor with an open suitcase half full of her clothes. Irina's suffering, her act of rebellion, had passed unnoticed, and her humiliation was complete.

In that moment Irina realised she was ridiculous to him and invisible as a real person. She was his wife but he had no inkling of her desires or wishes. And if he were to know how afraid and unhappy she was in Tomyator and within their marriage, she understood, in that second, that her feelings would be entirely inconsequential to him.

A roar of laughter sounded from the living room. Oleg had switched on the television and was watching a comedy show with a booming laugh track.

She examined the suitcase with a rising fury and knew then that she had no choice but to go.

She scrambled to her feet and pulled open the wardrobe and the sweaters and trousers rustled in the breeze she had caused. They were jostling and expectant. Pick me they seemed to say. She tried to imagine herself ascending the steps at Moscow Railway Station in any of them but they were a confusing jumble and she could not make them into outfits in her mind.

What did it matter? She would buy new clothes, reinvent herself. But she could hardly travel to Moscow naked so she dragged a few things off the hangers, barely caring what they were or if they would be practical or if this skirt had a matching sweater, and threw them into the suitcase.

What else? Shoes? Scarves?

The wardrobe stood in the corner of the room and the right door banged hard against the wall but she made no effort to hush it. She was glad. Jubilant. She took the door and threw it open again, as hard as she was able, grunting from the effort, and it made a gash in the plaster.

She caught sight of herself in the mirror and was startled by the hard slant of her eyes. Would they be sorry when she was gone? Who cared? Suddenly she inhabited herself entirely as all thoughts of Oleg and Vasily flew away and she felt, for the first time the sensation of being entirely in command of herself, now and in the future.

She was not running away from Oleg. She was going to Moscow.

It was an exhilarating thought and she felt her connection to Oleg break. The fact that he would not miss her was liberating, and she was filled with the quick lightness of relief

But she wasn't used to a rush of hot adrenaline like this; it was only a hair away from panic. She made her mouth into an 'O' and breathed out a steady stream of air to calm herself. She didn't recognise her own feelings or her body.

She heard Oleg's heavy, flat footed steps approaching the door, saw the handle dip down and heard the high squeak of the metal mechanism of the handle.

The bedroom door flew open again and Oleg stood with his fists clenched. She knew he would not hit her. His fists were a sign of his frustration. He knocked them against the door frame in time with his words.

'Stop. Fucking. Banging. Around,' he said. 'I can't hear my programme.'

Then he turned and went away again, slamming the door.

Oh how she hated him. And in admitting it to herself, really acknowledging it as a reality for the very first time, she began to feel like herself.

That night, Irina lay awake listening to Oleg snoring without irritation. Instead, she was filled with a bubbling excitement at the thought of her new life.

Twenty-One

C onfined, for now, within the four rooms of the small
apartment and muffled by the triple glazing, Irina
stood looking into the square. A faint, extra reflection of
her own face, trapped between the panes, floated like
barely realised doubt. Are you certain Irina?

The motel, a five eyed monster, occupied one full side of
the square. All of the lights were off, advertising its
emptiness to the town.

It would have hurt her once. Now it was a signal that she
had made the right decision.

Her eyes passed over the block formed by the old bar, the
pharmacy and the clothing store; all reclaimed by families
who lived, resigned to the inconvenience, inside the oddly
shaped rooms. The buildings were different heights and
made a clumsy row of utilitarian shapes, slopped over with
rough concrete coats. If they had anything in common it
was that they were squat, sharp cornered and seemingly
antagonistic to one another.

The light from the window of Alexi's store was the bright
spot in the scene and her eyes were drawn to it.

It spilled over his red buckets, illuminating them, so that

they resembled a row of braziers. It seemed like trickery, this illusion of warmth. Irina had not returned to the store since her humiliation and she closed her eyes, for a second, to wipe the unwelcome memory away.

How was it she had only noticed the brute, ugliness of the town now? Making the best of things, blinding herself to it, had seemed her only option she supposed. She shook her head. It was amazing to her, really astounding, that she had been able to tolerate it for so long.

She leaned forwards, holding a tea in her right hand, and with her left she gripped the cool, smooth edge of the sink. She held onto it tightly to steady herself. A faint trembling shook her, at the thought that she had almost wasted her whole life here. Almost.

A young woman emerged from Dr Nevsky's house. She hurried away, smiling in a private sort of way. Irina recognised her as one of the women who worked at the Sable Farm. Perhaps she's pregnant, Irina thought. Or not pregnant. Either way, it had been good news.

The woman walked across the square in the direction of the farm. The workers started early and Irina wondered what she would say to her boss about her late arrival.

The other women would already be busy in the low sheds, pushing the thrashing bundles of claws and teeth into chambers to be suffocated with carbon monoxide and waiting to pull their limp, newly compliant bodies from the other end for the furriers to slice open.

It wasn't a cruel death they said. Better than electrocution. Besides, it meant the fur was unmarked.

They collected the leftover meat for the pet food factory

in Omyscan. The excrement was scraped up and bagged for manure. Nothing was wasted in their little ecosystem. That was a good thing, of course. But, in thinking about the way everything was used up in the town, Irina felt the lack of surplus to be frightening. Finely balanced became, instead, precarious. If you had an extra need, it turned out there was nothing to spare.

She shuddered at the thought of those workers. Imagine a life spent in the semi-darkness, soaked in the rank smell and pierced by the shrill squeaks of the desperate, captive creatures. Others had it worse than her, she thought, and realised, with a start, how easily she could slip into her old way of thinking; making meek excuses for her life.

No more. She could not bear another year in Tomyator.

She knew that some of the farm women would appear at the end of their shift, to drink a hot chocolate with a friend at the café or to pick up some bits and pieces for dinner from Alexi. But that would be much later. For now, the square was as barren of life as the surface of a dead planet.

Irina took a sip of tea.

She and Oleg had watched a television programme about a motorised robot that had been sent all the way to Mars. It was such a cute little thing, like a friendly robot from a children's film. It rolled around on its chunky wheels, looking this way and that, sending ethereal photographs of impossibly empty landscapes back to the scientists in America. They were all very excited about it.

Until one morning, a wind swept across the surface to whip up a dust storm. It was impossible for the signal to get through. There was nothing they could do except wait.

A day or two later, when the wind had died away, they found that the little robot had stopped communicating with earth.

The scientists were devastated. This was their life's work after all. For a few days they had been hopeful that they might receive a signal. That this was just a glitch.

They sat in their control room with their ties undone and their headphones clamped to their ears, drinking coffee from paper cups and straining into the silence. But after a week they knew that the little robot was lost. They thought it would still be taking photographs but the transmitter had malfunctioned so that the images could not be received back on earth and they could not send instructions. The transmitter was the most sensitive part of the operation they said.

Irina thought about the little robot, still rolling about in the bleak silence, taking photographs and sending them into the stars. She imagined it listening for a contact from home and wondering why it never came.

Oleg had rolled his eyes at her. She'd cry about anything these days.

Her tea was stone cold now and she tipped it into the sink.

This place was hell on earth – that was the truth of it – and no amount of looking on the bright side would make a modicum of difference. Truth. She was energised by this new idea of truth.

She would confess to the engineer that she had been misstating the temperatures when they were settled on the train together. She would explain that she had no choice.

The survival of her business, of the whole town, had depended on it. Put, bluntly, like that, it all made sense. She would tell the truth and ask for forgiveness.

Irina knew that the engineer would listen and understand and that their friendship, that had built so quickly on the intimacies she had revealed to no one else, would be secure. It would withstand the truth. She had never felt so certain of anything or anyone.

She had been standing at the sink for a long time when she saw the sudden, sunshine flash of the engineer's coat.

At last. Any doubt, if that's even what it had been, flew from Irina's mind and she was charged up with a jolt of expectation.

Here she was, turning the corner from Libsky Street, and Irina laughed aloud at the scene. Gregor drove the snowmobile and the engineer, unable to squeeze in to sit behind him, was standing on the seat. She was carrying a narrow pole that she used to whip Gregor onwards. She shouted something in his ear so that he burst into laughter. Irina had never even seen him smile before and she rejoiced that she would be going, with this wonderful woman, to Moscow.

They stuttered to a halt and the engineer leapt off, leaning in to give Gregor a hug of thanks, before turning her attention to unloading the sled.

There had been much less to carry on the return journey. She had her cases of tools and the heater and the tent but the rolls of tubing, the temperature monitoring equipment and the solar panels had all been fitted, tested and were left to do their job.

There were no curious crowds to gather round now though. The town had lost interest in her.

'What have I done?' the engineer had asked Irina, with her eyebrows furrowed, 'I went into the store yesterday and everyone completely clammed up. They all started blowing their noses or examining the labels on their beans, as if they were fantastically interesting.'

Irina had tried to explain it to her.

They liked her. How could they not? And having become used to seeing her around, the locals were beginning to withdraw their affection, like lovers who knew there was a parting on its way. Not wanting to be hurt any more than they could help, they were taking steps to harden their hearts.

They would still nod at her if they passed her in the square but would only answer her greetings with one or two words, leaning away from her, ready to turn on their heels and leave as soon as they could.

They wouldn't be rude about it – rudeness was frowned upon in Tomyator – but there was a sense that their investment in the engineer would not be returned and that felt unfair somehow.

They were a little sheepish about their earlier excitement and affected a kind of unconcern about her departure. They were disappointed in a way; in her for leaving and in themselves for letting down their guard.

It was always the same story when someone was leaving. So although they knew she would be off in a day or two, they preferred not to know the precise details.

Irina watched the yellow beacon of the engineer's coat

from her kitchen window. It was a lighthouse. She gripped the edge of the sink and her heart thundered at the sight of it.

The engineer began to carry the boxes of tools into the garage, moving briskly in her angular, adolescent way. Gregor bent heavily over the sled to uncouple it from the back of the snowmobile.

There was an eagerness to the engineer; the bouncing, last minute, energy of someone on the home strait. She was confident on the icy path now and moved surely, like a local.

Irina rinsed her mug in the sink and dried it, with trembling hands, before putting it away again in the cupboard.

'Won't be long,' she said to the back of Oleg's head, he had forgotten yesterday's scene already, snatching her fur hat from the side cabinet in the living room and hurrying to the front door.

The engineer was not leaving until tomorrow morning – the jeep was due at ten – but Irina was suddenly overcome with a kind of panic that this would all be too late and she fumbled with her boots, hopping clumsily to shove them on in her haste.

It was suddenly urgent that she must see her.

She slammed her front door and hurried down the sixteen stairs, thinking she could hear her own heart over the sound of her feet on the concrete steps, and bumped her way heavily through the swing door of the apartment block. Thank goodness. The engineer was still busy with her treks back and forth. Of course she was. It had only taken a minute to get there.

She pushed down an urge to run across the square.

'You were right,' she called out to the engineer, waving. She was laughing and billowing vapour and she heard her own voice as muffled and muted from within the cloud.

The engineer straightened up from the sled and waved back.

'I'm always right,' she shouted.

She crouched down, made a snowball, and threw it towards Gregor who ducked as he drove away.

Irina approached, breathless, inadequately buttoned into her coat and bursting with her news.

'I'm losing my touch,' said the engineer, brushing the snow from her gloves. 'And what, in particular, am I right about?'

'Oleg and me. This life. Everything. What you said about choosing to be happy. I haven't stopped thinking about it.' Her words rebounded in the wind, but she would not take them back.

'I decided. Last night. I will come to Moscow.'

The engineer widened her eyes and tipped her head to one side. She lifted one of the heavy cases from the heap Gregor had left in the snow.

'Really? It's a big deal. Though I think it would be wonderful if you did. Can you imagine us commuting together on the Metro? We could drink cocktails by the Moskva if we were feeling fancy. Mostly, though, it would be extraordinary to see you in shoes Irina. It would be worth it just for that.'

'I have shoes,' she said, eagerly. Of course she had shoes.

'Good for you,' said the engineer. She smiled her open

mouthed, slant eyed smile and nodded towards the garage so that Irina picked up a case and they began to walk together.

The engineer had not been as surprised by the news as Irina had expected. Irina had the sense that here, at last, was someone who knew her better than she knew herself. Or, perhaps, she was just used to getting her own way.

Irina had seen her persuade the town to bend to her will, more than once, and effortlessly at that. It could be that Irina's agreement was entirely expected in that case. But as it was out of character for Irina to be so bold, reckless some people might think, she was disappointed that the engineer seemed not to acknowledge the magnitude of her decision.

Irina stretched her stride to match the engineer's, as she had on their first walk up to the Weather Station. The woman was moving quickly and Irina almost had to trot to keep up. She glanced sideways at her long profile and the calm, determined set of her mouth. Did she run around after the engineer like Oleg said? She felt a tremor of disquiet for a moment. How much of this decision had been hers and how much had been the engineer's?

In the end though it didn't matter. It was the right course of action, she was sure, and if the engineer had been the catalyst then so be it.

The engineer turned slightly to look at her once, and opened her mouth to speak, but smiled and closed it again. Irina knew she was thinking about getting home and the two of them in her little flat. They were a team. She felt the force of their friendship keeping them in step.

Twenty-Two

The morning really had arrived. She could barely believe it. How deceptively like every other morning it seemed.

A soft, grey suggestion of light still leaked from around the edges of the curtains.

She stretched her hand behind her under the covers. Oleg had gone but there was a warm space where he had lain. From the kitchen came the metallic chink of the kettle dropping onto the stove top, and then, a moment later, there was the smell of his first cigarette, drifting under the door.

He could smoke himself to death as far as she was concerned. She would not be here to watch it. She stretched, she felt lithe like a girl and light and delightfully free of responsibility for him.

Irina sat up and slid her feet into her slippers and went to the window, just as she always did, to pull apart the curtains. The material was coarse and unpleasant to touch and she frowned at the feel of it.

She placed a fingertip on the window where a smear of ice had found its way between the panes of the triple glazing. She studied it. It would wait there, patient, until the summer when it would melt and condense to form a blurred spot the size of a postage stamp at the edge of the frame. Come the winter it would freeze again and the outside would encroach a little further and the ice patch would grow.

She imagined herself, twenty years from now and old, and the window entirely obscured by a pane of ice.

There was no doubt she had thought this room so smart and modern once. The apartment was part furnished and the bed, brand new and with the mattress wrapped in thick plastic, crackled with promise.

Irina twisted around quickly to face it, trying to catch the room by surprise, to recapture her first impression, but she could not. Her optimism about this place had leaked away long ago.

She didn't quite hate the room but she was so damned weary of it. The familiarity of the tired wallpaper, a repeating pattern of amateurishly drawn leaves and the cream coloured tiles on the floor bored her.

The mattress was lumpy now and when she changed the bottom sheet there was a clear, brownish outline of Oleg's body, imprinted in sweat, on its roughened surface.

Oleg left marks of himself everywhere, sloughing off his skin to leave tiny grey rubbery threads in the bathtub and peppering his excrement around the toilet bowl and sometimes up in brown splashes under the seat.

His fingerprints, planted on the plastic cases that held the light switches, and on the wall surrounding them, seemed evidence of his disdain.

When he shaved he leaned towards the mirror and looked himself steadfastly in the eye and shook his razor sharply away from himself. Most of the stubble landed in the sink and could easily be wiped away later but Irina found the hairs, black hyphens, on the floor, and sometimes on her wash cloth so that she had wiped the hairs onto her own face before.

It seemed to her that his desire to exfoliate, to shed his skin, to expel his fluids and his smells and to spread the dusty filings from his fingernails around their home had the quality of anger.

The smear of grease on his pillow, an unapologetic fart at the dinner table, his tissues filled with sticky nose blowings beside the sofa and, in the old days, his semen inside her were all the ways he occupied this space, territorially, so that she, correspondingly, was forced to retreat further into herself to accommodate him.

A proprietorial dent in the sofa marked his place, even when he was not there.

She thought about the stained mattress and wrinkled her nose. She found it noxious and there was a relief to the idea that it would no longer be her responsibility.

He would have to manage on his own. She thought him pitiful rather than hateful for a moment and she supposed he couldn't help it. No one could help their own sweat. It had been her choice to tolerate it.

Irina took the end of the duvet in her hands and shook it out to make the bed and, at once, his presence was obliterated. It only took a moment. But she had an uneasy sense that if her defining characteristic was her ability to endure this shrunken life, to accommodate him and his excesses, then what kind of woman would she be once she had left it all behind?

She thought of their blank, Twilight Blush living room. What would she have to display of herself in her new life?

Irina had already packed the suitcase with as many clothes as could be crammed haphazardly into it, but had not given a thought to what she should wear today. She opened the wardrobe to see what was left that might be suitable. She didn't much care how she would look and she smiled at herself, at her newfound spontaneity. This was what life would be like all the time now.

She picked through the few remaining sweaters stacked on the shelf. She would not be reckless though, in her new life. There would be the long journey in the jeep, the wait at the cold station and the train ride to Moscow.

Be at least a little sensible Irina, she told herself. It's not a bad thing to look ahead. Wasn't that how she had survived Tomyator? Yes, it was important to dress warmly. She must make sure her excitement did not quite override her natural caution and practicality.

It was an unpredictable journey. A problem with the car might see them standing outside for a period. She would need to be properly wrapped up. But she could shed the unwanted layers on the train; tearing them off and flinging them out of the window as they drew towards Moscow and the air warmed and the sun shone.

Oh, she loved this idea of herself. She would do exactly as she pleased in her new life.

Irina looked at herself in the mirror on the inside of the

wardrobe door. She put her hands on her hips and turned her head to one side, with her small chin raised, and then flicked it the other way so that her hair bounced against her jawline. The mirror was fly-spotted and had the gentle, brownish hue of age. She knew her reflection was flatteringly softened but still, you're not bad Irina, she thought. I've seen worse.

She dragged on a pair of trousers, any trousers, and then pulled out a pair of fur-lined boots. They were bulky and water stained, entirely unsuitable for the city, but they were warm enough for now.

There was no possibility she would ever come back to Tomyator, she was certain of it, and she decided she would change into shoes – she couldn't wait to be in shoes – and dump these boots into a bin on the platform of the station in Moscow.

She and the engineer would laugh together about it.

It wasn't yet eight, too early to meet the engineer; she would still be showering and packing up and the jeep was not booked to arrive until ten. She hoped it would not be late. She couldn't bear the idea of a moment's delay.

There seemed nothing more to be done and Irina was restless. She paced up and down the room, tingling with supressed energy – it was almost a mania – and she went to the window and looked out at the square again, hoping for a distraction to make the time fly by quicker.

Zeena was standing in the illuminated window of the coffee shop with her hands twisting like snakes in front of her. Her head turned jerkily, flashing red, as she looked up and down, praying for customers.

There would be no proper goodbyes to anyone and she wondered, rubbing at the smear on the window with her thumb, whether she regretted it. This town had been her whole life for so long now. A goodbye, at least, would draw a line under her time at Tomyator.

Her hand fell back by her side. She didn't care about the damned smear or about the people.

Alexi darted out of the door of the store to drop some hunks of wrapped meat into a bucket, looked up and down for customers, and hurried back inside. Oleg would have no way to repay him the 95,000 Roubles. Any sympathy she had for Oleg flew away. He had bought this on himself.

As for Alexi, he could afford to lose the money. Irina scuffed at the skirting board. Let's see how much pity he could dredge up for poor Oleg once she was out of the picture she thought. She remembered his languid, down-turned eyes, as he informed Irina, so knowingly, that her husband was suffering and she clenched her jaw at the unfairness of it.

She would not be here to blame. The town, and all of its damnable people, could go to hell as far as she was concerned.

They would not miss her either. Irina was certain of it. That was the way they were. Her name might be mentioned for a month, maybe even two, with raised eyebrows and shrugs but then they would wipe their memory of her and in years to come might speak, in vague terms, of Oleg's wife who had disappeared.

Oleg had switched on the television. She heard the theme tune of the morning news followed by the rumble of self-important voices and she took a breath and began to gather herself to action.

Her plan had seemed so straightforward last night.

She would get dressed, drag out her suitcase from under the bed and march out without a word. Oleg was invariably stupefied in the mornings and would not think to try to stop her. It was unthinkable that he would chase after her, plead with her or demand an explanation.

Now that the time had arrived, the three steps between the bedroom and the front door seemed impossible.

She pulled on her hat and buttoned herself in to her coat. She bent to pick up her suitcase and felt that it was light, manageable. Her fingers slotted comfortably into the handle so that it felt like the most natural thing in the world.

Vasily would be in bed until lunchtime at least. She would write to him as soon as she was settled and explain as best she could.

She took a breath, paused, and opened the bedroom door.

The door to the living room was open. Irina looked across the corridor. Her view was of their sideboard that she knew to be filled with disappointing junk. The exhausted sofa. The television booming its opinions and news of other places more important than this, every hour of the day. She scrutinised it all through the softened air of Oleg's almost dispersed cigarette smoke and was ashamed she had waited so long to go.

Oleg did not look round or speak as she took the three steps from the bedroom, towards the front door. The whole scene seemed foolish, almost laughable, and she put her free hand to her mouth, in case a sound – what sort of sound she couldn't say – should burst from her.

She looked back over her shoulder at him. A fuzz of hairs ran around his ears and were illuminated against the glare from the TV screen. She had never noticed the hairs before. This is a fine time to be noticing something new Irina, she thought, but even that vulnerability, exposed, did not pierce her heart.

She ran her finger over the gash in the plaster made from the coat hook before unhooking the chain and flicking the catch to open the door.

'Milk,' said Oleg. 'We've run out.'

'Okay,' she said, and stepped into the corridor and closed the door quietly behind her.

She had expected the step over the threshold to be consequential and she took in a long breath and held it, gathering herself in preparation for a punch of emotion.

Would she be washed over with grief at the wasted years? Or regret that she was forty-five and her marriage had failed and she had everything she cared to carry away from her old life in a faded green suitcase.

But the corridor was the same as usual; a dimly lit khaki coloured passageway smelling of breakfasts and chilled concrete, and scuffed all along by pushchairs and shopping bags that had been pushed and dragged from one place to another, and back again, with a furious pointlessness.

It was too dull and deadening a space to allow for swelling emotions. It reminded her, instead, of why she had to leave.

Irina placed her palm on the wall and its surface was clammy and dusty at the same time.

She looked at her familiar feet planted in the usual way and knew they would carry her forward and away from this place. She hesitated, tentative, as if looking for a bruise after knocking into a table. But she was unscathed. Irina felt not an ounce of fear or guilt. The bubbling sensation in her chest was excitement and not trepidation.

It was all so easy.

Oh, but the keys. She had not thought about the keys. Should she post them back through the letterbox? It struck her as a melodramatic gesture and she felt herself to be in the right so had no need for it. Besides, Oleg might hear them clanking onto the floor and come to the door. There would be a conversation of some sort and that would just hold her up. She already thought of him, just the other side of the familiar door, as being in her past.

She put on her gloves, noticing the steadiness of her hands.

Behind each door a drama was playing out and she could hear voices, a toilet flushing and a child wailing and someone being called to breakfast and it seemed to her she was inside a giant box filled with unhappy stories and Irina could not wait to leave it all behind.

Twenty-Three

She counted the sixteen steps aloud on her way down, holding on to the metal handrail to steady herself because she had not bothered with breakfast and felt lightheaded all of a sudden.

It would be hours before they reached Omyskon in the jeep and she thought herself foolish not to have considered the length of the journey. She hoped the engineer would have saved some biscuits at least.

Biscuits were all she could face. The smells of fried bread and tea boiling were thick in the stairwell and she wrinkled her nose and swallowed, nauseous rather than truly hungry.

Beneath the rail, the muddy green walls had a line of grease running at about the height of a small child's hand and Irina ran her own, gloved, fingers along it. Children loved to touch everything. Irina felt she would like to touch and experience things again anew, like a child.

The suitcase was not heavy, she could manage it perfectly well with one hand, but it had sharp corners, tipped with metal, which scraped the edge of each step as she descended. She was glad of the noise. It had a definite quality that cut through the blur of unreality that overlaid this scene.

At the foot of the stairs, she scraped across the brush matting and swung out of the front door, for the last time. The skin across her cheeks hissed as the cells contracted against the icy cold and the sharp sensation snapped her back to Tomyator and its realities with a start.

It was bitter.

The wind galloped around the square at a furious speed, a brute, gathering the top layer of fine powder and flinging it up in quick, unexpected bursts, so that a sharp spray struck her in her eyes and she was blinded for a moment.

In her hurry, and knowing she had only a short distance to travel across the square to the motel, she had not taken care to fasten the flaps of her hat and the wind whooshed up and she felt the cold drilling into her ears, icy needles. A pain struck behind her eyes. She paused and pulled the hat down more firmly against the wind that seemed bullying and vindictive.

Then she thought, oh stop it Irina. Her habit of ascribing a will and a personality to the weather had made her feel less lonely in the past. No more. The wind had not been waiting for her. It had not, and she must face facts. She was inconsequential to it. Just as she was to Oleg and Vasily. The wind would rage and roar whether she was here or not. The ice would grip and then release the land season after season, long after she had been forgotten.

She hunched forward as she walked, as if shielding herself from a series of physical blows.

Nevertheless, even if it was pointless and purposeless,

the cold was hateful to her. Hateful. And she looked, from the sides of her narrowed eyes, in growing disbelief at the grey square squatting sullenly, enduring it all. It was unthinkable that people would choose to live here. Why had they come? It was hellish to be assaulted by the air and the cold and to have the ice and the snow biting and tearing at you for no reason at all.

She tucked the point of her small chin into her chest and gritted her teeth, grimacing. How contemptuous she was of the stubbornness and stupidity of the compliant people in their crumbling houses. How proud they were of their attempts to defy the elements but they wouldn't win, and she was sick, to the point of death, of battles that couldn't be won.

I pity you all, she thought. But it was not pity it was contempt.

Most of all, at that moment, she hated the ugly store, squatting there, filled with all the desperately mundane things people needed to keep themselves alive.

Through the window and between the metal shelves she could see that the store was already busy. She shuddered at the mass of bodies shuffling between the packets of tea and the long life milk and the tins of salmon in a dreary, inescapable ritual.

How could they stand it? The people of Tomyator huddled together in a circle of needless endurance, waiting for disaster to strike and being obstinately resolute every time it did. What else is there to do they asked each other and Irina was sickened by it and by their dumb acquiescence to a self-imposed purgatory. She would choose to be happy, she thought, and was so filled with scorn that she could have spat on the ground.

It was no more than two hundred metres to cross the square but she had not dressed as warmly as she should have and every step was a stiff, painful reminder of her life's struggle. She lifted her eyes to the single lit window in the motel and concentrated on it, hard.

Nearly there.

Not so far.

This was just the first stage of her journey and she reminded herself that the way would be hard. Irina knew it would be a test to begin everything again in a brand new city, even with the engineer, at the start of it at least.

She swopped the suitcase to her other hand, shaking out her wrist, and took a breath. She had done it before, here, in Tomyator. That must count in her favour.

But she had been young when she arrived and Irina felt the lost years flinging up into the sky and with them, a little of her strength.

The jeep had not arrived yet. It was still too early for it, but she was filled with panic that it would be delayed because, all of a sudden, she could not wait to escape. Irina began to move more quickly, almost running, so that the suitcase banged against her leg. She could not stay here a moment longer. Not a moment longer. Not one moment.

At the motel, she hooked the key out of her pocket. She was breathless now and she had a tremor in her hand. But the metal barrel was attached to a flat plastic rectangle that almost filled her palm and it was easy to slot it into the lock. The keys here were specially adapted to be manipulated with thickly gloved fingers. In Moscow she would have a set of neat, normal sized keys like everyone else and they would sit quietly in a pocket or in her handbag. There would be no need for endless ingenuity and effort to manage the everyday. Everything would be easier.

The heavy door to the motel corridor opened inwards so that it would not be caught by the wind and torn from its hinges. Irina looked down at the two notches in the door frame, a few centimetres from the floor, where the delivery men had tried to force the washing machine through it on the too-wide trolley.

She would not allow herself to be sentimental about those times.

She closed the door behind her so that the wind was quietened to a low groan. She did not flick on the light. The grey, breeze blocked corridor depressed her and she did not want to see it. The green glow from the fire exit sign was enough. She looked up at the stick man, fleeing at the point of an arrow and felt a grim allegiance to him.

Not yet though. The engineer's room was in the middle of the corridor, three doors along and the light spilled under the door, drawing Irina forward.

She rapped on the door, a bright and purposeful sound, and called, 'I hope you're decent,' before turning the round handle, trying to keep her smile small, because she could still feel shy around the engineer, even now.

But the engineer was occupied behind the closed door of the bathroom.

She had already tidied the room thoroughly in preparation for leaving. The bed was properly made with the top sheet folded neatly over the woollen over blanket and the pillow was plumped.

'We should pick up something from Zeena before we go,' she said, unbuttoning her coat and dropping it over the back of the chair 'I was too excited to think about eating this morning. I know, I know – like a big kid. But we'll need food for the trip.'

A couple of sandwiches and perhaps some scones. That would be plenty. Irina kicked herself for forgetting her flask. Hot coffees for the journey would have been a life saver but it was too late now. They would have to wait until they reached Omyskon. A hot drink would be blissful to them then.

Irina looked for the engineer's blue case, but it was not in its usual place under the window. She turned, a slow circle, bending slightly to peer under the desk, but no, not there either. She went to the wardrobe and pulled open both doors, but the suitcase was not inside it. All of the shelves were empty and the hangers, unclothed, shivered slightly together with the movement of the air.

'Where's your suitcase?' she called towards the bathroom.

Irina had left the door to the motel room open when she came in. She stepped back and pushed it closed, expecting to see the engineer's coat, a bright burst of yellow, hanging there as usual. But the hook was empty too.

In its place was the laminated sheet of fire safety instructions. She read them carefully, giving all of her attention to each word in turn. They were crisp and authoritative. Unequivocal. She held on to them to steady herself.

In case of a fire, guests were to leave the room immediately, by way of the nearest exit, and gather at Assembly Point One. There was a line drawing of the square with an X in the middle, next to the swings, indicating the point.

Irina stared at the X.

She bit down on her lip. She could hardly tear her eyes from the sign. Irina pushed down the sense that this was an emergency that was happening right now, and turned around to check the room again.

It was confusing. Everything was so out of step with her expectations that it was impossible to make sense of it. She felt as if she had opened the door into the wrong room.

She was blinking rapidly and she fluttered her fingers, trying to clutch at something that wasn't there.

On the bedside table, where the neat stack of six books should have been, there was a sheet of paper, torn roughly from a notebook, which had been folded untidily in two.

It was awful, the casual way the page was folded; the way the corners didn't meet.

It had her name, 'Irina' in large looping letters that looked scribbled as if in a hurry. She leaned towards it. The word slipped in and out of focus, as if Irina were looking down the lens of an old fashioned camera, twisting the barrel back and forth to make the picture sharp, turning it from a suggestion in a dream into real life.

She did not want to pick it up. She did not dare to, but she must. Irina hesitated, frozen. Her fingers tingled as she reached for it.

Irina,

You can't imagine how devastated I am to be leaving without a chance to properly say goodbye but Sergei is here with a too tempting offer of an earlier ride to the station. If we hurry I can catch the earlier train. It's awful of me to rush off – don't be mad with me – but I do feel we will be good friends for life. Don't you? I'm at Flat 9, The Print Works, Vozdvizhenka Street, 10, Moscow 125009. Thank you thank you thank you. Remember, if I ever hear that you've been to town and haven't called to see me then I shall be extremely and everlastingly cross with you.

Anya x

Irina turned the note over to see if there was more on the other side, but it was blank. It was a silly, contrived sort of gesture; like an actress in a film rather than a woman in real life. Perhaps she had been mistaken. She read it again, concentrating on each word to search for a hidden meaning. Was the engineer suggesting she take the later train? That might be why she had included her address.

Yes. The Print Works, Vozdvizhenka Street. She was signalling that Irina should come. She cast about the room looking for another clue the engineer may have left her. But every surface was empty.

Then she smiled and put her hand to her mouth. The engineer was teasing her and was waiting in the bathroom with her case packed and her coat buttoned, wrapped up and ready to go. It was a cruel trick to play but she could forgive her.

Irina, not daring to consider that this was not the case, because knowing would be the end for her, held her breath in an uncomfortable lump in her throat and crept, full of dreadful expectation, to the bathroom door.

She turned the small metal handle and pushed the door slowly open, preparing to be cross with the engineer and to scold her. 'That wasn't even a bit funny,' she would say to her.

It was empty, as she knew it would be. The white tiles stared back at her. They were heartless. The shower dripped, echoing their indifference.

She could not understand it. She had been invited and she had accepted. Irina had been clear that she would leave her family and the town and make a new start in Moscow. Was that just something city people said? Was that the way they talked? Abandon your husband and your son. Come and stay with me. Start a new life.

Irina gave a small, choking cry and yanked the door closed.

It wasn't right.

It was not possible that this friendship, the most consequential of her life, had not been important to the engineer. Remember how they had talked and talked and the engineer had listened to Irina in that special way she had; stopping what she was doing so that all of her attention was directed at Irina so that she could absorb her words fully. Who had listened to Irina like that before?

Irina refolded the note, making a new crease so that the edges lined up properly, and replaced it. There was a misunderstanding somehow. Her breath came fast and shallow and the lightheaded feeling from the stairwell swooped back so that the room seemed to rock on its shallow foundations.

Irina had been honest with her. She had gradually, willingly, unravelled her intimate thoughts and her secret feelings about her life and exposed herself to this woman's gaze entirely. Perhaps the engineer had not liked what she had seen. Irina's cheeks flared suddenly with shame.

The engineer had not believed her to be sincere in her acceptance. Or she had assessed Irina and judged her too weak to carry through her plan. Another thought floated on the periphery of her mind, but it was too awful to examine, that Irina was inconsequential to the engineer. She simply didn't care.

Irina turned on the spot and pulled open the desk drawer so sharply that it flew out of its slot entirely and fell to the floor and a panel of wood cracked away from the drawer itself. Now that the drawer was exposed she saw it was shamefully and cheaply constructed with thin baslsa wood and glued together roughly and it had disintegrated under the merest strain.

It was like everything in this awful room that she hated with a savage passion. How could people be expected to pay good money for such an ugly, flimsy room? Irina rushed to the window and dragged at the thin curtains that had no lining and were made from a brownish fabric that was crisp to the touch, as if it were half paper and half nylon.

The curtains were fixed to the plastic strip of curtain rail by thin plastic clips. She had longed for wooden poles with proper curtain rings made of metal that would slide elegantly along the pole but Oleg had said 'no, no' these were cheaper and easier to fit and that was that and she had brooded about their nasty, flimsy, insubstantial nature until she felt tormented by it.

When no one came to the motel Oleg would say, 'well, it's a good job we didn't buy those curtains you were so desperate for isn't it because we'd been even more in the shit if we'd listened to you Irina.'

When he said her name he twisted his mouth as if tasting something bitter and looked away from her and around the apartment, spreading his arms at the small, out-of-date television and the sofa in a kind of triumph at their threadbare life together and what she had reduced him to with her foolish, womanly decisions.

When she pulled at the curtains the clips flicked off in rapid succession and landed soundlessly on the brown nylon carpet, making even her terrible rising anger into a subdued and supressed feminine thing that was of no consequence. She made no sound and barely a ripple, even in anger, and she was swept with an impotent self-pity. She wanted to smash the room to bits but was too feeble.

She snatched at the note and balled it up tight in her hand. She threw it onto the floor with all of her strength where it bounced once, lightly, and rolled, meekly under the writing desk.

She clawed at the covers on the bed but the blankets were tightly tucked and the rough material burned against her fingertips but did not yield so she pounded her outstretched palms on the mattress, over and over and was startled by a raw, groaning noise that she realised, horrified, came from her.

Irina couldn't guess at how long she had sat on the engineer's bed. The snow had blown itself out and a pale trail of light through the window made a stripe on the wall that showed where the edges of the lining paper had begun to unpeel.

It must have been a while. The cold from inactivity had thickened her blood and she knew, without moving, that her muscles would be stiff when she stood up from the bed. Her hat was on the floor. Had it fallen or had she thrown it there?

She wondered if the engineer was already on the train. Tapping on her laptop. She might have bought a coffee in a polystyrene cup and be balancing it on her table, careful that it didn't spill onto her precious papers.

Or she would be talking to someone new in the carriage, leaning across the aisle with her elbows on her knees and her chin in her hands, all the better to listen. She would be smiling and enthusiastic. She would be busy making a new friend.

As the train tracks spooled away and the thread between them stretched, Irina saw the countryside unfolding and the ice melting as the engineer sped towards the green fields and countryside of Moscow. She would never catch her. Irina's eyes were filled with tears that blurred the memory of the engineer's face into soft outlines and unknowable expressions.

Twenty-Four

Frumpy. That was exactly the right word thought Maia. She watched from the window of the coffee shop as Irina crossed the square, dragging a green suitcase behind her as if she hated its guts.

Those boots had seen better days. You could see that, even through the condensation. And that awful old coat!

Maia touched her coppery hair. You couldn't blame Oleg for some harmless flirting if that's what he had to put up with at home. She smiled into her cup. He did have a way of making a story seem funny.

She lifted her biscuit, preparing to wave it in greeting to Irina as she passed by the window but she didn't look in her direction. Was she talking to herself? Goodness! Maia sighed. Poor Oleg. She licked her forefinger and returned to flicking at the pages of a magazine.

Irina didn't notice her small gesture. She turned her face up and into the malicious wind, enduring it. Was this the worst that it could muster? The punishing cold, clawing at her face presented a physical discomfort to focus on. And that was so much easier to bear than her feelings. She welcomed it; the way it forced the terrible thoughts from her head. There was a relief in it.

She had thrown on her coat too carelessly in the motel room, leaving the lower three buttons of it undone. The front of the coat flapped in the gusts, slapping sharply against her shins, like thin sticks beating on them.

She could not have stopped and removed her gloves to fasten the coat even if she had wanted to. He fingers would have been stiff and useless within moments and so she bore it. What choice did she have?

The wind insinuated itself inside the folds of the coat and crept upwards, wrapping quick circles around her waist and gripping it suddenly, with a nasty glee.

Her muscles shuddered and then snapped tight at the touch.

Even though her scarf lay forgotten on the floor of the engineer's room and her neck was fully exposed, she did not tuck her chin down into her chest. She would not shrink from it. She bore the cruelty of the cold with a resignation that recognised the hopelessness of resistance.

She may have been crying. She didn't know. But if there were tears they were blasted from her eyes and turned to ice before they had the chance to form and fall.

Damn this suitcase. It dragged her backwards. It weighed twice as much as it had just an hour or two ago. It was filled with her things, useless things. She would not have cared if she never saw those things again. She did not want the suitcase, but it was her burden and she was condemned to haul it with her through the square.

The oil truck was here again. The driver, waiting in his cab with the engine running, recognised Irina as the woman who ran the motel. That was probably what the suitcase was all about. He flashed his headlights in greeting, but she winced and turned her head away from him with her mouth set in a line, sharp, like the blade of a knife.

There was nowhere else to go but back to the apartment block.

Irina put her shoulder to the door and pushed though into the vestibule. There was a silence as it closed behind her and she stopped to catch her breath. The shrieks of the wind were muted enough that she could hear her own rapid breathing. She was panting. Each intake of new air sent a sharp pain running across her ribs.

The door opened behind her, with a yelp of the wind, and a man came crashing inside, banging together his hands and scraping the snow from his feet. She could hardly stand the brush-brush noise of the matting and the way he nearly knocked against her so that she curled her face away from him with an expression of revulsion.

'What a day,' he said, beating his hands together again and he laughed in a mirthless 'ha-ha-ha' kind of way for no reason.

He hesitated. He had seen the case straightaway and thought he would offer to carry it up for her. It was a good deed and he was eager for it. He would tell his wife all about it, exaggerating its weight and the difficulty of the climb a little to make a more interesting story, and she would be pleased to hear about it. But he was put out that Irina was not responding. Especially when he was going out of his way to be so friendly.

She looked away, rounding her back at him, still silent. He cleared his throat. It was difficult to know what to say in a situation like this, they were neighbours after all, and he scraped his boots on the bristled mat some more and made a 'bbrrrr' sound to cover up his awkwardness.

'More to come I reckon,' he said, but still Irina could not summon the strength or the will to reply.

So he thought, suit yourself then, if that's the way you want to play it. And he hurried off through the next door and up the stairs, feeling embarrassed and hurt. He would think about Irina, on and off, for the rest of the day.

Time had passed, the way it did, she supposed, but Irina did not know how long she had been standing there. No one else had come in or out of the building. Her breathing had stilled. There was no rumble from the engine of the oil truck. But what did it mater?

She looked out through the rectangle of thick, greenish glass. That was it. She would just leave her useless case behind – it would only slow her down – and begin to walk.

First through the square, following in the footsteps of the people who had trekked back and forth already on their countless, pointless journeys. She would be sheltered from the worst of the wind at the beginning by the huddled, hunched over buildings.

She would cut through the narrow passageway between Alexi's store and the silent, shuttered garage next door. The snow would be trampled down in the alley and translucent, sliced through with cellophane from cigarette packets, dropped lists and wrappers torn eagerly from chocolate bars. It was gloomy, even on a clear day, and she would head towards the beckoning rectangle of light at its end.

Emerging, with the small, primeval, relief that comes from escaping small spaces, Irina would take in the widened view.

The land that looped behind the square was studded with wooden houses on stilts, set apart from each other and in a broad ring that was, perhaps, three or four houses deep. Each had its own outhouse, squatting in its shadow.

They were close enough to each other that a shout of greeting from the top step would arrive, faintly, in the ear of a neighbour pottering on their own verandah, if the wind were in the right direction. But they were far enough apart that raised voices inside the house kept their domestic battles private. They had a loitering quality; guarding their privacy but watchful in case they should be overlooked.

These houses considered themselves, very much, to be 'in town'. The occupants could see the square clearly, albeit the backs of the buildings, and were no more than five minutes' walk from the store, even in the worst of the weather.

Irina would skirt the boundaries of their land, most marked with fences, and anyone glancing from their window would remark to themselves, 'That looks like Irina. Where's she off to in such a hurry?'

It would take her just a few minutes before the town was properly behind her and she would be on the edge of the plain and passing the last two or three remote homesteads.

These houses invariably had single occupants; suspicious

eccentrics who had chosen their exile and expected no pity for it. They were tough people. They were too far from Tomyator to hear its sounds and probably glad of it. They were largely ignored out here and felt no need to spruce up their paintwork or knock the icicles from the eaves. Their rubbish and junk spilled out of the front of their houses and accumulated there, without apology.

She would continue past, taking high-kneed steps because the snow blew into drifts here, and she would approach what seemed to be a small hill, the only raised feature of the landscape.

This was Tomyator's dump. It was unofficial but, as the Region charged each household for taking away the rubbish, bigger items that would have filled up the bins often found their way out here. It was a burial mound of dead car batteries, broken televisions, empty tins of paint and rusted oven trays. Under the cover of snow there would be a rug that had become too stained and threadbare even for Tomyator and plastic toys that the children had loved once, but were tired of now.

And then, soon after, there would come a great flattening of the world so that she could believe the earth to be a vast white disc, and that she was picking her way across its shimmering surface towards its edge. If she could keep walking and walking, she would be able to move beyond the periphery of her own life, heading towards, well, where? The precipice? Perhaps she would meet an enormous, out of scale, smiling walrus. Look how far away I am, she could say to him.

Irina rubbed at the smeared glass with her mitten. Even

with all of her buttons properly fastened, and if she had remembered her scarf and with her hat pulled firmly down, she would not survive more than a fistful of hours out there.

She turned to the inner door instead and drifted into thoughts of the triple-glazed, hot apartment, where she could barely stretch out her arms without brushing her fingertips against a cupboard that jutted awkwardly into a room and, unless she was careful, she would knock her knee, painfully, on the wooden frame of the sofa or on the small tables scattered around their cramped living room.

She, Vasily and Oleg moved restlessly around each other in the apartment with the unnameable discontent of zoo animals that had only known captivity. It was a life spent prowling back and forth between your place on the sofa, your chair at the kitchen table, your side of the bed, to stake your claim in your tiny territory. Having scented freedom, it seemed too awful a prospect for her to bear.

She felt herself undecided and between two worlds. She doubted she could survive in either.

But she could not stand here forever so she picked up the suitcase. She must have put it on the floor at some point, and it was hateful to her. It banged against her leg and pulled on her shoulder so that it ached, but life demanded of her that she move forward so she pushed open the second door and into the stale, stewed air of the stairwell.

Sixteen steps. They were insurmountable. Dizzying. Yet up she went. Each step an effort of will that threatened to exhaust her so entirely that she felt she might sink down at any moment and surrender to oblivion.

She did not know how she managed to climb those terrible stairs.

At the top she waited, staring down the familiar khaki corridor that was, at once, entirely strange to her. There was a throbbing heaviness in her legs so that she was conscious of the effort involved in every step. Irina felt like an astronaut who, having returned to earth, found herself surprised by the sensation of gravity.

I'm back again, she thought as she reached her front door and she could not make sense of how it had happened or why she had arrived here. This had not been what she planned and she was bewildered.

She shook her head.

Irina took off her mittens, pulled out her keys and examined them. It was an effort to understand what they were or how they might be manipulated.

They were keys of course. Just ordinary keys. When she slid the right key into the lock, the metallic, scraping sound chilled her.

Oleg didn't look round. He was watching football now, sitting forward on the sofa and leaning towards the screen with his shoulders rounded and flexed in concentration. His round head bobbed stupidly in time with the action as if he were taking part in the game, and she loathed him.

She unbuttoned her coat with a series of unthinking, automatic movements and hung it on the hook, running her finger in the gash it had created in the wall.

'You took your time,' he said, without looking round.

She felt out of time, like a ghost visiting her own past and she held up her hands and examined them, the backs and then the palms, to see if she were solid and real.

She moved to the doorway of the kitchen and flicked on the light.

Everything was spick and span, just as she'd left it, but there was no pleasure to be had from the neat surfaces. The labels on her spices faced the same way on their rack and all of the bottles were wiped clean of grease. Her Dualit toaster was brightly polished. She knew that there would be few crumbs in its little metal drawer because she had emptied it, and wiped it with a cloth, just yesterday. It felt as if it could have been a year ago.

This kitchen is showing its age she thought, as if she were a visitor observing someone else's home. The laminate on the counter top had begun to bubble up at the edge where it met the sink and the tiles behind the stove were stained brown from the heat of the burners. Irina had scrubbed and scrubbed at the stain but had never been able to remove it completely. She hated that stain and the way it always drew her eyes to it.

On the table a plastic ketchup bottle lay on its side and a dusting of salt made a trail showing the course of a meal. She leaned against the doorframe and rested her head against it because suddenly it was too heavy for her neck to support.

She wondered if she would ever summon the strength to lift it upright again and she wished she could sink to the floor and sleep.

Then she thought, this won't get you anywhere, Irina. She turned to study Oleg's profile. He licked his thickened purple lips in excitement at the game, jutting out his rounded jaw and then wiping his moist forehead with his palm, before rubbing it on the front of his vest.

I hate you, she thought.

She slid open a drawer so that the cutlery shivered together. How neatly the knives and forks and spoons sat in their plastic compartments. This cutlery set had been a wedding gift from Oleg's parents and she remembered how grown up and sophisticated she had felt, dropping them into place in their ready made slots in her beautiful new apartment.

She had been contented then.

Next to the plastic cutlery tray lay the loose knives. There was her bread knife, made from a single piece of brushed steel, with a ferociously serrated edge. It made light work of the black bread from the store. It tore through the tough crusts with a brutish, eager sound, spraying crumbs.

The cleaver was large and heavy to handle, and they bought their meat ready-cut these days, so the blade had retained its bright potential. If she had needed to, she could have held it with two hands and brought it down, with all of her strength, to crunch through the densest bone.

The knife Irina used for meat, for carving slices of ham, teasing a chicken wing from the carcass, or trimming the fat from a chop, was, maybe, twenty centimetres long, including the black plastic handle. It had a thick, raised lip on its hilt to prevent wet hands from slipping and causing a nasty accident.

It had a firm, thick blade that swooped inwards from its

widest end to make a sharp point. At least, it had once. She held it up and frowned at the squared off tip. Oleg had snapped the end under the stubborn lid of a jar of pickles.

She slid it back into the drawer and pulled out her filleting knife; it was surprisingly light considering the length of the blade. Its flat back could be dragged along the gleaming bodies of fish to tear off their scales. The delicate give in the long, lean shaft meant it could curve around the spine of the fish to slice paper-thin, translucent slivers of the flesh. It had a resting tension in her hand. She remembered that this had been an expensive knife. 'Professional standard' they called it in the shop in Yakutsk and it had come in a presentation box.

Here though, this was her favourite knife. A short, robust, tool. She used it for slicing carrots and dicing beetroot. She could jab out the eye of a potato or trace the tight, dry seam of a leathery fava pod so that it could be split open to disgorge the flat beans intact. It scored the length of a plump salami before she peeled off the papery skin and then pushed through the fat-speckled meat to make dense, even slices.

It was quiet and unassuming and perfectly suited to its task. She kept it sharp on a stone.

Irina weighed it in her hand, feeling the familiar press of the steel handle tucking snugly into the soft crease of her palm. It felt like it had been made for her.

Her hands were cold and the chilling sensation, she thought, seemed to be creeping over her like the sea freezing. It was welcome in a way, this numbness that came over her.

Then she went to the wooden crate, covered with a cloth, next to the fridge, and picked out an onion.

She peeled away the crisp brown skin and began to slice; methodically, automatically, inevitably.

Lunch wouldn't make itself, would it Irina?

She must endure this life.

What else was there for her to do?